TATA McDONALD

MONROVIA
THE CITY OF LOVERS,
LIFE & THIEVES

A Novel About 21st Century Monrovia

Clarke Herring Publishing
New Jersey & Liberia

Monrovia: The City of Lovers, Liars, & Thieves is a work of fiction or faction (a mixture of fact and fiction), but references to all work of art, cities, counties, towns and villages, in Liberia are all real or factual. Names, Characters, incidents either are the products of the author's imagination or are used fictitiously.

2017 Clarke Herring Publishing Group Fiction Edition

Copyright © by Tata McDonald

Published in the United States of America by Clarke Herring Publishing Fiction Edition, an imprint of Clarke Herring Publishing & Consulting Group, LLC. Hamilton, New Jersey.

ISBN: 978-0-9898042-8-8

Cover designed by Emmanuel Clarke
Cover photograph taken from http://www.naijanewsplus.com

Printed in the United State of America
Published simultaneously in United States of America and Liberia

https://www.clarkepulbish.com

2 4 6 8 9 7 5 3 2 1

This book is for people like you and me. Thanks for the love you forever have in your heart for the city of Monrovia and its transformative power on us all.

And as always and forever, to my children, Regnia, Eukey, Emmaree, and Luah

TATA McDONALD

MONROVIA
THE CITY OF LOVERS,
LIFE & THIEVES

A Novel About 21st Century Monrovia

ABOUT THE AUTHOR

Tata McDonald is a Liberian author whom love for country radiates in everything she does. Born and raised in Monrovia, Tata's love for writing started at the age of six when she was a student at the Monrovia Demonstration Elementary School, MDES on Clay Street. Upon graduating from MDES, she was enrolled at the St. Peters Lutheran School, SPLS on 14th Street in Sinkor, Monrovia. While at SPLS, she was introduced to several Mills & Boon romance novels by some of her classmates. Since diving into the emotionally sensual world of romance, Tata has never stopped reading and writing her own collection of romantic stories.

Tata is a graduate of the Williams V.S. Tubman High School on 12th Street in Sinkor, Monrovia. After spending a few semesters at the University of Liberia, she was forced to flee Monrovia for neighboring Sierra Leone, and then, the Republic of Guinea during the Liberian Civil Wars. Tata currently lives in Winston Salem North Carolina in the United States of America with her husband and four loving children. She is also a graduate of the New Jersey Institute of Technology in Newark, New Jersey. She is an avid reader and writer. This debut novel, *Monrovia: The City of Lovers, Liars, and Thieves* is a testament of her passion for the art. Tata is currently working on a follow up title to this book.

"THEN THEY TORE MY LAPPA ON BROAD STREET"

BY:COMFORT MARTIN-LEECO

I was just a little girl walking on the streets innocent of it all;
then they tore my lappa on Broad Street.
My parents couldn't afford just anything when they tore my
lappa on Broad Street.
The man told me he would give me money and fine things;
then they tore my lappa on Broad Street.

I saw all the beautiful things and good food
and pretty hair wraps girls of my age had so;
they tore my lappa on Broad Street.
Sometimes the man forced me, sometimes he begged me.

Sometimes he gave me those fine things;
then they tore my lappa on Broad Street.
I yelled, he gave Mama money.
I screamed , he gave Papa money;
then they tore my lappa on Broad Street.

Sometimes Mama said no. Sometimes Papa said no.
I started accepting it as my life.
I was hopeless;
then they tore my lappa on Broad Street.

Nobody cared.
They called me "little prostitute".

They told their children "don't play with her".
My heart, my life, my soul was captured;
and they tore my lappa on Broad Street.

One day, I thought I smelled freedom.
Someone saw me. Yes, I am free!
No, I was wrong!
Then they tore my lappa on Broad Street.

They stripped me off my clothes,
captured my captives
and gave me fifty lashes on Broad Street;
then they tore my lappa on Broad Street.

Some booed, some cheered.
Some agonized my situation.
The ones I had asked God to save me.
But they tore my lappa on Broad Street!

CHAPTER 1

A loud bang from a flash of lightning and thunder jolted Stanley out of his thoughts, or perhaps one of his many daydreams. Like Usain Bolt, the great Jamaican olympic sprinter, he bolted toward the opened windows and quickly closed it shut to keep the rainwater out of his home office. He could not believe that after so many days of drought, it was finally raining. Stanley stopped and stood beside the half-parted curtains of the second window he had just shut closed and took a long silence look at the skylines of the city of Monrovia—a city that has so many stories to tell. As he stood there listening intently to the sounds of raindrops against the roof of his house and on nearby houses, and the smell of dry red earth being provoked by the drenching water hitting its surface with fierce force, produced that intoxicating smell. *"Will this outburst of unexpected rain trigger the usual torrential flood around the city that we are now getting used to?"*, Stanley said to himself followed by a light bite on his lower lip. He knew that the city and its surrounding boroughs have been badly managed by the central government seated up on Capitol Hill, in Monrovia. For being vilified by the establishment, he didn't want to further ruffle any feather with his politically-charged writings. Rather, he wanted to sit and be quietly effective without raising much suspicions. As quickly as he had bolted to the window, Stanley returned to his desk. As he sat down, his mind shifted on his personal struggles rather than that of the characters in his story.

Monrovia always had a way of invoking his creative juices. This is what he loves and missed about the city he loves so dearly....

...This city which sits humble like an abandoned but forgiving mother on the edge of the Atlantic Ocean, once epitomized everything the wanting strangers and her residents longed for back in the 19th and 20th Centuries—smiles and romance, freedom and justice, hope and peace, a promise of a better tomorrow, and a life filled with grace and mirth. Though she was built back then as a home for a quarter million people, but since the dawn of the 21st Century, she has become a haven for more than a million of her citizens and strangers—making her streets crammed and dangerous at night, and her land flood prone during the annual raining season. Her welcoming radiant smile once shone as a beacon of hope for so many wanderers and fleeing Jews during the time of a great war which cast a dark shadow on a world that was made for love and peace. Not even a long fought internal civil war and an Ebola virus outbreak could quench her flame that draws so many people from across the globe onto her shiny gates. This great shiny city which sits up on a peninsula along the Atlantic Ocean with a soft Bint el Sudan (Bindu Sudan) like gaze, has dealt me and many others before us, our shares of what she has in her bosom—the good, the bad, and the unexpected. Like a loving mother, she has also become a home for everyone who had entered her gates—lovers and haters, sinners and saints, hustlers and thieves, prostitutes and their johns, backstabbers and their victims, fickle politicians and myself. I love my beautiful city to death. But, for her residents and thousands of her sons and daughters, I have come to learn a bitter truth about them. Many of them are ungrateful, fickle, and hopeless lovers of themselves and of everything. Most of them are like foxes, they are wicked, liars and deceivers who shun danger, but are greedy for profit and prestige. Often, they are not prepared to keep their words to you, therefore, you too should never keep their words to them,

especially when it is at your disadvantage to do so. For the most part, many Monrovians have moved to the far-left of human existence—many have removed the ethical dimension out of everyday living because they have become liars, thieves, sexually exploitative, they lack the fear of God within their hearts, and hold no loyalty to anyone . Like those that rule over them, they will flatter and deceive you with sweet flowery words that they do not truly mean. Like the deceivers they are, they will always find some good-hearted and willing victims to deceive. This is the enigma and the complexity of the great city of Monrovia, this shining city on the hill which sits at the edge of the Atlantic Ocean and the Mesuardo River. On the other hand, if you are honest, and perfect in all your actions and want to survive in the city of Monrovia, then you must learn Monrovians' behaviors, and also learn how to be able not to be good! I say these things not out of spike for my city or for anyone, but based on my direct experience with people in this once quiet city that we love so much. Of all the good and unkind things Monrovia and her corrupt and sugar-coated tongue politicians along with her deceptive religious leaders have done to me, I still have faith in her unending love for us all, and my destiny of a happy tomorrow. I will never give up on Monrovia, a place which is the most beautiful city in all the world. This city is filled with smiling faces and hopeless lovers that have the willpower to survive against wars and injustice, Ebola and deaths… Stanley let out a faint smile at his soul-searching thoughts. He ran his manicured right hand over his soft dark hair and laughed at all the craziness that were brewing inside his head about the city of Monrovia and its people.

Though his thoughts may sound crazy to him, but for people who know the history of Monrovia, they will tell you that he was speaking the brutal truth to power. The facts were glaring—since the end of political turmoil in the late 1990s and early 2000s, the city of Monrovia has become a model of systemic political failure for every successive government she had played host to—many of its residents are living in abject poverty while the city swims in a sea of wealth and abundance with politicians and dishonest businessmen being the benefactors. If a true patriot and a son of the city does not emerge soon to save her, she would die under her own weight. For decades now, lies and deceptions have been the order of the day; and unfortunately, Monrovia is a place seen by citizens living in other parts of the country as the beginning of everything—the good, the bad, and the ugly. Stanley knows the big shakers and movers that are living within the city, many of whom are trying to repel him for being critical of their deeds and misdeeds. Understandably, many of the city's residents, especially the political and business elites do not hold loyalty to the city because many of them are urban migrants who had only come to Monrovia to acquire wealth, power and prestige. The dilapidating state of the can sometimes weight heavily on Stanley's mind—making him to fall out of favor with friends and love ones. Like a man without hope, Stanley has become a man with a hopeless longing for love and romance, peace and security. While Stanley may not be able to live to see the best of his beloved Monrovia, but her best days are still far ahead of her.

As he sat at his home office desk that early afternoon with rain pouring outside his home like a floodgate that had burst open, he could not stop himself from wondering why life had been so unkind to him for the past five years. He could not conjure up in his mind any modicum of explanation as to why so many good people closed to him had died of the Ebola virus epidemic more than two year earlier. He could not stop blaming the government and other self-serving politicians for not stopping the virus at the borders from where it crossed over into Liberia and down to Monrovia where it wreaked havoc with more than four thousand eight hundred deaths. He had come to develop a deep-seated hatred for the government, especially for the death of his former-wife.

She died after being infected by patients she was caring for. Though they were divorced, but he dearly loved and cherished her more than anything in his world. Her death brought a recurring nightmare of her unwilling divorce to him.

...Where are you my true love? I want to reach out and hold you. In the unlikely that is called hope, I know there is nothing false about true love. True love is like a mysterious female who brings smiles onto the lips of her dying lover. True love never sees any wrong in the actions of the beloved. True love triumphs where no one expects her to. She falls onto the ground at times; but like a prize fighter, she gets back up to continue slugging it out against the odds. True love bears it all with every pain and joy life throws at her, even to the edge of doom. True love knows neither the past because she lives within the immediate present, as she looks into the unforeseen future for a better tomorrow. Not even the enemy of love has strong hands over true love. I think it was true love that made some relatives of the infected to have looked into the cold eyes of Mr. Ebola and death, and said, "Though he or she may have Ebola, but I will care for him or her." Stanley eyes welled up with tears. He reflects on how his beloved city was once plagued with deaths from the world's deadliest Ebola virus outbreak that killed thousands of his fellow citizens. He let out a deep sigh as he playfully moved the mouse pointer around on his notebook computer's screen as more thoughts clouded his insatiably fragile mind.

...True love is a faceless, colorless, odorless, and tasteless conundrum that has become humanity's greatest nemesis as well as its hopeful liberator. True love is the rock upon which the Golden Rule of Relationships was built—love me unconditionally. Like me, true love will never be understood by those who never loved another living soul because she is something someone has to experience and embrace before believing in her true transforming powers. Indeed, it was because of true love that families and love ones died while caring for their sick and infected love ones and relatives during

the Ebola nightmare. With all that I know now, here I am, suffering in comfort. Hmmmm......

......How can I forget that one thing that made me who I am today? How can I live my life then, so I cannot be that person everyone wants me to be...mean, unkind, inhumane, and hateful of the city that I love? How can I make this depression go away forever with the passion that I have deep inside of me? Huh? How can I make my heart feel youthful, so I can love and be loved once again? How can I control this intense desire that has consumed me like an eternal flame? Why can't these cycles of rejections end so I can be that person that I used to be? Where is that self-esteem that I once had, which made me walk tall like a giant, fled and gone to? Ummmm...... Hmmm? Stanley thought of his present state of being as he once more stared blindly at the blinking cursor on the computer's screen in front of him as thousands of thoughts raced through his mind for the second time. For he had been bemoaned by grieves since returning home from the United Stathes of America after the deadly Ebola flare which snatched thousands of lives from mostly poor people that were ill-informed about the disease. For Stanley, it was not only the death of his personal doctor, Samuel Brisbane who died during the height of the virus crisis that broke his heart, it was the death of his first love—the only woman he once loved and still loves even in death. Her death had robbed him of any hope of finding another soul who he could truly love without him living in his past. The hope he once had of returning to the only woman he loved after their divorce was shattered by the virus that caused her death. She was one of those unsung heroines whom death never made the news headlines—she had gone to the Phebee Hospital in Bong County to volunteer as a nurse practitioner prior to the viral outbreak. At night, if Stanley was not sitting at his desk writing, he would lay in his bed and cry himself to sleep.

...When will I find that special person of my dream, so I can

be well again? Like a lust in my soul, I've cried myself to sleep and back from sleep. I've strived the hardest in maintaining my sense of balance; even when everyone around me has lost theirs. Like my beloved city, Monrovia that has been in search of a true lover who will restore her lost glory, I too have searched for so long to find that special someone who will bring peace and joy to my broken heart and revive my dying spirit. But here I am, still lonely, still looking, and still praying to find and be found by that precious love of my life who may be sitting in some solitary corner of Mother Earth's bowel; like myself, praying for her Prince Charming to come along and rescue her from her lonely castle of despair and hopelessness onto a beautiful and a peaceful shore of everlasting romance and true love. Why can't I be understood, though, by the people I love and care for the most?" Stanley said out loud as he locked teary and itchy eyes with the writings on his computer's screen for a third time. He was now wondering if his sensual erotica romance writings were affecting his social life, though he was heralded by millions of young millennial readers at home and abroad for his great talent, but was ridiculed by corrupt local politicians and religious leaders for what they termed as "corrupting the minds of the youth". 'Nimrod', as Stanley refers to those persecuting him, he thinks his prosecutors were enslaved to their own inner desires whether they knew it or not. An established fact is that, many of them are checkbooks and brown envelopes seekers who only preach the politics and gospels of anything goes because they all lacked the willpower to resist the temptation of the quick money making schemes that have led to the backwardness of the city of Monrovia and the country she represents.

Prior to the civil war and the Ebola outbreak along with the Internet revolution of the 1990s, sex was always a very sensitive topic that was rarely discussed openly in Monrovia and in many parts of Liberia and Africa. More often, discussion was reserved for procreation between married couples in doctors' or pastors' offices, or inside half-lit bedrooms across Liberia and the rest of the Dark African Continent. Unlike in the 1970s when the William R. Tolbert administration proposed that the consent for sex with girls be set at the age 13, it was the first time the topic of sex took a center stage in Monrovia, the nation's capital. For the most part, sex has always been a backroom conversation in the now sleepless little city. For the American educated Stanley Kla Nimely, his line of work has transformed him into a celebrity among young millennial readers and a reviled villain to many conservative readers in the deceitfully religious oceanfront city and in many parts of the country. For fearlessly venturing in an unchartered water of political romance writing about people that are highly placed and their sexual exploitative behaviors in his homeland, Stanley was forced to deal with a counterculture of deceit and marginalization from mainstream society while he was being celebrated by a younger generation of audience for openly discussing subject such as love, sexual exploitation of young men and underage girls by wealthy government officials and powerful businessmen and women. Due to his writing style, the establishment labelled him as a troublemaker and a misfit. This accusation was an affront to justice which was aimed at silencing Stanley for shedding lights on sensitive issues like teenage pregnancy, institutionalized corruption, prostitution, political backstabbing in which sex is used by nefarious politicians against their rivals as a weapon, and sexually transmitted opportunistic diseases that were ravaging the country like wildfire since the end of a 14-year civil war and the recent viral outbreak. Many of Stanley's novels are filled with honesty of everyday social problems, but are provocatively laced with open sexual contents and various public displays of erotica affections that have angered cherry-picking religious rights groups within the small country and other parts of the African continent. For his style of writing, he painfully lost a marriage to his now deceased beautiful ex-wife of twelve years due to pressure from her church; but Stanley believed he would find true love again someday.

The loss of the woman he once loved, played hard on his mind. Since his return home following the end of the Ebola outbreak, his ex-wife's death robbed him of his self-esteem and any positive outlook he may have had for romance, and finding a lifetime partner. Though they were divorced and drifted worlds apart, but she had remained the center of his universe whether she knew it or not. At one point, he was the only man in the world she wanted to spend the rest of her life with, but religious pressure brought about their separation and subsequent divorce. With the advice of her church's pastors, she had put forth a precondition to returning to the only man who once gave her everything a good woman deserves—love, laughter, luxurious lifestyle and cars, a big house, endless vacations, gold and diamond, and a life only made for a queen. On the other hand, Stanley's passion and his male alter ego of believing in his work, and his philosophy of individualism would not bring him to a romantic compromise. Like a zealous and a doomed dictator who never sees a reason to compromise—he never stopped writing sensual and political romance novels for the sake of pleasing his wife and the pastors of her church, Winners' Chapel International in Oldest Congo Town, outside of Monrovia. His stands of not letting go of his writing or backing out on a talent God had endowed him with was based on his principles and his firmed believe in being a free-thinking creation of God Almighty whom his late ex-wife also worshiped at the Nigerian-based church. Like Andrew Jackson and many of the founding fathers of the United States of America whom believed that the creator of humankind, created everyone with certain inalienable rights. Stanley strongly believed that two of those inalienable rights were the right to think freely, and the right to write politically incorrect books that tell the story of Monrovia and sensual romance books that warmed the bedrooms of every lover and also put back spice into any dying relationship. For these reasons, he was going to allow no one to infringe on his God's given rights for the sake of adhering to some temporary social and religious agreement called 'MARRIAGE'. He never stopped writing and he never ceased thinking about his former wife up to the time he heard of her unexpected death in 2014.

Overwhelmed by grief during their divorce, Stanley, being a man of faith due to his religious upbringing, asked a pastor friend of his, the Right Reverend A.T. Miller the following questions that had burned him for most of his adult life, about his line of work, *"I have a question for you my dear reverend. Am I wrong for writing all the stuff I write? If God didn't want us to think or write books about humans' behaviors and humans' sexuality, then why did He create the desire within us, and why did he create the desire for lies and sex in the first place? If God didn't want me to write love and erotica novels for a living, then why would He give me such a great talent only to be ridiculed, prosecuted, and bastardized by a few group of people who happened to find themselves in a temporary position of authority, wealth, and many of whom live double lives in the dark of night and in broad daylight? Isn't it true that God never makes mistakes because He does everything for a reason, even if we humankind do not understand or accept it as His will? Am I right, my Dear Reverend?"* Stanley asked to the astonishment of his longtime friend who was the head pastor of the African Methodist Episcopal Church on Camp Johnson Road in Monrovia. The man of God only laughed at Stanley's question, but later told him to take it to the Lord in prayer because, God never makes mistakes—for He is faithful and just in all of His actions.

Stanley's ideology of his God's given rights cost him dearly, though writing politically incorrect and dirty books of sensual romance for a living was all he had earnestly prayed to the Father of Creation to be able to do. From the tender and innocent age of ten, it was something he'd been passionate and motivated about. Growing up in Monrovia had its ups and downs—for Stanley; Monrovia is the greatest and most beautiful city in all the world. Like many Liberians living in the Diaspora that are ardent lovers of the city of Monrovia, Stanley believes that the city of Monrovia is the only place on Earth that makes him and his fellow compatriots feel like human beings—that's the reason people from overseas and other faraway places flock into the small city to vacation in December of every year. For many of the Diasporan Liberians, this beloved city is the only place that makes them walk tall like Goliath. Monrovia is the city that give them something to look forward to while away from their country of birth. Though the city keeps expanding outward and imploding under its own weight because of political uncertainty, Monrovia is that light in the darkness for both foreigners and Liberians looking for wealth, relevance, freedom of speech, and self-actualization. Monrovia is the place that gave birth to Stanley's writing career—no wonder he holds the city very dearly to his heart.

It all began when Stanley's two best friends, Adolphus Porte and Moses Dekai along with him, secretly took an X-rated Hustler Magazine out of their neighbor, J.N. Elliot's apartment one Saturday afternoon while they were still living on McDonald Street in Central Monrovia. After he and the other teenagers browsed throw the book's explicit pages which were filled with dirty nude pictures of exotic women, after burning the images of women's vaginas deep within his brain, after hearing Adolphus and Moses narrate how pleasurable it is when a boy inserts his rock-hard penis into a girl's warmed, soft, and fleshy vagina, he was sold out. He wanted a firsthand experience of all he'd heard from his best friends—he wanted to run his fingers over the mound of a female's vagina and kiss her like the men in the Hustler Magazine did. Stanley wanted so badly to plunge his hard and curious penis deep inside Connie's warm vagina—for she was his neighborhood crush. She was the first woman he saw early in the morning whenever he awoke, and the last woman he saw before he went to bed—they lived right opposite each other on the small street. At one time, she was the girl of his dream. From the day he was exposed to pornography to the day he had his first kiss with a girl at the Monrovia Demonstration Elementary School's bathroom on Clay Street, all Stanley wanted to be able to do was to write and tell stories of eroticisms and human sexual pleasures, especially the behaviors of people living in and around the city of Monrovia.

As a young elementary school student, his artwork and stories found in his third-grade exercise books reflected his inner most desire and true passion. Often, his class teachers invited his parents to conferences at the city's pride elementary school in order to discuss their son's unusual behavior and artworks. Punishments and other forms of chastising did not alter Stanley's rare behaviors—the more he was disciplined and reprimanded for his drawings and boyhood fantasy stories, the better he got at drawing and narrating them on pages. When asked why he only sketched and wrote explicit story about humans' sexuality, he informed his parents that, those were images that came to him naturally and the stories were all works of his imagination. Like any good and concerned father would, his father feared that his only child had been exposed to the wrong crowd or he'd been involved in voyeurism just like many boys of his age did in and around the city. He and his wife sincerely wanted their child to desist from his habit at all cost. The more they tried to discipline him, the more recalcitrant he became. His worried mother believed that her only child's mind had been overtaken by evil forces, and the only way to save him from destruction was for her to fast and pray to God for deliverance. Even fasting and praying did not alter Stanley's behavior—he continued on his path of writing stories and sketching lurid images.

For Stanley staying true to his unusual talent at such a young age, his angry and worried father took him to one of Monrovia's leading psychologists and psychotherapists, Miatta Roberts to see if should could diagnose his rare behavior that had both his teachers and parents' concerns. When she could not help the young boy, his father then took him to the priest at the Sacred Heart Cathedral Catholic Church up on Broad Street so he could help deliver his only son from the power of the devil whom Mr. Nimely also believed had taken over his son's mind, body and soul. When all of his good efforts failed, Jay Blamo Toe Nimely, Stanley's loving father, then gave him up to follow his devilish desire of his imagination before labeling him a reprobate. Little did he know that his son had a raw talent that needed no religious intervention or psychotherapy. Rather, he needed the enabling environment that would let him thrive and take his craft to the next level.

After receiving a Liberian government's sponsored scholarship to travel to the United States to further his education at Princeton University, Mr. Nimely took young Stanley and his mother along to the land of enormous opportunities and endless possibilities. Without a doubt, Stanley's writing took another level when he was exposed to the American-way of life. When Stanley graduated from high school in East Windsor, New Jersey, he had already published more than two-dozen short stories in various magazines and journals. In college, he majored in Creative Writing and Classical English. His first book, 'Love at First Sight: When East Meets West' took the publishing world by surprise—it sold more than seventy-three thousand copies within six months. Stanley was a natural talent—he blended his African experience with the American-way of life in many of his early writings. Without a shred of doubt, he was successful at his craft. His fanbase was evident of his enormous success as a politically incorrect sensual romance writer. In Monrovia

alone, Stanley had more than a million fans and admirers
of varying ages. Worldwide, he was regarded as a fearlessly
evolving writer who defied traditions and broke down cultural
barriers by writing about everyday issues people in his
homeland and in other cultures considered taboos. Female
Genital Mutilation, FGM which is a culturally sensitive issue
in Liberia and many African societies was one of Stanley's
focuses—he hated seeing the scars in the vaginas of local
women he has had sexual encounter with as well as hearing
stories about how uneducated women only referred to as Zoes
were destroying young girls' sexual organs by severing off
their clitoris and Labia Minora with crude knives and other
forms of cutting instruments only with the intent of lowering
the victim's sexual appetite. From his research and what one
of his cousins, Nyempu told him about her experience in the
secret sect which is often referred to in Liberia and Sierra
Leone as Sandy Bush, he knew this practice complicated
childbirth for many of these women who underwent the cruel
and in humane practice of FGM. He and other local women's
rights advocates had been on the frontlines in campaiging
to stop this ancient practice in Liberia, Sierra Leone and
elsewhere on the dark African continent, but they often
meet stiffed resistance from people in government and in the
community.

Stanley cried the day his cousin, Nyempu who was
from his mother side of his family narrated her experience
during her genital mutilation exercise several decades back.
*"The pain was so much, especially when I saw my own aunty
who had raised me helped the other women to pin me on
the dirty ground as the ugly old lady cut pieces of my vagina
away,"* Stanley recalls his cousin's words. *"I could hear her
rhythmically cutting away pieces of my flesh with that dull knife
which she had used on other girls before my turn came for my
untouched vagina to be destroyed. Oh, it hurt so much, cousin,
Stanley. I could feel my blood running down my legs as the old*

lady cut away my clitoris and then my labia. The pain was so great that I was only praying for it to stop but it seemed like it took forever before I could be set free from the women's strong restraints. I still get nightmares from that terror 35 years later. That day, I cried for my aunt to save me from those women, but she instead helped to hold me down and told the Zoe to continue with her work. FGM has brought an everlasting division between the only woman who I once called 'mommy' because of her adherence to a stupid tradition that only lowers a girl's self-esteem instead of boosting it," Stanley recalled. For Stanley, he believes that a long-held tradition that does not advance human development or social mobility needs not to be practiced at all. He and other rights advocates wanted to have the practice of FGM bastardized and outlawed through legislation with the help of local politicians, but they were up against a force that has reigned for millenniums in an Africa that is somehow evolving technologically, but selective in its embracement of modernity. Many of its leaders are lip serving only to get voted into political offices by their victims.

With all the successes and accolades Stanley enjoyed, the one thing that was evident in his own life was his lonely state. Like the city of Monrovia that was once known as the greatest and most radiant city in Africa back in the 19th Century, but was now in a lonely, depressive and dilapidated state, Stanley felt lonely and somehow unhappy. He could also relate to the fate of his beloved city whom smile had disappeared by the passage of time and the actions of her sons and daughters. He felt alone in a city with more than a million people. It seemed like the divorce and the death of his former wife, along with the government's continuous harassments of him had thrown everything life had in its bosom at him. For these reasons, Stanley became a man 'Without'. Though he had over two hundred and fifty thousand followers within his own country, yet he lived a life of a loner. He was often in the midst of people, but no one was there for him or understood the man, Stanley Kla Nimely outside of the books he wrote. As a result, he was suffering in comfort; he felt alone while in the company of thousands. This is the kind of aloneness and lonely state many depressed and mentally ill people all over the world experience on a daily basis—being in a throng of thousands and in a world of billions, but without having anyone to care for you or anyone to call your true friend.

On the contrary, Stanley Nimely was not really a depressed writer, he felt lonely for the fact that he wanted to have someone to call his own—he wanted that special person to not only share his bed and wealth with. Rather, he wanted someone he could befriend and cherish just as he had done with his now deceased ex-wife, Taisue Morris. Like the city of Monrovia that now lies in a depressed and dilapidated state and needs a true partner who can restore her fading glory, Stanley too wants a partner who will learn about him and will get used to his temperament, and not to be judgmental of him for his line of work. He longs for a partner who will respect his true passion for life—writing sensual romance and politically incorrect books for a living. For the past three years, the city he calls home, and the only place that makes him enjoy all that he has become became unlivable for him due to government's persecution—the government wanted to silence him for exposing systemic corruption and the government's incompetence in fighting briberies, corruptions and financial thieveries that were being orchestrated by appointed officials right under the nose of the president. Due to the harassments, he turned to a life of a bohemian—spending most of his time travelling around the world and making new friends in strange places like the Islands of Micronesia, Solomon Island, Polynesia, Lesotho, Cape of Good Hope, Mongolia, and in dozens other faraway and exotic places around the world.

Now a single man back on the dating scene, and having gotten the entire country's attention after defeating the government in a lawsuit brought against him by the state and some civic rights groups, Stanley struggled to find inner peace and the perfect woman who would take him as he is, as well as finding his true voice in order to complete his new political romance novel which he thinks would become an instant best seller upon publication. For more than four months, he had experienced a writer's block on this new novel which he'd loosely titled, 'The Black Mamba: A Secret Weapon of The Black Man'. As he sat at his home office computer desk that early afternoon thinking about his pending blind date that had been arranged by one of his friend's, something suddenly clicked within his brain, he finally found his voice as ideas for the story begun to pour out of him like a broken waterpipe.

...It was a sweltering summer night in Monrovia, the small historic oceanfront city on the West African Coast that had successfully defected the world's deadliest Ebola Virus Disease that killed thousands of people more than three year earlier. Following the end of the outbreak, many people living in the city are now taking the necessary safety measures in preventing another viral infection by not making personal contact with strangers and by constantly washing their hands with disinfectants. During the outbreak, it was difficult to control many of the city's youthful residents' socializing or clubbing habits. For loners and other pleasure seekers like Tony, Ebola could not prevent them from having a good time in a beer joint or in a crowded nightclub. With his arm resting on the bar's countertop, Tony gave Elizabeth one of his lustful smoldering glances, the kind that kept her and her silver bullet-vibrator company when she was alone in bed at night, lustfully dreaming of him. As far as Elizabeth knew, Tony was the most handsome man she had ever met within the city of Monrovia—he had the height to go with his masculinity and his boyish look. After four and a half years of platonic friendship, after a painful decade of hearing about every voluptuous and apple-bottom shaped woman who had passed in and out of Tony's bed, Elizabeth

*knew it was time for things to change. Her version of change
was not the kind one often heard being preached at political
rallies by sugar-coated tongues politicians or even the former
President of the United States of America, Barack Obama. It
is the kind of bold and radical romantic change a woman with
years of crush on a man is able to make by mustering up the
courage within her to tell that man how she felt about him
and how badly she wanted him. But again, in hypocritically
cultures influenced Africa which Liberia is an integral part of,
it is difficult for a self-serving woman to tell a man how much
she loves him when there exists no relationship between them.
People in Monrovia and many backward African societies often
frowned on such a behavior; and this behavior is often regarded
as immoral westerners' culture. For Elizabeth, it didn't matter
what the world would think of her? As she normally tells her
close friends, "The President of Liberia and the President of the
United States, both get their grooves on every now and then".*

*Maybe her new confidence came from the three shots
of Hennessy, mixed with the 8 PM Indian Royal Whisky
she'd already gulped down. Maybe it was because they were
celebrating her promotion to Senior Loan Manager at Ecobank's
Headquarters in Monrovia, and she was giddy with her
newfound power. Whatever the reason was, Elizabeth Mason
simply didn't care about anything else in the world tonight, outside
of the promise she read in Tony's deep penetrating brown eyes.*

*Like a dirty-minded and sexually active high school girl, she
was uncrossing her long, fishnet stockings covered supple legs,
and then re-crossing them slowly for impact. She scooted to the
edge of her barstool and leaned in close to Tony in the steamy
bar. Keeping her eyes trained on his lips, she found the courage
hiding deep within herself and said, "If I have to look at your
juicy lips for one more second without tasting them, I think I'm
going to go crazy." A tingle of urge for him shot through her body
like a thunderbolt as dirty thoughts of slutty quickie sex clouded
her mind. If there were any second thought of her female pride*

preserving warning left in the further reaches of her conscience, that too might had been thrown out of the window of her mind and replaced with her feminine lust and the urge for Tony, the only man in the whole world she wanted to bed so badly.

Tony's eyes didn't widen in shock. He didn't faltered, and he didn't make things any easier for her by leaning in to kiss her like he normally does with women who come at him like Elizabeth had just done. Instead, he raised an eyebrow, puckered his luscious lips slightly in a half-smile, and said, "Prove it. Prove how badly you want to taste them like Joyce Johnson did to Charles G. Taylor in Congo Town."

The heat between Elizabeth's legs increased several degrees and her nipples grew hard beneath her sexy silk top. For once in her life it was time to feel, not think. She was one of the lucky people who was never affected by the Ebola Virus Disease that killed thousands of people in Liberia, Sierra Leon and Guinea. Elizabeth stole a quick look around at people in the hot bar before leaning forward until she was so close she could feel his breath on her lips, she reached up with her thumb and gently stroked Tony's bottom lip. A shiver ran through her, and she felt as if her nipples were going to break through the fine silk of her bra and top. She wondered if anyone else in the bar had noticed how incredibly turned on she was, but she forced the thought aside. She wasn't going to ruin her one chance at seducing the only man she'd ever loved because of what some strangers thought about her. In fact, she always remembers the words of her late mother whenever she tried to suppress her emotions for the opposite sex, "No matter what you do, be it good or bad, people will still talk about you. Therefore, live your life without any apology, my child."

She had imagined feeling his lips on her breasts so many times, just touching them with her fingers was almost enough to make her spontaneously come in her seat. His lips were almost soft to the touch, and she wanted to explore every square millimeter of skin, from the corner where his upper and lower lips met so exquisitely, to the incredibly sexy, yet masculine bow in the middle of his upper lip. Oh, how she had fervently said many secret prayers to God for a moment like this. For an answered prayer or perhaps, by a stroke of luck, she has decided to make the maximum use of the once in a lifetime opportunity God or maybe fate has given her tonight.

Part of her wanted to go as slow as possible, to savor the sensations already washing through her in waves. The other part of her, the part that made her vagina lips drenched and her nipples hot like fire, wanted nothing more than to straddle Tony, right then and there at the bar, to sink down on his manhood one inch at a time until she was on the edge of the best orgasm of her life. Women in Monrovia and the Diaspora that have had sexual intercourse with Tony Kromah had nicknamed him, 'The Black Mamba'. He was one of those few Liberian men that were well endowed. His peers called him, "God's Gift', for they believed God had blessed him with an extra large third leg that made women to flock on him like bees on honey. But for Tony, he was always modest and dismissive about his look and his natural ability to sexually please a woman's desire and her every fantasy. Whenever a friend brought up his penis size and gigolo behavior, he would aptly brush the topic aside with statements like, "For many females, size doesn't really matter. It is how you treat a woman that's what matters, and not how massive one's manhood is or how much money you have in your bank account to throw at her. I think women should be treated like a precious stone or a special wine glass forged from the finest sand mined out of the heart of the Earth which needs to be protected from breaking." Tony believes it is not only a big penis that satisfies a female. Rather, it is how the monster is used to bring that female to the biggest orgasm of her life. During one of those awkward conversations, Tony once told a friend of his that even a guy's tongue and his pinky finger can satisfy a female's sexual appetite. That is, with a soft and tender tongue movement around a female's clitoris along with a good rhythmical finger thrusting in and out of the vagina, a female can be brought to a massive orgasm better than any man can imagine.

Lighter than a feather, Tony darted his tongue against her thumb. Elizabeth groaned, practically in sweet pain, her need for him was so great. Grasping her wrist with his strong, warm hands, he held the fleshy part of her palm up to his mouth and nipped at her sensitive skin. Elizabeth was shaking now and hornier than she'd ever been. Her womanhood was soaked wet with her own juices, all without one single kiss. But then again, just thinking of Tony had always been enough to bring her right to the brink of orgasm.

She was so caught up in her need, she barely heard Tony whisper, "Taste me." Trying to break out of her fog, she moved to obey his command as quickly as she could, just as Jewel once did for her now imprisoned husband. Closing the distance between them, taking his breath as her own, she licked at the middle of his lower lip with the tip of her tongue, the same place she had already memorized with her thumb. Tony winced with pleasure—he smile and stole a quick look at people around the room. He didn't want inquisitive people in the bar knowing about he and Elizabeth. Monrovia being the small city it is, everybody knows everybody. There is a cliché in Monrovia that everyone is having sex with everyone. And gossip is a way of life in and around Liberia. Often, people talk things before they can even think about the implications thereof. As a result, Tony did not want to send out the wrong signal to the wrong people in the hot club. Caution has been one of his guiding principles. Though he was not morally straight, but he was a man of class and taste. Elizabeth was just one of those females who did not actually cross his mind at night or while under his shower beating off himself, but he wouldn't hesitate an encounter with the career banker.

"What flavor Am I?" Tony asked her, again so softly she

could barely make out his words.

Her head was spinning and she could hardly speak. "I need another sample, another taste", she said almost whisperingly, and captured his incredible mouth in hers, tasting every inch of him, relishing in the feel of his tongue against hers. In her wildest dreams, she never knew a kiss could be so hot and so sweet. She'd give up her vibrator forever for a lifetime supply of kisses from Tony. God knew, if he kept it up, she was going to be moaning so loud everyone in the newly constructed Sky Bar in the Murex Plaza on 10th Street Tubman Boulevard would be forced to stop their conversations to watch the live sex show happening right in front of them.

Tony pulled away from her and threw a $20 bill on the bar for the bartender. Before the bartender could tell him about his change, he said, "Keep the change, I have work to do." Grabbing her hand, he pulled her off the seat and almost dragged her through the teeming crowd toward the elevator. Her skin was so inflamed in a sensual hype such that, every time her nipples rubbed up against some stranger she had to bite her lower lip to keep her from crying out. In the back of her mind, she wondered if she should be embarrassed that she was feeling so incredibly sexual for a man who has slept with more than eight dozen other women in a city of more than one million people, three quarters of whom were beautiful and exotic women of varying ages, sizes and shapes.

No, she told herself. I'm going to take tonight as far as it can go. Tomorrow I'll go back to being the straight-laced banker many Liberians and the world think I am. Sometimes in life, one may not have a second chance to get what they've longed awaited. Tonight, I'm a sex goddess and no turning back!

Tony got them down the stairs and out the front door in record time and into the balmy December summer night ocean air. He led them toward the beach side of 10th Street. Within seconds, the damp sea breeze made Elizabeth's silk top cling to her like a second skin. Tony promptly directed them down the nearest alley toward the back of the plaza, nearly running in haste. The swelling that was now forming in his pants was evident of his desires for her, though she hasn't been a figment of his sexual imagination like many of his Liberian and foreign sex-mates were. He wanted to quickly have his immediate urge and need met without hindrance. Loss in the moment, his heart raced faster and faster as more blood pumped into his corpus— the sacks within the penis walls the hold the blood that causes erection in men.

Elizabeth was breathing hard, but not from their quick paces. She knew what was about to happen, and on the verge of every single one of her dreams coming true. She was working hard not to hyperventilate in fervent expectation of what was about to happen under the clothes of darkness. Turning down another alley, this one even darker due to the shadow cast on nearby buildings by the plaza along with flower bushes, this alley was narrower than the first. Tony stopped abruptly and pushed her against the cool cement brick wall. Reaching his hands under her shirt, he cupped her full, high breasts and squeezed her nipples while he leaned his head down to devour the pulse of her neck with his mouth and teeth. Deep down within him, he knew what was about to happen in the dark alley behind the plaza would cause an embarrassment if they're caught—but again, he was at the point of no-return. As careful as he is, he was now surrendering his moral judgment to his immediate desire. Like the popular Liberian proverb that says, "Enjoy now and worry later—eat sweet and forget about toothache." He was going to enjoy the best few minutes he had at hand and then worry about whatever ramification that would follow if they are caught in the act.

"Anthony," she moaned, wrapping one of her long legs around him, trying to pull him in closer to her. She pleaded, "Fuck me now, I can't wait another second. Please fuck meeeee!"

He reached down to her short skirt and pulled the hem up to her hips. His hands searched for her panties to take them off, but all he found were moist, brown lips, readier for him than they had ever been. Tony heart skipped several beats as his finger slipped deep inside Elizabeth's wet vagina.

"You're not wearing any panties," he growled into her mouth, consuming her lips once again as he slid two fingers deeper into her wet and juicy slit. "You're so wet," he said reverently against her lips, the bulge in his pants growing even huger against her thigh.

Elizabeth grounded her hips into his hand, on the verge of exploding, and began to scream as an orgasm ripped through her. Tony covered her mouth with his, taking in her scream, muting it with his tongue so no one hears her. For he was aware that the night does have ears and gossips were the main career for the idle minded and the unemployed in Monrovia and many parts of Liberia.

As wave after wave or orgasms coursed through her, Tony unzipped his pants and pulled out his massive thirteen-inch manhood. Wrapping her right hand around it, she was amazed at the mere size of the meat she was holding in her hand which was about to split her vagina wide open like the Ancient of Days did to the Red Sea during the Exodus of His children out of Egypt. "Wow, your dick is very big, Tony," she declared. Tony's legend is really true. This Mandingo man is a woman's filler, she thought. Tony said, "I want you to guide me into you. Every single inch." Tony's words made her wetter as she moved the tip of Tony's massive pipe against her drenching wet pussy lips and clitoris in order to get the head wet for ease of penetration. The sensation from the rubbing and moving made Tony to get harder as his dick grew few inches longer in length and girth.

Elizabeth's eyes widened. Though she has heard of Tony's massiveness, but she did not know his length extended more *than she had ever imagined. She always suspected he was big, but even in her wildest imagination she couldn't have come up with his exact length and width. His dick was thirteen inches long and three inches across in diameter. Her dildo wasn't even this big and for a brief second, she worried that she wouldn't be able to take all of him inside or even if she could manage, she would not be able to walk like she normally does. But again, she was not letting size to dissuade her of enjoying something she had craved for many years to have. In fact, a good sex is a combination of pains and pleasures, she thought. With Tony Kromah, she would settled for both and nothing else.*

Tony must have sensed her reluctance, because he said, "Don't worry, baby. You're so wet this bad boy is going to slide right in without you even feeling an ounce of pain." In most parts of the African Continent, Monrovia included, women love good sex, but unlike women in the West, many of the African women ignorantly fear big dick—they do not know the pleasures and pains a big dick brings during sexual intercourse. "Ok, Tony. You can have me. I'm all yours tonight," she moaned and kissed his exposed chest.

Grabbing her ass with his hands, he added, "Wrap your legs around me." Doing just that, suspended her in midair, she positioned the tip of his now wet dick at the entrance to her pussy lips. Waiting for barely a second, wanting to remember the sensation of his huge penis entering her for the first time, she slid his head around on her lips, on her swollen clit, until his dick was drenched with her pussy juices. She could tell he wanted to plunge himself into her as hard and fast as he could, and she admired his self-restraint and the way he let her pace their lovemaking in the dark corner.

Slowly, painstakingly, Elizabeth slid the first three inches of him inside of her, and as the walls of her vagina stretched to accommodate his incoming monstrous trunk, she felt herself on the verge of another orgasm. Trying to contain her need, she slid in another inch and felt herself slipping and sliding along Tony's skin. Drenched in sweat, Tony managed to keep his hold on her, holding her up against the wall, poised on his dick as if she weighed no more than a feather. It was more than a moment of truth—he had to live up to the tale the many women he had been with told about him. For Anthony Kromah, a good love-maker does not have a second chance to make a first impression—he has to pleasure himself as well as the woman he's making love to. He was about to give Elizabeth the best fuck of her life.

Unable to wait another second, she allowed gravity to pull her down and she fed the last nine inches of his powerful dick into her moist and drenching wet pussy. Nothing had ever felt so good to her in her whole life and she fell into quick spasm and the third biggest orgasm she'd ever had as Tony squeezed her ass cheeks while lifting her up and down, sliding his massive dick in and out of her with powerful thrust after thrust like a heavyweight boxer in the biggest fight of his career.

Pulling his head back to look deep into her eyes in the dark alley, he said, "I've always loved you though we're worlds apart," and then pumped hard into her, all the way to the hilt, rocking back and forth rapidly as he shot his warm load of come deep inside of her. Elizabeth went straight from three orgasms into four and then five, as her heart was filled with the biggest and deepest joy she'd ever known.

All the while this action was going on between Tony and Elizabeth, unknowingly to them, their voices had attracted three local thieves that had gone to a nearby house to rob its occupants. Knowing how easy and soft a target Tony and Elizabeth were, the thieves hid themselves behind a nearby shrub until Tony and Elizabeth could finish what they had gone into the dark alley to do. When the two horny birds were done making love and were lying against the cool wall of the parameter fence, a grouchy male voice, who happened to be the leader of the robbers broke the silence in the dark, "You two stay right there and turn your faces to the damn wall." He pointed a rusty AK 47 in Tony's face before reaching into his pocket for his wallet and his expensive wristwatch was then snatched off his hand by a second raggedy looking robber. The other thieve armed with a large double-edges machete quickly snatched Elizabeth's Michael Kors hand bag containing cash, cell phone, and other personal effects. "Please don't hurt us, please… please," Elizabeth yelled with her hands covering her mouth. "Shut up, woman! Keep your face to the damn wall," the leader of the robbers said as they disappeared in the dark, just as they had appeared. Frantic about what had just occurred, Elizabeth screamed, "Oh my God, we had just been robbed, Tony……

Stanley saved the updated file on his computer's hard drive and rubbed the tired muscles on the back of his neck with his right hand. *"Too bad real life can't be like my books,"* he muttered, trying to remember when the last time was since he returned home after the Ebola virus epidemic ended more than three years ago, he'd actually had a good romantic sex with someone he truly loves. If Stanley had told any female, that he hasn't had sex for more than eleven months, three weeks, four days, and fourteen hours, they would not believe him. Like his led character, Anthony Kromah, he was writing about, he was most females' fantasy. He was highly successful as a writer, he owned a beautiful home in the Paynesville suburb of Monrovia, he was good looking, a six-footer, owns a fleet of luxury cars including BMW, Mercedes Benz, Porsche, and others. Above all, he was rich according to Liberians and many Africans living standards. But on the female front, he was not successful. He was not lucky to find a woman of his taste since his divorce from his late beautiful ex-wife. He had been on a female search ever since the divorce proceeding ended.

"That's another ancient history," he grunted as he got up from his home office chair and headed into the shower. He

had another blind date that late evening, but he didn't have any higher hopes for that one than the multitude of other dates he'd been on in the past three and a half years just before the Ebola virus outbreak met him out of the country which killed thousands of people in the country. He met the woman in question on Facebook through the suggestion of his friend, Sean Edmond Cheeks more than two months ago. Adhering to government's warning, he'd avoided physical contacts with females since returning home from Paris in the aftermath of the worse Ebola viral epidemic in modern human history. He also avoided the Ebola orphans that lived behind his beautiful. The two abandoned children's story were a part of the larger Monrovia's narrative, though he hated seeing how the 12-year-old orphan boy struggled to care for his five-year-old brother. For now, his focus was himself and his blind date.

In fact, he was not too sure if he would take his date to another level if he ever got lucky tonight. Also, he wouldn't be surprised if all of the single women in Monrovia had been spreading the word of his pickiness, to warn each other off, in a show of females' solidarity which may be viewed by single Monrovia men as a conspiracy against single men. Many of the women thought they were not in his league due to how Stanley had been selective about the women he goes out in public with. He had traveled all over the world including the Far East and Near East, the Middle East, Asia, the United States, Europe and many African countries on vacations, but had not been lucky to have found the woman of his taste and dream.

As Stanley showered in preparation for his date that evening, he let the scalding stream of hot water pulsate against his hairy chest as he tried to shake off his depression. *"She's out there. I know she's out there somewhere. It is just a matter of being in the right place and at the right time. I'm not giving up on love, and I know love has not given up on me either,"* he said aloud, his words reverberating against the tiled shower walls.

Drying off and dressing quickly in a blue jean and a white polo shirt, he slipped on his solid-platinum Movado watch and grabbed his wallet and keys to one of his seven cars and ran out the front door.

Carefully driving through the anxious crowds at the ELWA Junction section of Paynesville, many of whom were passengers flagging down commercial cars to take them home to their various home. While driving in the slowed moving traffic, Stanley noticed a low-level thief stealing the gas cap cover off the SUV driven by a senator from Grand Cape Mount County who was also a big-time lawyer in the city. Flabbergasted by the thief's brazen act, he drove slowly behind the thief and the vehicle. Finally catching up with the thief who was about to disappear within the busy crowd, Stanley signaled to him so he could come over to his car.

"Why did you do that?" Stanley asked the drugged-up looking young thief.

"Why did I do what, Bra Bee?" the young man asked in replied with a question of his own.

"I just saw you breaking the gas cap cover from that senator's SUV," Stanley replied.

"Big Brother, those are the people that got us suffering in this country. They're stealing all the government's money and making us to suffer like Hebrew Slaves," the thief retorted.

"But if you steal from him, it is going to give him the courage to keep on stealing the money that should be used for the development of his country and for you as well," Stanley said as he locked a deep penetrating look at the thief.

"Papay…..I am really hungry. I took this thing to sell it to the Nigerian guys that are selling car parts down there. I need to survive too, Big Brother," He said in an honest tone.

"Okay, let's stop the blame games and get straight to business. How much do you want for it," Stanley asked to the

thief's disbelief?

"Anything, I will take anything you give me Bra Bee, I am begging you. I just need to buy something to eat, and to buy my baby's rubber draws," The thief replied, almost apologetically.

"Okay, fair enough. I will give you $10.00 for it," Stanley offered.

"That one is plenty for me, Big Brother. I thank you plenty," the thief said as he reached into his pocket to hand the gas cap cover to Stanley after seeing him pull out a crisp $10.00 note from this pocket.

"You need to stop this behavior and try to find something to do, my son," Stanley grabbed the gas cap cover from the thief and drove in the direction he and the senator were headed. After several failed attempts in flagging down the proud senator's SUV, he quickly overtook the honorable vehicle and pullout the gas cover after rolling down his window. Halfway past former Liberian President Charles Taylor's resident, Stanley pullover and the senator pullup right behind his car. A young man dressed in a police uniform disembarked from the rear passenger door and walked over to Stanley's parked vehicle.

"How can we help you," the office asked.

"I think this is from your car. Someone just tried to steal it from the vehicle," Stanley replied as he handed the gas cap to the policeman.

"Oh....wow," the officer said with a surprisingly look on his face. Hee quickly snatched the gas cap cover from Stanley left hand and quickly walked back to the waiting SUV without thanking Stanley for his kind gesture.

"At least a thank you would have been better," Stanley said after the policeman before driving off to meet his blind date.

Stanley could not believe how quickly his beloved city had bounced back almost one year after the Ebola epidemic that killed thousands of people in Monrovia alone. He noticed that the people were mostly in jubilant moods—many of the pedestrians he drove past on the side of the road wore big smiles on their faces. Everything about Monrovia was appealing to Stanley, but the one thing he hated was the garbage that were now overtaking the city. Few years earlier, the city was sparkling clean during the leadership of the most controversial City Mayors Monrovia had ever had since it was renamed from Christopolis to Monrovia in 1824. He was a strong supporter of the Mayor, Mary T. Broh who was forced out of office for enforcing straighter city ordinances. Her aggressive actions in transforming the city from being a garbage dump to a vibrant one had angered many of the politicians who represented underdeveloped counties and cities around the country.

As he drove to his blind date that early evening, he was worried that he would be late because of the heavy traffic congestion he encountered earlier at the ELWA Junction in Paynesville after his encounter with the gas cap cover thief. Stanley is one of the few Liberian men that respected and had value for time as a scarce commodity. He believes time and money were two conjoin twin brothers from the same parents and that one could not live without the other. Maybe it was because of his American upbringing—he completed Hightstown High School in East Windsor, New Jersey where he began his writing career. Like his father, he also graduated from Princeton University in Princeton, New Jersey with a degree in Creative Writing and Classical English. After beating the evening traffic At ELWA Junction and SKD Boulevard, he came into two more traffic congestions one at the Nigerian Embassy in Congo Town. The second traffic was about two miles long—it went back as far as Catholic Hospital all the way pas Lonestar Cell MTN and Club Gossip. After beating the last traffic congestions, he made a hard left turn by VAMOMA House onto Airfield New Road. Right on time, he pulled into the parking lot at PA's Rib House in Airfield, Sinkor. As he walked through the glass door leading into the restaurant, he was pleased when he saw the cute brown-skin lady sitting alone at a corner table by the window of the newly constructed fast food restaurant. He walked into the restaurant and directly up to his date and held out his right hand in greeting.

"Hi. I'm Stanley, Stanley Nimely. Are you Theresa Urey?"

The beautiful lady nodded happily. *"I sure am,"* she drawled in a beautiful light Nigerian accent. She smiles faintly letting out a pair of perfect pearl white teeth beneath a black gum line. Stanley forced a quick smile at the beautiful creature in front of him as thousands of thoughts raced through his mind. Due to government's prohibition on handshakes in the country which was largely due to the past Ebola epidemic that killed thousands, they didn't mind to risk a friendly handshake followed by a beautiful exchange of friendly of smiles.

After pulling out a chair at the opposite end of the table, they ordered the first round of red Naufragar wine and chatted as they sipped their drinks, beginning the process of getting to know each other better. Stanley could tell that Theresa liked what she'd seen so far. He too somehow liked what he'd seen, especially her pair of queen-size breasts with her nipples rubbing against her tan shirt. She wasn't so bad herself, and he hoped that she would be more open-minded than the last fifty something women he'd dated since his divorce. One thing was clear with Theresa Urey though, she was not the drop-dead gorgeously beautiful type Stanley would fight to please and keep beyond the first two dates. On the other hand, she had something Stanley could work with, big ass and full breasts. Stanley was more of an ass man, as he often jokingly calls himself. He thought she needed a bit more refining if he ever wanted to keep her as a partner. *"A wife!?.....*

Hell no!" he thought to himself.

"*So,*" she asked coyly, "*what do you do all day? Your friend Sean who suggested I befriend you on Facebook didn't tell me much about your line of work. Is it some kind of top secret job that you do? Are you spying for the CIA here in Liberia?*" she asked hopefully, all the while eyeing the platinum band of his watch, taking in the expensive Ralph Lauren label on his polo shirt, and the faded leather of his $500 Italian loafers on his feet. Stanley has great taste when it comes to clothes and some times, women. It was odd that he could not find the perfect woman of his dream being a familiar face locally as well as internationally.

Stanley smiled engagingly. "*But my Facebook profile says it all,*" He let out another gorgeous smile before continuing to speak "*I'm a writer.*" His thought was that Sean, who highly respected his controversial line of work, didn't bother telling the beautiful woman what Stanley did for a living. Sean might have left out the details so he could fill her in with them. Sean is one of those friends who admired and highly respected Stanley. Both men have been friends for more than thirty years. Only that Sean had been married for more than twenty years with two beautiful daughters.

"*Ooohhh....wow,*" she said expectantly. "*How exciting. What do you write? Christian books? How To? Mysteries? Actions?*"...... "*Sports? or political news?*"

"*Actually,*" he said, striving for a confident tone, "*I write sensual romance novel. The kinds of books that awaken a person's sexual appetites and romantic emotions. These are the types of books that put back sparks into people's dying relationship and keep the bedroom warm and steamy for lovers and for all those who have never given up on love.*"

"*Wow!*" Theresa said almost unbelievable to Stanley as she stared around the restaurant to see if anyone was listening to their conversation. The silence was deafening. Not bothering to hide her sneer, his blind date said, *"You're a porno writer? You know God hates that kind of writing, right? Also, you could be arrested for these types of books, knowing full well that Liberia is on a path of becoming the first Christian nation in all of Africa—."*

"I can explain it better, maybe you don't understand," Stanley interrupted his date, but before he could continue, she interjected.

"I don't even want to hear any lamed explanation for something this immoral. Do you even go to church? Do you even know that God destroyed a whole city because of immoralities? Remember, Africa is not like America where everything is possible and anything is accepted, Jack!" Theresa said frankly.

Stanley cleared his throat. *"No, I write politically sensual romance novels. Women make up 75% of my reading audience. It's really quite—"*

Before he could get another word out, his date stood up, and said, *"You pervert! You need Jesus Christ and His plan of salvation for your life,"* and splashed her entire glass of ice water in his face. Then she grabbed her purse and stomped out the door on her seven-inch stiletto heels pump shoes with her big cocked-ass wiggling under her knee-length flowery dress in outrage all the way down the parking lot toward her old beat up 1994 red Honda Civic.

"Damn! That's the problem with you 100% Nigerian women. You all damn well take things out of context. Damnnnnn!?" he yelled out after her as he forces a disappointing smile, perhaps at himself. People from nearby tables stared at him embarrassingly. Since rumors were people's breakfast, lunch, and dinner in Monrovia, Stanley knew that the news would soon spread out of proportion in this close-knit city.

Stanley quickly wiped the shards of ice off his face and

chest, while few of the guests and the wait staff's supervisor, Eva Wallace, who was a personal friend of his, openly laughed at him. Embarrassed and stupefied, Stanley laughed right back at the people within the room.

"Wow. That's a first since I've been this dating business," he muttered to himself as he stood up and headed for his car after paying for their ill-fated first date drinks. Usually many of his blind dates were satisfied with looking scandalized and making flimsy excuses about getting home early because their great grandfather or babysitter which never exists in many quarters in Liberian society called with an emergency. At the very least, he had to give Theresa points for originality. She was out of his lead—he never would've considered her for a blind date had Sean told him about her religious views—a Pentecostal church going, Heavenly tongue speaking, and Holy Ghost filled woman. Many of whom think God Himself will send the man from their prayers directly from Heaven straight into their laps or into their bedrooms for marriage. Due to this stupid and foolish supernatural miracle seeking notion, many young men and women do church hopping in a bid to find the right man or woman after God's heart without giving destiny a chance to do its work. Due to this anti-modern belief, his beloved city, Monrovia has gotten her share of the proliferations of Nigerian-based miracle working, Holy Ghost filled, and tongue speaking churches all over the city within the last ten years. During the Ebola virus outbreak, some of these churches were accused of trying to pray for the healing of Ebola infected people at the height of the viral onslaught. For Stanley, Theresa, like many of the women before her, she was a bad karma—he was never lucky with women who did not understand his line of work. He had decided against doing what everyone was doing in religious craze Liberia, seeking miracles by going to churches to find a woman or man to marry. It was not his fault that Theresa disrespected him; he thought she was probably brought up

in one of those straight-jacketed African religious household and was doing all she could do to keep her religious virtue. Or perhaps, she was not exposed or even well read to understand the diversity and complexities of human being in regards to how globalized our world has become. One fact worth considering is that technology has dramatically changed the world, this included Monrovia and some of the remotest places in Africa and around the world.

As he drove off the restaurant's parking lot to head back home, he tried blaming himself for failing to know more about Theresa instead of being excited about her physical structure—small in the waistline and big at the bottom. He remembers the writing on her Facebook wall that said, 'The God of Bishop Oyedepo is My God'. After putting one and two thoughts together, Stanley realized the Bishop was the founder of Winners Chapel International Church which is headquartered in Nigeria with many satellite branches in Monrovia and all over the world. It is the same religious-craze church that caused him his marriage. Realizing the insanity and absurdity of his situation, he frustratingly pressed hard on the gas pedal of the vehicle that caused it to almost speed out of control. "It's all my fault. I shouldn't have even gone out on a date with such a person had I know more about her. She's not open minded and not my first choice for a partner anyway. Her tunnel vision will not get her anywhere, not even closer to finding a date or as a spouse anyway." He hissed as he brought the out of control car under control. Upon reaching Oldest Congo Town, he stopped by Musu's Business Center, formerly called Musu's Spot to chill out for the rest of the evening.

No matter how hard he tried to frame the situation, he was sure of one thing: he wasn't getting any closer to finding the woman of his tastes. One thing was evident in his quest for a partner—nothing was going to stop him from finding that special woman of his dream and his wishes for a happy life. Not even a cold glass of water thrown at him within a crowded restaurant with laughing bystanders could stop him, nor an Ebola virus outbreak that have cause many single women to be cautious when in the proximity of a strange man. Holding his favorite cold bottle of Club Beer in his hand while sitting alone at a corner table at the entertainment center, he finally said, *"I will not leave my fate in destiny's hands, I will find her no matter what, when, where and how. I will find her! She's out there somewhere waiting for me, just like Monrovia is waiting for the right son or daughter to rescue her from her deplorable state."*

Ironically, sex has become one of the cheapest commodities in Liberia and many of the surrounding neighboring countries. Often, government official, businessmen and women and other wealthy Liberians took advantage of the economic situation of poor young girls and boys and sexually exploited them of their youthfulness. Sex tourists and other vacationers looking for cheap sex would sometimes pick up a girl or a boy as young as 13 or 15 years of age at local nightclub or off the streets and took them home or to a local motel for their sexual pleasure. As part of the underground sex trade that is going on in Monrovia, government officials and lawmakers would sometimes hire the service of financially stranded girls at their private parties and flash them with a few hundred dollars bills to entertain them and their guest with striptease and other sensually exotic African dances or twerking.

There were several incidents of sexual exploitation reported by the local media, one of which was a report of a lawmaker hiring the service of a local college student to perform topless during a private wedding ceremony. Unfair to the lawmaker, the situation went out of proportion because he had a lot of political frenemies—for striptease and threesome are common things in Monrovia. As it is, many teenagers and other sex workers charged these big shots and wealthy clients as little as $5 for a short sex time or $20 to spend the night. As for Stanley, being a man who prides himself on his reputation and morality never paid cash for sex to anyone in the thriving sex market that was an open secret in Monrovia and in many parts of country. Because of the low price of sex in Monrovia, the country has become a destination for sex tourists looking to fulfil their sexual desires and fantasies. Men and women in the Diaspora flood the country, especially Monrovia daily to engage in a threesome or foursome sex with young women or men. Many of these poor young men and women looking to make a quick cash, are sometimes infected with various types of sexually transmitted disease, or STD. No wonder HIV and AIDS and other sexually transmitted opportunistic diseases are on the rise in the Monrovia, and other parts of the country. Though the Ebola virus somehow put a temporary dent in the sex trade during the outbreak, the country has now found itself at a critical juncture with more and more young men and women flooding nightclubs with the hope of finding someone from overseas that will take them out of their miseries and hardship to a life of stability, whether in the United States of America, common known by Liberians as the Great Land of Opportunities or Europe where their lives will change forever.

CHAPTER 2

No matter how badly the situation is for most residents of Monrovia, the city still attracts people to its gates. Stanley knows the contagiousness of his beloved city. Once a person visits the city, they can never leave—their heart, body, mind, and soul would always remain in Monrovia. But again, there is something electrifyingly enigmatic about life in the city. The city has more poor people than its rich residents like Stanley and the president, along with the speaker of the House of Representative or even the President of the Liberian Senate. No matter where one traveled within the city, the people of Monrovia exhibits warm and friendly behaviors that concealed their daily struggles. Often, they would let outs such radiant smile regardless of their impoverished conditions or their rich lifestyles. Most often, people gravitated to the city in search of wealth and power, education and dreams. Unlike the United State where Stanley grew up and schooled, and where it didn't matter where one lives in order to make it in life, Monrovia is the center of everything for the small West African nation, Liberia. Most people come from faraway and nearby villages as well as from distant foreign countries to Monrovia to find gainful employment, business opportunities, wealth, presidential and legislative powers, and spouses. The overcrowding of Monrovia, has caused many of its residents to become unethical—many have become liars, thieves, self-centered, and corrupt at the expense of the city and its poor residents. Amidst all of these competing forces and sentiments, Stanley still believes that Monrovia's best days are still ahead of her as he struggles to find his own path within the city.

On the thirteenth day of the following month, Stanley Nimely who happens to be a lead mentor to a local literary writers group that meets once a month to read and critique the creative writings of its members at the We Care Library on Carey Street in Midtown Monrovia, had just recovered from another month's disastrous date with Theresa Urey, the four foot something woman who humiliated him in the restaurant. To put the whole Theresa Urey's incident behind him, he had come to sit and chitchat with some of the promising writers around Monrovia and from other parts of the country. As the premier romance author in the country, amateur writers of all ages looked up to him for guidance and support in developing their skills into a craft.

This amateur writers' event is usually sponsored by one of Liberia's leading book publishing companies, Clarke Herring Publishing, CHP. On this late evening in the reading room of the library, Stanley's attention was drawn to a particular work from one of the newest members in attendance, Ernestine Johnson. According to her profile on the group's blog, she had mainly been focused on the slowly evolving young adolescence writings market, but it was her hoped to make it in the highly competitive and critically selective global romance market. Many people on the African content have not fully embraced romance or sensual erotica books due to misinformation coupled with various religious and cultural reasons. On this night, Ernestine's story was similar to a book Stanley had published two years earlier, but he somehow loved the twist she had weaved into her storyline.

Ernestine was one of the more than ten dozen frustrated romance writers that had not made a successful break into the highly selective world of romance publishing. Reason being—people in the highly illiterate, but semi technologically advanced country did not understand the true nature of sensual erotica novel beyond its explicit contents that are often criticized by the few educated readers and religious leaders within the various community around the country. For many pundits and conservative cynics in Liberia and other places on the African continent, it was widely believed that the continent was not yet ready for erotica genres beyond what old school writers had been publishing for decades. For people like Stanley Kla Nimely, Ernestine, and the host of other emerging authors, they believe that there couldn't be a better time than now to write books the explore human sexuality and discuss sensitive subjects like teenage prostitution and pregnancy, unprotected sex that often leads to sexually transmitted infection, STI, that sometimes lead to HIV and AIDS as well as other opportunistic infections that were slowly crippling younger generation of Liberians and elsewhere across the African Continent.

After being interrupted with a *"Hi folks, I am Stanley. I am your mentor tonight"* by Stanley who was late in coming to meet members of the group that evening because of his prior engagement with other groups within the small and shabby library, Ernestine continued to read as most of her peers listened carefully. Stanley's second mild interruption of, *"…Sorry guys, I am a little late"* didn't stop Ernestine from continuing to read the story she had been perfecting for several weeks.

…..For Melvin, it had been a long way coming. He cried so bitterly for most of the time during the ceremonies at the church. Having lost both parents to the recent Ebola virus epidemic that spiraled out of control in the impoverished country, he was very sad knowing he was taking this special journey all alone. To see an only male child transition into manhood was every parent's dream to be a part of. Oh, how he wished his parents were alive to see him walk his beautiful bride down the aisle. With the day

behind him, and their guests gone, Melvin laid Fatu against the specially made Kente bed sheets and stood back to admire the way the setting sunlight drifting through the window danced off her creamy-brown skin. She was the sweetest girl in the whole world, and he'd been waiting years for this moment to arrive.

Fatu's cheeks were rosy and she nervously licked her pink, delicious lips as she stared back at Melvin. "Are you going to take your clothes off too?" she asked him innocently.

Melvin smiled and kneeled at the side of the bed between her legs, sliding her body across the Kente sheets so that his face was mere inches from her sweet vagina, the special part of her body he had wanted to see, touch and explore from the first day he saw Fatu. He didn't want to frighten her any more than she already was, but he was having a hell of a time trying to rein in his passion. He had to tame that Liberian animal within him that usually does not waste time with a vagina they have sought for a while when given the opportunity. In fact, she was his queen and he was her king.

It pleased him immeasurably to know that Fatu was still a virgin, and that she had been saving herself for him, for their wedding night. In 21st Century Monrovia which is heavily influenced by MTV, along with the Nigerians and Ghanaians movies industries, there are not that many virgins left in the city. Melvin had waited so long for this night, for her to finally grow up and come of age. Of course, even though he had spent the past several years walking away from their chaste kisses and straight into taking cold baths whenever there were any, he had been with his fair share of available and ready-to-sleep women. He always knew no matter how good the sex was with these other women, he was simply releasing pent-up steam and honing his skills for the one and only woman who really mattered. Fatu Kemokai's parents had been keeping her for Melvin Gibson. On this night, they would consummate everything that love and marriage had to offer—Fatu had been anxiously looking forward to this day, this moment, this hour, this minute and the slowly passing seconds. She was anxious as well as a little afraid of the unknown. She had read and heard scores of stories from friends of how painful a first-time sexual intercourse is. At the same time, she had heard about how memorable the first time is for a virgin whenever they make love to a person whom they are really in love with, especially if that person loves them in return.

"I am, sweetheart," he said, stroking her hand lightly with his own. "But first, I want you to experience deep pleasure. Something only you can relate to. Not your mother, not your father or even the President of Liberia who is living in the Executive Mansion or the angels that protect you and me at night and everywhere we go."

"Oooooh, I have Melvin. Your kisses alone are incredible," she sighed, trying to sit up so that she could kiss him some more.

Getting up onto one knee, he leaned toward her and captured her mouth in a passionate, scintillating kiss. "Kissing is only the beginning. There is more to kissing, my love," he said, with a big promise in his eyes.

Fatu opened her mouth into a darling "o" and blushed prettily. "Should I be doing anything?" she asked hesitantly, and Melvin was touched by how much she wanted to please him. He knew right there and then that she was born to please and love him. She was the woman of his dream, and he knew that his honest prayers to his maker had been answered.

"Oh my darling," he said, pushing his hands into her silky soft black hair. "Just lay back against those pillows and I'll do the rest. Tonight is your night and I promise to make it a memorable one that would last for a lifetime." Kissing her again lightly, he said, "And remember, there's nothing to be afraid of, because I love you so very much and this is how I want to share that eternal love with you." He whispered, using the popular jab-line often used by Monrovia boys to get into young girls panties

or under their dresses.

Fatu followed his instructions and laid back against the pillows. He ran soft kisses down her neck and got caught up in worshiping her breasts. Her breasts were unlike anything he had ever seen—for they were simply beautiful and extraordinary. A full queen-size succulent firm breast of a Liberian virgin. Just like the breast of his first love, Teemon Dennis, whom was snatched away from him and was forced to marry someone whom she really didn't love. Back then, he would toy with Teemon's bouncy and juicy breast for uncountable numbers of hours. Melvin's youthfulness and lack of experience back then, made him believe that Teemon was different from other women and he was going to do whatever it took to make her his wife. When she was snitched away from him by her now husband who is twice their ages, depression took control of him. He once contemplated suicide due to the incident. From the day he met his Fatu, it was like Heaven had send her to rescue him from his moments of despair onto an everlasting life of love and ecstasy. He had come to love her more than he had loved Teemon whom he now refers to as Pendora. Like in Greek mythology, Melvin believed Teemon was his punishment from God—for she had come and seduced him with her love and left him lonely without looking back. The one thing that she never took away from Melvin was hope or his inner god that gave him strengths to go on day after day. The experience made him to love and cherish Fatu more than anything in the world.

He marveled at the sensual picture she presented. Her nipples were rosy red and had formed into tight buds as he neared them. Even the swell of her breasts had a delicate pinkish flush, proving that she was as aroused as he was.

Fatu was most Liberian men's dream girl—smart, intelligent, and she was also a Mulatto or biracial as her kinds are referred to in the West Indies. Her father was a Swede and her mother was a Liberian. She had been raised in Robert Sport, Grand Cape Mont County by her stern maternal grandfather and grandmother. She was raise to keep her female virtue for the man who would one day marry her.

Cupping her breasts gently in his large hands, Melvin ran his thumbs over her taut nipples and blew warm air across them. Fatu gasped and he bent down to rain soft kisses all over her mounds, making sure he stayed away from the place she needed him to touch most. It wasn't until she was writhing on the bed in torment that he took pity on her and slowly took one nipple into his warmed mouth, swirling the nub with his tongue, tasting her on his lips. Like a good performer, Melvin was doing all he could do to impress his newlywed wife. He'd plan to take his own time to make this encounter count, last a lifetime or to be one of a kind that Fatu will ever remember.

At that moment, Fatu arched her back into him, pushing her breast even more deeply into his mouth and he nearly lost control of himself, more ready than ever to rip his clothes off and mount her like a Monrovia street-boy jumping into a parked taxicab for a ride home after a long day of hustle under the scorching sun. Pulling from a deeper well of control than he knew he possessed, he continued to give loving attention onto her other breast, making her moan louder with pleasure and needs.

Barely managing to pull himself away from her breasts, he nipped and kissed her flushed skin across her tight athletic belly, while running his hands up and down her quivering thighs. He slowly parted her legs and softly ran kisses in her left thigh, and then the right until he could almost feel her pleads from him to do what she thought he wanted the most. Sensing the urge that had already built within her, he relaxed his romantic assaults. His attention was soon wholly focused on the soft, wet mound before him.

Her black, curly pubic hair was wet with her juice, and her scent was intoxicating. He ran his opened hand down her stomach. Lightly, he slid his finger between her lips and then slowly into her incredibly tight vagina.

"Melvin," she moaned, her head thrashing back and forth on the bed.

"Oh baby," he said, his voice thick with lust and emotion for her. "You have the sweetest pussy in the whole world." He saw her eyes widen and slipped his finger back out, and stood up partly to kiss her again. "You're so beautiful that there is nothing I can compare you to, Fatu. Am I making you feel good? I am so lucky to have you as my wife. I want to spend the rest of my life with you, be it good or bad, in wealth or in poverty, in wellness or in sickness. You were made by God for me. I hope life will treat us kind in this marriage."

Blushing again, Fatu replied, "I've never felt like this before. Is it normal? It feels like I am dreaming or on a beautiful island with a big waterfall. Just like the one in Bong County, in Kpatawe."

Melvin laughed softly and brushed the hair out of her eyes. "What we have is so amazing. It's so amazing to be love by some you're in love with. Trust me baby, I will take you all the way to the sky up above," he added, "and I'll take you all the way beyond your Earthly imagination."

Fatu swallowed, and then said, "I do trust you, Melvin. And I know you will. I want you to please teach me everything you know about love, sex and relationship. I've come to you with my heart in my hands, and I want you to protect it more than you've been doing over the past years. You're the man that God had sent for me."

Laying her back down, he knelt between her legs again. This time, he couldn't help himself, and he leaned in and tasted her wetness with his tongue. She nearly bucked off the bed, but he held her thighs firmly with his powerful hands to keep her vagina right where he wanted it—in his mouth and in full view.

He plunged his tongue into her vagina several times before focusing on her swollen clitoris. Taking it into his mouth, he *swirled his tongue around once, slowly. Then, taking the utmost care, he swirled it again and again. At a snail's pace, he teased her clit, savoring every moment of his fantasy becoming real. He dug his long tongue several more times deep into her slippery and wet penis glove as far as it could go. Pulling it out with her juices dripping off, he tantalized her swollen clitoris several more times and gently wrapped his lips around it. After several seconds of sucking her clits, he then inserted his tongue back into her warmed, tight and wet honeycomb.*

Fatu got an out of world feeling from what Melvin was doing. She softly said, "Where did you learn to do this, Melvin? It feels so strange, but very good to me. I don't want you to stop what you're doing. Please continue."

Fatu grabbed the back of his head to push his face down harder into her mound and he knew she was on the verge of coming. He abruptly changed tactics and flicked her clit rapidly and firmly until she was crying out with his name and with joy. Within that moment, her spasms took over her body for a long while. She was now having a full female internal ejaculation without physically squirting out. This was typical of many females in this part of Africa—they exhibited their true feelings inside the bedroom and not outdoor. Their mothers often told them to act like ladies when out in the streets, but should never act like a stranger whenever they're making love to a man they truly love—that freak in them should unleashed in its full force.

Melvin stood to remove his clothes as quickly as possible. Even the mere friction of fabric rubbing against his penis was almost more than he could bear, and he wanted to divest himself of his clothes and sink himself deep and far into Fatu as quickly as was humanly possible. But again, he reminded himself that this was not his moment; rather, it was Fatu's. He had to do everything to please her, not himself. He would have enough time with her now that they have survived the deadliest Ebola outbreak that had delayed their wedding several months.

He was greatly pleased when Fatu pushed herself up into a

sitting position and began to rip off his clothes in haste. Once they had pulled off his slacks together and were taking off his boxers, she stilled as if a ghost had suddenly appeared from nowhere.

Looking up at him, she said, "I'm afraid, Melvin. Do you think that thing is going to fit inside of me?"

He cupped her face in his hands, kissing her thoroughly, getting her used to her own sweet taste from between her legs, he said, "I promise you FK, it will only hurt the first time. Only until you get used to having me inside of you, boo, boo. In fact, the pain lasts only for a few seconds and the rest is pleasure and an everlasting thrill of joy that you will never regret."

Fatu nodded and slowly reached for the waistband of his boxer, pulling it down his hips with excruciating slowness. When his monster sprang free from the boxer, she gasped.

"Oh my God, you're so huge! I don't think this is going to fit inside my nunu, Melvin," she exclaimed for a second time.

Melvin chuckled softly, thrilled that she was so impressed with his big penis. "And I'm all yours, sweetheart. It will fit right in without much pains," he said as he took her small, soft hand in his and wrapped it around his fat and rock-hard rod. This alone was scary enough for a first-timer. It was different here— she was now his wife. In fact, this is something she would have to get used to as part of her marital duties.

"Mmmm," Fatu said. "You're hard, long and big too." She ran her hand up and down his length, getting used to the feel of his manhood.

Melvin couldn't take any more teasing, so he gently pushed her back into the Kente bed sheets and pulled himself up and over her, careful not to lean too much of his weight onto her. Placing the head of his dick at the entrance to her nookie, he gently probed her wetness to get the tip of his penis moist with her juices for ease of entry.

The way Fatu was wriggling underneath him made him want to ram into her without waiting even one more second, but he wanted her first time to be perfect, so he governed his lust. Pushing in no more than an inch, then two, he heard her swift intake of breath and felt the barrier that guarded her most precious gift expand to accommodate his incoming pleasure machine.

Poised above her, gazing deeply into her eyes, he said, "I never want to hurt you again," and then forced himself to push past her barrier, until he was practically touching her womb. She cried out softly in pain, but within moments, he knew her virgin's muscles had adjusted to the size and feel of him as she began to rock her hips back and forth, left and right in an age-old rhythm of love and ecstasy.

Her body eagerly swallowed his dick and Melvin lost all control, pumping hard and fast into her. Beneath him, Fatu met every powerful thrust and together they cried out in a magical simultaneous orgasm. "Oh, oh, oh, oh, oooooohhhhhhhh, shiiiiii iiiiiiittttttttttttttttt!"

For Melvin and Fatu, their wedding night was the beginning of a lifetime of love, sex and ecstasy, better than anything they could have ever conjured up in their dreams. Not even Mr. Ebola could quench the love and pleasure they share with each other....

Ernestine finished reading the final words of her chapter and looked up at the faces of her new writing group's members expectantly. The silence was heavy in the library's meeting room. She couldn't miss the shocked expressions on the faces of her fellow writers. "Was it really that bad," she asked herself questioningly.

Several people cleared their throats, and to get the ball rolling, Ernestine said, *"I'd love to get some feedbacks on the ending of my story. I just finalized it yesterday, so it feels pretty much fresh to me."*

Sixty long, painful seconds ticked by before one of the older ladies spoke up. *"Ernestine, I'm very disappointed in you. I am really not sure about the, Uhmm, appropriateness of the passage you just read us. I expected something uplifting in this post Ebola Liberian's Literary Renaissance and not something more of a shocker."*

"The appropriateness, are you kidding me? You can't be serious, right?" Ernestine exclaimed, almost crying. *"It's erotica! It's a sensual romance, for Christ's sake. I'd say a sex scene is pretty damn appropriate for an erotica and for a mature audience like we have here tonight."* She searched the eyes of the other members of the group for some support, but only found one.

"I love it, I love it very much, my dear. It is very much appropriate for a sensual romance though not a lot of people would want to agree with me. I want you to know that it was very clever and would become a masterpiece once completed," Stanley exclaimed in solidarity.

"We all know you would love it because that's your life and your specialty, Mr. Nimely. We're talking about sensual or erotica stories that are appropriate for a general audience not an X-rated story like the one she just read," another older lady scolded Stanley.

"I am sorry if it offended anyone here, but in my honest opinion, it is a very beautiful piece of story that needs a little-bit of fleshing out and fine-tuning. Keep up the good work, Ernestine. And I want you to know that Jesus Christ too was hated by his fellow Jews and was crucified by the Romans. Here in Liberia, please note that we have Liberian Jews and Nigerian and Ghanaian Romans too," the vituperative and highly controversial erotica king chimed in. Everyone in the group laughed, the older women did not laugh.

Exasperated, Ernestine said, *"I thought I made myself unequivocally clear with all of you before joining this group. I write erotica. Sexually explicit romantic fictions. That means there are sex scenes in them. And you all said you were okay with it. Everyone in this group is having some kind of sex, be it solo, dual or group. Why are you all having problems with me now? Jesus Christ, you people are something else! That's why Liberia is the way it is, and people like you all are here making it worse."*

During the intense interaction, a man and a woman excused themselves from the room and walked toward the library entrance where the only restroom was located. A fortyish man spoke up. *"I thought it was an excellent passage, Ernestine. You perfectly captured your hero's deep feelings for the heroine. It was incredible and smartly crafted. I also think your characters' interaction brought to an end a long anticipated emotion they both had for each other neither the Ebola viral disease nor God could have stopped. I personally do not have any problem with it. I love it!"*

"Thank you," Ernestine said, flashing a smile at him as well as Stanley, but before she could feel better about her evening, an old hag who had just contributed a story about her nephew living in the United States said, *"I will not stand for such dirt! I think you should not be in this group with decent people like us. I think we should take a vote right now to determine your fate. Who here wants to listen to this trashy porn that people in this Christian nation of ours or anywhere else in the world will not waste their precious time reading or listening to someone read to them?"*

Only Stanley raised his hand, but the middle-aged man half-raised his hand, giving Ernestine a sheepish grin, and she had the awful feeling that he was only voting for her because he thought she was easy to get.

Looking smug, the ringleader asked, *"And who wants her and her trashy writing to leave our group immediately?"* Everyone else excluding Stanley and the middle-age man raised their hands while their eyes shot daggers at Ernestine.

The vote was a classic case of democracy at work in a public library—only that this form of democracy was not truly being practiced in the current government that runs the impoverished nation of almost four million people.

"*Fine,*" Ernestine said, calmly slipping her papers back into her brown leather bag. Swinging it up onto her shoulder, she stood up, after taking a hard look at those who wanted her out of the group, she gave Stanley a faint smile and left the room without a backward glance.

She was not too surprised when she heard footsteps behind her in the stairway and turned to see her middle-age supporter hurrying to catch up with her.

"*Ernestine,*" he said, slightly out of breath. "*I feel terrible about what these folks are doing to you, my dear.*"

"*I'm sure you do, but that's life, right,*" she said questioningly, a slight twinge of bitterness lacing her words.

"*Even though this didn't work out, I was hoping that, ah, maybe I could take you out for lunch next Saturday at Omoko's Restaurant or Evelyn's.*" He looked intently at her expecting a positive answer.

Ernestine acted like she was considering his words carefully. Forcing a coy look onto her face she asked, "*Is that all you want from me?*"

Giving her a sleazy smile, he leaned in until she could smell his bad breath, and said, "*I'm opened to the idea of helping you try out some of your new scenes, anytime you want.*"

Ernestine was bubbling with anger, but she worked hard to keep her hands firmly at her sides. He wasn't the first guy she'd wanted to slap in the face, and he wouldn't be the last. From between gritted teeth she said, "*I don't know why every guy who meets me thinks all I want to do is fuck his brains out simply because I write sensual romance or have a big round ass behind me. Because I wouldn't have sex with you if you were the last man on this Earth."*

Clearly upset by her slam, he looked her up and down and disdainfully and said, *"Then maybe you should stop begging for it, you damn slut, wata police, hopo joe,"* then ran back up the stairs to the library's meeting room, slamming the door behind him.

Standing in the stairway, stunned by her latest bad experience, Ernestine heard the distinct sounds of lovemaking coming from the bathroom. A minute later, the two people who had left the room right after she read her chapter emerged, clothes in slight disarray, and sneaked back off toward the meeting room, thinking no one was that wiser to have noticed or perhaps heard their sounds. She let out a faint smile and then shook her head in disbelief.

Ernestine smiled momentarily some more. *"I guess that means it was a darn good chapter,"* she said. But then, feeling despondent again over the difficulties of her new writing direction, she added, *"At least some people are having a good night. Liberians got some freaks in them. It would be good only if they will remain true to their feelings instead of hiding behind some 18th Century belief of "Plying Church" brought into Africa by white Christian missionaries from the U.S. and Europe."*

Trying not to be too down about the events of the evening, she headed out to her car which was parked at the intersection of Gurley and Carey Streets, so as to go home for another lonely night curled up on her couch with a paperback novel by K. Moses Nagbe, where she could dream about having a perfect life with a wealthy young man, like the character, Joan in "Tugging Whisper".

CHAPTER 3

Stanley stood at his living room window as he looked down at the abandoned Ebola orphaned boy and his little brother that live next to his home. He often does this during weekdays when he was not in his home office perfecting his work. This morning, the twelve-year-old was getting his brother ready for school. After bathing him with a barely cleaned water from a polluted well in their neighborhood, he dried him off using a tattered piece of cloth that resembles a floor rag. He then lotion up the child with burned palm oil that was in a small bottle. Stanley watched the 12 year-old boy throws a dingy blue and white uniform on his little brother.

"Damn! Why can't someone come to these children's aid? What has happened to our moral compass in this city?" Stanley said to himself as he watched the two children from the window of his beautiful home.

After readying himself for school, the 12 year-old brought out a small cup filled with Lipton Tea and a loaf of bread that was not enough for the two of them. Breaking the loaf of bread in half, the boy gave the bigger piece to his little brother to eat and pretended to eat his half of the bread. He sat back and watch his little brother as he ate his share of the bread and drank the tea. He in turn would pretend to take a bite off his share of bread and would also pretend to drink the tea in the cup just as his little brother was doing. After every pretentious bite, the 12 year-old boy would hide the bread behind him with his right hand. In less that two minutes, the little boy was done eating the piece of bread. Realizing his little brother was done eating his share and didn't seem fulled, the 12 year-old would then pretend to magically produce the extra piece of bread from behind him. He would then give it to his little brother to eat in a show of love and care for his only sibling and family. Seeing what was playing out in front of him, Stanley became emotional as his eyes welled with tears. "Oh God, please help them. I can't bear it any longer," Stanley Whispered to himself. He wanted to help but didn't know where to start. He was aware that there was no safety net in Monrovia for the poor, the destitute, and the orphans. The government and its self-serving officials only looked out for themselves and not the citizens of the country or the residents of Monrovia, a city in which she operates. For the most part, poverty reigned supreme; there was nothing Stanley and other well mean Liberia with a heart of gold could do about plight of the people without the right government in executive mansion that has the right interventionist strategy.

Trying to get out of the depressing fog after watching the boy that morning, Stanley shifted his thoughts back to the incident that took place during his mentorship several weeks ago at the We Care Library. Ever since the encounter at the library, Stanley had never gotten the young woman he'd met that night out of his mind for some unknown reason. He thought there was something familiarly special about her writing style that turned the people against her. He reflected back at how critical the other writers were of Ernestine's writing as well as how dismissive they were of her enormous talent. For the most part, Stanley felt her pains. He knew she felt dejected and betrayed by the very people that supposed to be her only means of support and relief from the hypocritical Liberian readers. She was in the same position as the city of Monrovia that is in so much pain because of the social and political neglect she feels. He knew that their actions would be a dream killer to the up and coming romance writer if nothing was done to avert the negative energy that had been directed at her. He remembered as a young and promising writer still living in Liberia, this was something he encountered and later learned to deal with. Stanley often attributed his success to being opportune to have gone to the United States of America which he refers to as the land of limitless possibilities and countless opportunities only the smart and the brave can see. He remember how his parents had taken him to several churches and traditional healers to deliver him from the power of demons they believed had taken control of him at such a young age. Being misunderstood was something he wanted to encourage Ernestine and other young writers to learn to deal with as they transform their passions of writing into a trade that they can live off of. He had planned that the next time he sees the young woman to inform her and other writers' wannabes of society's ugly venom and the culture of deceit in Liberia and many parts of the world.

For Stanley, being a guru of societal criticism is different from being a rookie writer under the lens of society's enmity as Ernestine and others were. One thing he had learned to deal with as a writer and as a human being is the hypocrisies that permeate within Liberian society and everywhere on the African continent. Stanley wanted to educate young writers of the social deceits that are part of the psychs of many of the residents of his beautiful city, Monrovia. Many of the people who publically abhor eroticisms and other forms of sensual writings are the same people that practice threesome, teenage sex, homosexuality, and femdom in the dark of night. Many of them are avid consumers of pornographic materials from various websites on the Internet, and sex club that were sprouting up around Monrovia and in many parts of the post Ebola nation. As a result, people who ridicule and labelled him as a social dissident, some of whom were top government officials, politicians, clergymen and women often used the religious or the morality card to divert public attention from their own immoral lives and behaviors. Several years ago, it was the very people that threw him under the bus when he tried to shed lights on their dirty habits of sexual misconduct. In many societies the world over, this tactic of diversion has always worked and Stanley knew how to rise above the tide when his passion come under attack. He hated the head of the nation's House of Representative and the Senate—he knew of their dirty sexual deeds after dark. Stanley had secret e-mails and text messages from dozen of young girls these powerful men were having sex with. He had records of the total numbers of government officials, members of the national legislature that were sponsoring young girls and boys at the African Methodist Episcopal University, United Methodist University, African Methodist Episcopal Zion University, The Adventist University of West Africa, Starz College of Technology, the University of Liberia, and various education institutions around the country. Stanley was aware of the pervasive corrupt acts that were pulverizing his beloved city of Monrovia like cancer. Due to his unchanging love for his city, he had been on a campaign of exposing public servants since he came in the limelight more than 10 years ago.

Stanley remembered an incident that took place more than three year ago when someone from the Liberian Council of Churches and an officials at the government's Ministry of Information Culture and Tourism took his complaint to the Ministry of Justice for writing explicit books and other flaming or offensive materials they claimed were perverting and damaging the minds of young people. In Stanley's view, over 95% of the youth he was accuse of corrupting were not being cared about by their government and lip-serving politicians. For the allegation, he was subsequently charged with perversion of the youth and promotion of indecency by the government of Liberia. The charges against him were something the government would later come to regret. For

Stanley, it was something that was long overdue. He had so
many weapons within his writer's arsenal that he used to
his own defense during the trial which made government
prosecutors to appear incompetent in the eyes of millions
of Liberians and other regional and international observers.
During the trial, he wrote daily articles in many of the
leading newspapers operating in the country. These articles
were about life after dark in Monrovia and many parts of
the Liberia. In many of his articles, he wrote of the sexual
behaviors of top government officials, lawmakers, ministers
of the Gospel of Jesus Christ, Imams of leading mosques in
Monrovia and around the country, powerful businessmen and
women, heads of NGOs and diplomats that were involved in
illicit sexual activities with underage girls and boys within
Monrovia and around the country.

These daily newspapers articles were wildly read by
members of the reading public both in Liberia and in the
Diaspora. Frontpasgeafrica.com which is an online news
source, was one of the few places he got a huge notoriety. His
satirically pungent articles got the attention of the President
and the Executive Mansion in Monrovia. To avoid further
embarrassments to the administration, the President and
members of executive mansion's inner cycle asked that all
charges brought against Mr. Nimely be dropped and that
the case be thrown out of court for lack of evidence. As
radical as Stanley is, he demanded a public apology from the
government and those involved. As would any government
that operates in a half-illuminated environment while its
members acted differently in the dark of night, the apologies
he demanded in public never happened. Rather, he was
called to a private fence-mending conference at the Executive
Mansion in Monrovia by the President who was also a great
admirer of his work. A week later, he was invited at the Justice
Ministry, and was offered the apologies he had long wanted
behind closed door. For him, it was the validation he had long

awaited from the establishment. It was the bargaining chip he had sought to give his career the final thrusts it needed in the country. In fact, the case gave him such a huge following and a quick career boost that his books were flying off bookshelves around the country and in online bookstores around the world like hot and juicy chocolate cake.

In many of the daily articles Stanley wrote during the trail, he highlighted many of the phony behaviors of the very people that prosecuted him in public, but lived a double lifestyle in the dark of night. In his Friday Februar 16, 2017, edition of 'Life After Dark', he wrote of one of the opened prostitution scenes he was a witnessed to on Gurley Street, in Central Monrovia at the famous Club Exodus Nightclub which is commonly called "Facebook" by many Monrovians…..

….It was fast approaching midnight, but the club was just beginning to get crowded. The reason for the crowd was due to the closure of schools and colleges for the Christmas and New Year holidays. Gurley Street was blaring with loud music and people were all mixed up in a big frenzy of excitement— good and bad, old and young, rich and poor, politicians and clergymen, thieves and hustlers, prostitutes and their johns, undercover officers and drug dealers, just to name a few people that were out having fun that night. Hundreds of cars lined the side of the street with people walking back and forth, and dancing to the sound of one of David Mell's. songs coming out of the nightclub's powerful speakers. Curious to learn more about the nightclub I have heard so much about, I too came out to do my usual investigation for my 'Life After Dark' article. Unlike the many people that had come out to have fun, I pretended to be out for fun as well. Before heading to the club that night, I wore a slack khaki pants with a slim fit blue checkerboard button down Ralph Lauren shirt and threw a $50 bill into my pocket just in case I ran into some friend I have not seen. According to the reputation of Club Exodus, it is a place you *might see a friend you have not seen for years, no wonder it is ironically called 'Facebook', a place where the world meets, make friends, and fall in love. My curiosity, anticipation, and excitement soon took a dramatic turn when I suddenly ran into an honorable representative from Capitol Hill and a young girl having a conversation.*

"Short time is $20 U.S., Papay," a youthful looking girl said to the man sitting in the backseat of the REP plated black Toyota 4runner. The lawmaker rolled down the back-passenger's window of the SUV some more to solicit the girl who was somewhere in her mid-teens. A sad but acceptable fact is that prostitution is an open secret in Monrovia and other parts of our country. The President had unofficially endorsed the business by the current administration's lack of policy to get young boys and girls out of the streets. The rich and powerful are often left alone to have their feast and field-day with the poor and hopeless youth of our country. For me, I do not think things should be the way they are for our young people in my beloved city of Monrovia which I love so much. This is a city so many politicians pretend to have love for, but uses her to profit for themselves. I know with a slight change in priority at the executive level, I think this Monrovia and our country can give a decent shot at life to all the young men and women that are selling their bodies for a bottle of Heineken or $5 United States Dollars in the name of entertainment and survival.

This night, the girl in conversation with the honorable representative wore a pretty low red flowery dress which was cut high above her knees that complemented the Brazilian hair she wore on her head. She was about five feet four inches, weighing about a hundred and twenty pounds. She was perfectly shaped up, with a fine firm queen-size breast and a coco cola bottom. Her bust size might had been about 36B cup. In fact, she wore one of those Pushup or Miracle bras which is commonly known in Monrovia and other parts of Africa as, "Fool the Minister Bras". She was light in complexion, perhaps naturally or through artificial bleaching, which made her an easy target for men looking for an exhilarating sex with a young but not too much of an innocent teen. She stood about ten feet away from the rest of her pals on the sidewalk opposite the nightclub. She danced as she talked with the honorable lawmaker. Ironically, the Ministry of Gender which had been cracking down on prostitution in the country was located a quarter mile down the road from the famous nightclub on Gurley Street.

Many people, I included, do not believe if this ministry is functioning at all or should even be a part of government's bureaucracy. Several months ago, the Ministry of Gender in conjunction with the Liberian National Police, LNP, launched vigorous campaigns to get young prostitutes out of the ghettoes and streets in Monrovia and other sex trading places around the country. For me, I wouldn't be surprised if these efforts exacerbated prostitutions among many jobless residents of Monrovia and in other parts of the country. Though these campaigns were deemed successful from the Ministry of Gender's perspectives due to the arrest of local prostitutes in various ghettoes and whore houses in and around Monrovia and other places around the country, but the campaign failed to address the root causes of prostitution among cities dweller and young people in this impoverished nation. In poverty stricken Liberia, selling drugs and exchanging sex for cash are the only two easy means by which many of the unemployed young citizens are surviving.

With a government dominated by chauvinistic males, many of whom use sex and bribery as preconditions to employment, raiding girls off the streets and ghettoes was a threat to their sexual gratification and leisure. At first, many Liberians blamed the West African peacekeepers, and then the United Nations Military Mission in Liberia, UNMIL for exploiting our young men and women sexually. As we have all seen now than ever before, the government is a co-conspirator to supporting prostitution and corruption in the country. Just the other day, it was reported that one of our lawmakers encourage a young woman to strip naked at a private gatherings just for the entertainment of his guests. Many of these official usually have threesome orgies with both young men and women every day. No matter the social outcry for religious quarter, the fact is, sex is very cheap in my beloved Monrovia and in other parts of Liberia and Africa. For an official of government to get sex from any unemployed or under privileged teenager is as easy as snapping his or her fingers. Honestly, I do not think people and our government should blame me for exposing the secret sex life of power people and government officials after dark. The fact of the matter is, the darkness belongs to everybody; this includes, the rich, the poor, the young and old, angels and devils, vanquish and victor, and even a hated writer like me.

"Damn, fine girl, why are you asking for a whole $20 U.S.? What do you have on your pussy, gold or diamond? I'll take you and your friend over there for the night for $20 U.S. I will give you girls free food to eat, free liquor to drink, free place to sleep, and a nice bathroom to bathe in," the man said with his counter offer.

"But I will give you it in both places. I will rock your world tonight, honorable," the young girl countered.

"Okay, I will round it up to $30 for you and your friend. That's the max I can go. The balance will be on credit which I will pay next week when the government pays me," the lawmaker declared. Not wanting to miss-out on the opportunity at hand, the girl excused herself of the honorable lawmaker and walked over to her friends. After a few minutes of chat with one of the girls whom the lawmaker had pointed at in the group, she and the girl walked back to the waiting vehicle and both girls jumped into the backseat alongside the big shot. Moment later, the SUV slowly drove off, toward United Nations Drive to its destination with the honorable representative and his two catch for the night. Only God knew what he was up to and what he was about to do to those two poor young girls that have taken

the life of prostitution as a means-to-an-end.

"Cheap ass mother fucker. Two innocent girls he's going to use and abuse all night for only thirty fucking United States Dollars. What an asshole of a representative he is," I cussed in disgust at the honorable lawmaker's exploitation of my fellow Monrovians. Slowing my pace to almost a turtle-like walk due to the crowd, I found my way deeper into the throng of club goers. After that episode, I knew I was in for a big surprise that night, I knew I was going to see things straight out of the movies. I knew my eyes would be opened to more of the things that happened after dark in my beloved city, Monrovia, where we are all pledging allegiance to the red, white and blue, and hoping for a better day to emerge…

Liberian and African males' insatiable sexual chauvinistic behavior was one of the things that saddened Stanley Kla Nimely when it came to how some government officials, top business executives, corporate lawyers, religious leaders, educators and listless others that used their finances and social statuses to exploit the youths of their youthfulness, especially their sexual prides. But again, how could he judge others as he was as well guilty of the very same act of exploitation? How could he champion the liberation of young Liberian women when he writes books that deals with human sexual pleasure? How could Stanley separate himself from something he had come to meet, sex, exploitation and manipulation, lies and corruption, hatred and jealousy and many other vices the post Ebola city was currently dealing with. Of all the two hundred plus women Stanley had had sexual intercourse with, none were in their teens. For he loves only smart, and mature women that had something to offer beyond the bedroom. The only regret he had was that his books were being read by thousands of girls and boys in their teens. Come to think of the situation, it was something he had no control over. In fact, the government had used the issue of teens reading his books in their deposition against him court. For the most part, he was misunderstood by some of his audiences and the government when he wrote the book titled, 'Teenage Sex: The Good, The Bad, The Ugly'. According to Stanley, the book was actually aimed at cautioning teenagers about the dangers of teenage sex and not to glorify teen sex as it was misinterpreted by the government and rights organizations within the country. In that book, he criticized President William R. Tolbert's Age of Consent Proposition made back in the 1970s. In that proposition, the President wanted the age of consent for sex to be set at age 13, which Stanley thought was inhumane and a violation of human rights and the rights of the Liberian child. Just imagine seeing a 13 year old child being sexually involved with an older man or woman. Though Stanley loves sex, but he loves safe and mature sex. No wonder finding the perfect woman had become his Achilles Heel which he had not given up on overcoming.

......That night following the encounter between the girls and the honorable representative at the club on Gurley Street, I decided to move further into the throng of joy-seeking club goers. Pushing my way through the crowd, with some smelly odors from the armpits some of the patrons, I managed to come to the mean entrance of the jammed packed club. After several 'hellos' with some acquaintances, I soon bumped into several of my old elementary school classmates whom I hadn't seen for more than six years. The three men were seated in the far left corner of the hot nightclub surrounded by three younger but very beautifully dressed women. By this time, the music was so loud that one had to yell before being heard or understood by the person they are speaking with. I hate the club scene and everything that comes with it, but here, I was on a mission to uncover the nightlife of deceptive people who loved to act like moral police in the light of day while living like the devil behind the veil of darkness.

"Hey, Augustus A. Michelson, aka, Sample......long time, bro," I shook my old friend's hand. Abel now looks like he was

*approaching his fifty though we were all in our mid-forties. For
he was now leaned with a lot of gray in his beard and on his
head. Abel was one of those kids I admired very much when
we were all kids. He had everything a young boy could ever
dream of. As the only child for his parents, he was given not only
the love some of us didn't get from our parents, he was given
anything a teenage boy could ever think of; toys, clothes, money,
I mean, he got anything he ever ask his parents for. Along with
his fortune, he had the look that made him the chick's magnet
as we used to tease him. Due to his handsomeness and flashy
attitudes, some of the other kids envied him, but I was always
his friend. Abel loved me like a brother, and I loved him back.
Our brotherly relationship remained until this day. Abel and I
causally refer to each other as "Cousooo", which means, Cousin
in our Liberian slang.*

*"Hey Smart Ass, long time no see. How have you been after
all these years? I thought you were out of this country again,
bro," he said, letting out his usual boyish smile, followed by a
slap on my back. I tapped him on the shoulder after a warmed
and quick handshake and a shoulder hug.*

*I then slowly walked over to greet the young lady who sat
next to Abel and introduced myself, "I am Stan."*

*"I am Lovel……Lovel Myers, I know you. We've bracketed at
Gbedze Resort in Marshall before," she said to my amazement.*

*"You two know each other, Stan? I wouldn't be surprised
because Lovel is into sensual romance and all kinds of strange
sexual and freaky things," Abel laughed as he shook my hand a
second time.*

*"I love your last book, 'The G Spot'. I read it more than
eight times. Each time I read it, I learned something new. I must
admit, I am sold out to you, I am a big fan of yours," Lovel said
animatedly.*

*"WOW! I didn't know that, but thank you. I wrote that
book when I was going through a midlife crisis. I put everything*

that I had internal into that book," I said looking at my other old friends. "We will talk some more, sweetie," I told her before turning to shake hands with my other friends.

"Look at this old ass, Sampson Manyongar Zangai, the Bassa King, what's up my broda.....long time no see. I heard you're now a banker. Damn, what a big change," I said as both of us hugged, followed by slaps on the backs.

After chatting with Sampson for about a minute or two, I methodically walked across the table to shake hands with our other buddy whom I noticed was putting his hand between the legs of the young lady sitting in front of him wearing a mini dress. The short dress gave him an easy access to her honeycomb. I can tell you with certainty that his fingers were buried deep inside that young lady's wet pit. Trying to avoid the self-created embarrassment, he quickly removed his hand from under the young lady's dress and pretended to looking for his cell phone. She looked very young, perhaps, she was somewhere in her upper-teens.

"Damn Stan.....you haven't changed much. I always send you requests and birthday wishes whenever I am on air at the station," he said as he stretched his hand to shake mine.

"What's up Chriso, I seriously lost your contact. How are the little people and my sister-in-law, Tee? I heard there was a new addition to the family. Congratulations, bro," I said, giving my friend Christopher Nah a fist bump instead of the handshake he had sub-conscientiously requested. In fact, how could I have given him a full handshake knowing what he had been up to? At that moment, I allowed sanity to be my guard. I didn't want to have the juices and smell of a strange woman's vagina all over my good and Jesus Christ-like hand.

"S.K. Nimely, you've been missing in action, bro. How is everything with you and your beautiful wife," he asked.

"My late ex-wife, you mean," I was quick to correct my friend with a question.

"What!? Since when she became late or your ex?" Chris was surprised upon hearing the news of the death of my former wife who died during the height of Ebola epidemic that killed more than thousand people in Liberia alone.

"She gave up her ghost during the last Ebola assault. I wish I was around to have gotten her the necessary helps she desperately needed," I replied.

"WOW! I am very sorry Stan. I didn't even know you guys have divorced or T had passed," Chris quipped with condolences as the others looked on in disbelief.

"Since when?" Abel asked sub-conscientiously, "I mean the divorce?"

"It is going to three years now. We remain good friends up to the day she died, bro. I even heard she was crying out on my name when she was on her death bed," I told the group to their outmost surprise. Often in Monrovia and many parts of the world, when a couple divorces, they sometimes become sworn enemies, even if there were children produced during the marriage. Often, they do not see eye-to-eye due to grudges each of them hold against the other.

"WOW! I thought you and Taisue would have loved, lived and died together, Stan. From elementary school bro, that's some bullshit right there with these days' women. Why will she pull out of something she desperately wanted? Why are some women like that, man…that's some deep shit I just cannot get my mind to understand," Chris lamented.

I was kind of surprised to have heard these words from a man who himself had just been orally stimulating a young girl twice his junior, and was about to take her to some dirty motel on the outskirt of town or even in the backseat of his car and feast on her like a wild beast, just like many of the men in Monrovia do while their wives lied in bed and awaited them to come home for the night. How dare he speaks of me and my late ex-wife as though he was morally straight or ethically sound?

As people normally say, "This Too is Liberia". The only country where anything is possible and everything is acceptable—even driving on the opposite side of the road into incoming traffic, corruption with impunity, and the exploitation of the country with less than four million people by its citizens as well as foreigners from faraway places.

"That's why they called it marriage, Chris. I am very sorry that she had to die to an epidemic that should have been halted by that inept government when it initially showed up at our doorsteps. Chris, you may not know this, but marriage is a temporary commitment that's easily broken nowadays. People need to understand that marriage is just a contract made between two loving people from two different backgrounds with the hope of each person upholding their side of the bargain. The end could be forever or never," I told my stupefied friend.

"Those are very powerful words from the master of love and relationship himself. No wonder why you have army of followers out here that believe in your words and many of whom use your books as the ultimate relationship guide. I am very much one of those diehard fans of yours. You know exactly what to say, when to say it, and you know very much how to say it," Lovel said sardonically, but with a truthful undertone.

"Thanks, Lovel. Anyway, what are you guys up to tonight," I asked, turning to Sampson, as I tried to switch the topic from my failed marriage and my wife's death to a more general one that required less personal data or information. This tactic of conversational diversion has often worked for me. It has always worked in cases where I didn't want to be the subject, verb, and predicate of a cordial conversation in a public gathering.

"But…but don't you feel lonely and sad having been in a marriage with someone that you once cherished and loved wholeheartedly? Doesn't it affect your personal outlook of things and the people you care about the most," Lovel said questioningly. By this time, everyone's attention was focused on me, perhaps to hear me say something ridiculous or reveal a *deep-seated secret about love and relationship.*

I smile faintly and said, "Lovel you see, happiness does not lies in the institution of marriage. Self-respect in solitude is not loneliness. It is a virtue and a celebration of a person's individuality or self ruling, especially when the former couple remain friends after the divorce. In as much as I am contemplating on finding my better half, I must remain truthful to my real self, acknowledging all my weaknesses why relying on my inner strengths to serve as my relationship guide. For some, marriage has brought them a lifetime of happiness, and for others, it has becomes a nightmare that they cannot seem to wake up from. The former is what everyone prays for, while the latter is what every human being, I included, must divorce from no matter the situation. Life being short as it is, should be lived with happiness and mirth, my friends."

"WOW! That some deep and very powerful shit right there, Stan," Sampson said, almost yelling.

"What are you doing here all by yourself tonight, my brother? I hope you're not here looking for your missing better half," Abel asked as everyone laughed at his question.

"I don't think here is the right place to find my better half, Cousooo. Maybe I could try in a church, a library, or at a classical music concert where only the prayerful, God fearing, smart, intelligent and highly potential frequent." I continued.

"I am actually out here doing research. I am sure you guys are aware of the lawsuit the government has against me," I replied as I locked eyes with Abel, and then with Chris.

"Oh yes...I am actually following the case as well as your "Life After Dark" articles. Are those articles really true," Lovel said followed by a question.

"Yes, they are. Everything you read in those newspapers are all true," I replied. Right there, I noticed how the facial expressions of the men in the group changed.

"You're not going to write about us, right," Lovel and Sampson asked in unison.

"Well, that depends and you can never tell. I may or I may not. I just witnessed something interesting a few moment ago, right before I ran into you guys. I saw a man in a REP. government—plated SUV negotiating price for sex with two very young girls below the legal sex age. Just image that," I said.

"You mean the black Toyota 4Runner? That man is one of the representatives of Montserrado County. He's a regular around here. He often takes home girls in their teens and feast on them like a hungry man eating boil peanuts. That man often pays the girls he uses little to nothing after sleeping with them all night. He is a bad news for many of the girls out her looking for survival through the selling of their bodies. That man credited one of my friend's pussy and refused to pay her after using her for a whole weekend. It is not only he alone that does that. Several of our so called senators and government officials always come here to shopping for pussy. I even heard that he is HIV positive and he have sex with those girls without using condoms," the young girl sitting next to Sampson interjected with a long narration.

"Are you one of their regulars around here for them, too," Sampson asked jokingly. We all laughed at the insanity and absurdity being exhibited by people we expect to know better but really lacked the common sense they need.

"Hell, NO! God forbids. Many of those men are sick with HIV and AIDS. I can never risk my life for a few Grief Bearing United States Dollars that may bring me an everlasting worry that will ultimately lead me to my early grave. I once loved to the former Minister of Information. That was a relationship I regretted because he used to like fucking me and three other prostitutes at the same time. What I hated about that stupid minister was his constant habits of fucking me up in the ass all the time. That man only used to fuck us in our butts whenever *we were making love to him," the young lady snapped back as everyone sitting at the table laughed and listen to her sad, but true story about the former government official.*

"TMI," I said to myself in sympathy with the young lady's sexual ordeals with the honorable minister. These stories were all common among many young and unemployed Liberian girls and boys, especially those that live in Monrovia, the capital. As Miatta Fahnbulleh or Aunty Miatta as she is called often says, "Prostitution among young men and women can only be eradicated if you give the prostitute who is a victim of choice something to do as well as punish the perpetrators." But can this be done when the perpetrators are those in high places? How can the police or enforcers police themselves? This is the question that remains to be answered by everyone who loves this country and the people of Monrovia which is the hot seat for everything.

"WOW! Who was this minister?" Sampson snapped back, "And how many times did he fucked you in your butt. That's some serious shit because you can't even allow me to pass my fingers around your asshole, let alone stick my dick up in there. That's some bullshit right there, Alfreda."

"Do you think I used to like being abused or sodomized by someone for chicken change, Sampson? If you guys see many of these young girls out here in the streets selling the bodies for few American bucks, you all need not judge them. Many of them are doing these things just to survive due to the hardship in this country and the lack of jobs or the basic social cushions they need to fall back on in times of economic hardship. This fucking country is too damn fucking hard when you don't have the financial support or family backing…" The young lady narrated her story of her Monrovia experience as we listened on.

"…Do you think I used to like having sex with strange men, many of whom smelled like Billy Goats? God knows, I hated

*when some of those men released their sink sperm inside of
me. Due to some of these experiences, I hated myself for what
life was putting me through, and I hated Liberian men to the
extent that I killed every romantic desire that I had within my
heart and replaced it with X-ray eyes for the contents of men's
pockets. For the most part, many of the local men in Monrovia
only use our young girls and boys for their sexual pleasure,
but are not willing to lift them up or to help push them to get
a firm footing in life even if they had a truckload of stolen
money." She continued as everyone listened to her, "Honestly,
do you guys know why I had sex with strange men in some of
the strangest places? I did it because it was a means to an end
for me. I am sure it is the same reason thousands of these boys
and girls are doing what they are doing right now. Look at me
now, I just turned nineteen years old, three weeks ago; I now
have my own little business from which I am trying to build
my first home without a penny from you, Sampson or from any
man's pocket for that matter," the young lady blasted out her
frustrations. "This corrupt government is doing nothing to serve
those who are in need of the most help, rather, the government is
paying incompetent people big salaries to sit in air conditioned
offices and do nothing, while calling us young people that are
struggling for survival prostitutes, drug users and Zokos. The
government and its officials are the prostitutes and Zokos. They
are the criminals that are destroying this very country and
that are contributing to the backward state of this damn dirty
Monrovia. To hell with them. To hell with the damn president,
and fuck whoever tries to bring us down further. They can go to
hell and tell the damn fucking devil that I sent them!"*

*"You're right about everything you said, Alfreda. I think you
should also let me hit that ass one day; just like you did that
damn fucking minister," Sampson said followed by his usual
stupid scornful laugh which no one laughed to.*

*"That was strangely romantic, Sampson. The young lady just
spilled her heart out a few seconds ago and I think we need to*

applaud her for her strength of courage," I said. "You see, those things she just mentioned are the identical issues I normally write about in my articles, "Life After Dark". I write about the lies and deceptions that pervade the Liberian society. I write about the systemic correction that is slowly moving this country over the steep cleft of destruction. I tried to bring to light some of the ills that have given a good country like Liberia a bad name around the world. I am not an angel, nor Am I a moral police, but I will work very hard to expose these numb nuts and make them infamously famous for their actions and behaviors against poor and innocent people that are the victims of their venoms. I will keep exposing the president and LISCR money laundering criminal syndicate that is robbing this country out of millions of dollars in tax revenue," I barked as people on adjacent tables turned the heads and stared our way. By this time, a music of one of Liberia's newest artist, Geno was just ending on the powerful speakers at the club's sound systems.

"One more thing I want to tell you guys, please hear me out. I am by no means try to be disrespect to Liberian men by what I said or I am about to say. You see, 90% of Liberian men will never help an unmarried or even married female who is not a family member of theirs without asking for sex from that female in return for that favor," Alfreda continued. "Liberian men are very wicked and self-centered many of whom are corrupt from birth and unrepentant at death. I think when they die, they will not see God's face," she said before being interrupted by another female.

"Excuse me Mr. Nimely….," Lovel said. Seemed somehow unsure of what she wanted to say. "The other day I read your article about some people in the President's inner cycle being homosexuals as well as how some of them are having sex with young boys around the country and how they are giving these children jobs for sex. To be frank with you, I was really glad you brought up this social issues in that article. For a fact, these are open secrets around here. People talk about these things in

barbershops, beauty salons, and even in drinking stalls all the time. What I wasn't too sure of is how vividly you described how one senior government official groped a young boy's ass right in your presence. I also liked how you exposed big shot from the National Oil Company, NOCAL when you saw him kissing a young man in his car. How sick have these men gotten around here? I wonder what is wrong with us women that our men are now going after young boys to get sexual pleasure when we were made to please our men."

"What about the women too…lesbianism has become a way of life right here in Monrovia. I don't understand why our women are turning to other young women to seek sexual pleasure." Sampson was quick to snap back at Lovel with a question of his own.

Often in my beautiful city of Monrovia, at dinner tables, at bible studies, and in mosques, many residents pounder over these questionable sexual behaviors of some residents of the city. While I may not have the right answer for them, I usually tell people that these things happen when East meets West—when the chickens come home to roost.

"Well, it is not my place to judge anyone. Like what I saw here tonight with the honorable representative bargaining price for sex, I was lucky to have been present when those things were happening. It was through a mere double coincidence of wants that I was on the beach that night when the president's confidant and his young lover walked behind the parked vehicles in the parking lot. It was there I saw them in the act of making out. The young boys I wrote about in that particular article you mentioned who was with the fellow from NOCAL is my nephew, Moses. What I want you all to understand is that, my writings are not about blackmailing anyone or bashing gay or lesbianism in Liberia. As for me, I think we need to accept people for who they are rather than passing judgments on them for what they are or their sexual preferences. Here in Liberia and many parts of Africa, we have gay and lesbian friends all *over the place, churches, mosques, in government, you name it. What we need to understand is that, people might have either chosen to be homosexual, bisexual, transsexual, or they might have been gays or lesbians due to genetic predisposition. I think those of us that are educated about the gay lifestyle, need to be open minded when we discuss this social issues that is somehow affecting less than two percent of the Liberian population. I was surprised to have learned from my nephew that he thinks his body is not aligning with is brain. He believes society is telling me to be a male, but his body tells him that he is a female. Now, how can one judge a person like Moses who is having this experience of living in a body that feels foreign to him while the larger society that does not understand what he is going through wants him to fit into their perception of accepting his physical attribute?" I continued narrating as my friends looked on with interests.*

"Now, back to the incident at Golden Beach, just imagine a senior member of the administration who happens to be a closed aid to the President doing such a thing in public. For many uninformed Liberians, I think this public display of offensive affection casts a bad shadow for the executive mansion because our Liberian and African population are not well educated or informed about homosexual lifestyle—we are all aware of the reactions Leroy Archie Ponpon got when he tried to advocate gay rights in this city a few years ago. I am sure the President is aware of all the things that are happening, but nothing can be done about it because the Executive Mansion in Monrovia often listens to the voices coming from up Benson Street and from 1600 Pennsylvania Avenue in Washington DC. From what I have heard many of you saying around here about the president needing to take the moral high ground in addressing some of the issues of immoralities, we all need to be careful; especially when many of us are guilty of those very things we're accusing others of doing." I informed the group. Sampson, Chris, and Abel and their lady—friends all looked at me almost begging me to hear more of what I have seen around my beloved city of Monrovia.

I said to their amazement, "You see, I have so many weapons within my arsenal that can bring these stupid and corrupt people down who are persecuting me because of their hates for what I write about their dirty lifestyles. My writings are like mirrors—many of these criminal minded bastards see themselves in things I am writing about daily. Due to this, they are trying to silence me forever just like they tried to do Rodney Sieh of Front Page Africa Newspaper several years ago. But you know what, as Ralph Waldo Emerson once said, "I ought to go upright and vital, and speak the rude truth in all ways. If malice and vanity wear the coat of philanthropy, shall that pass?" I will not compromise my principles because of badges or some kind of title that my detractors are awarding me, I will keep preaching the truths. I will keep advocating the rights of the downtrodden even to the day I draw in my last breath. Politicians in Monrovia and the world over, are all pretenders. Many of these gravy seekers and suit wearing rogues that are bad-mothing me are hiding behind the veil of their social statuses to exploit the poor and the voiceless or our society. Though we all point fingers at people in leadership, but some of my fellow Monrovians are not trustworthy. Monrovians and Liberians of all ages, backgrounds, ethnicities, and creeds, use and abuse people that are not like them. Many residents of this city have become liars, and thieves. As a word of advice to you, I want you to not ever trust any one of the highly placed in Monrovia because they will never keep their words to you. Liberians, especially Monrovia politicians are exploiters. They will say anything to the poorest of the poor for power. This act of exploiting the less-powerful among us are often perpetrated by some church leaders that preach one thing and do things contrary to what they preach, lawyers that institute justice on behalf of the rich, but abuse the constitutional rights of others, just to name a few. So is members of the executive branch of government, the legislature, judiciary and even many of the officials that are deceptively preaching morality in the light of day or are becoming moral police while they're morally bankrupt and functionally inept..."

"But Stan…..Stan…please hear me out, though," Chris interrupted before I could end my story.

"Go right ahead, bro," I said.

"Isn't this a normal part of life for people to have sex how, when, and with whomever they want to without people intruding into their private affairs," Chris inquired.

"Of course they have the rights to do so, as long as they are not having sex with underage boys and girls around here. As for me, I will continue to meddle into the affairs of those people that are bigshots in our society using their positions to rub our youth of their sexual youthfulness. One thing I would like to remind you of is that, if you're in the public's eyes and want to criticize others because you think you have the rights to do so or are threatened by them, be it in government, church or even in corporate, your private life becomes a public tool for scrutiny. For example, I may not write about how your fingers were just buried deep inside this young and beautiful lady's vagina a moment ago when I walked in because you are not an official of government, but rather, an honest and peace loving private citizen trying to have a good time without judging me," I said to everyone's surprise. At that moment, the young girl sitting next to Chris quickly closed her partly opened legs and brought down her short-length dress which gave Chris an easy access to her honeycomb. When she did, we all laugh and looked at one another's faces.

"WOW! You're crazy, Stan. Who told you I was fingering fucking Princess? I was just…I mean, I was, ummm," Chris was stunned as he continued to stutter.

"Princess, was I fingering you, sweetheart," he turned and asked the young girl who seemed somehow embarrassed by the exposure.

"Take me out of your damn conversation. I told you to stop what you were doing when you started in the first place," the young lady somehow angry, pushed Chris' hand aside and

moved her chair a few feet away from his. We all laughed at the theatrics a second time.

From that point onward, the conversation took another turn—my friends and their female friends somehow felt my plight. They understood that I was being falsely accused by the establishment and its agents for writing books that did not have any negative consequence on Liberian youth. Come to think of it, the elites of our society and the financially capable are the ones corrupting and exploiting the youth. They are exploiting the young men and women of their sexual youthfulness just for their sexual gratification. I think I am right for writing and exposing their behaviors, and their misdeeds. They are darn wrong in the harshest form for prosecuting me. More to come next week, when I bring you the 'The Night Life of Liberian Pastors, Imams and other religious Leaders" in, "Life After Dark".

This was one of the many articles and topics Stanley dealt with during his trial for the charges of sedition and perversion of the youth. For a man who was hated for speaking the truth, Stanley's appearance on the national stage during the case created a media frenzy. Each time he appeared in court, the courtroom was filled with fans and many admirers from across the world. His case was comparable to that of O. J. Simpson's 1995 murder case in the U.S. Among his supporter were Members of the Liberia Association of Writer, LAW, The Press Union of Liberia led by its president. Former government's officials that had fallen from grace also came to court in show of support for the beleaguered writer. At the end of it all, the government withdrew the case and dropped the case and he somehow became the victor. Stanley's lawyer, Counselor, Flomo demanded a public apology from the state for the public humiliation and pains it caused him. Though his legal fees were paid, but he did not get the public apology he demanded, but at least he got the public relation, PR he deserved. The PR really boosted his writing career on both the local and international stage as it did Rodney D. Sieh of Front Page Africa news media. After the failed lawsuit, Stanley's books became a hot commodities. Many of his books went global. As for his "Life After Dark" articles that featured the night life of Liberian Pastors, Imams, and religious leaders, it was a topic of discussion in Liberia for more than 10 months once it was published by five of the local newspapers in the country.

CHAPTER 4

It has been another tumultuous week in Monrovia with political jabs being thrown at current and former government's officials for stealing public funds and engaging in briberies and other forms of corrupt acts. As has always been, this acquisition was nothing new to the struggling residents of the overcrowded city of Monrovia. As Stanley listened to the newscaster voice on the radio informing Monrovians about the officials misconducts, he wonder if those accused will ever be brought to justice.....

".......There we go again with another corruption and bribery allegation with these dishonest people calling themselves lawmakers and government's officials," Stanley said to himself after taking a deep breath. He walked toward the window where he usually stands to watch the orphan boy and his little brother carry out their daily activities.

"What more does Varney Sherman and Alex J. Tyler want with all the money they have accumulated over the years? Why don't these people realize the curse behind ill-gotten wealth? Look at the lives of former government's officials and their children today....Ummm," he said aloud. Stanley lamented the sad situation as the newscaster continued to read the news and the names of the officials involved in the Sable Mining Company's bribery charges. He knows that this allegation will not go anywhere because nobody will be imprisoned or forced to pay back the bribe that was taken in order for the company

to cheat the country out of badly needed revenue.

"Are we Liberians born as criminals or are we made into criminal by our environments? Are we just suit wearing criminals in this country we have made poor by using our education to rob the very country we profess to love and care about? What is wrong with us in this 21ˢᵗ Century Liberia? It is very sad to seen people that we so admired and love involving themselves into criminal activities," Stanley said to himself as he walked away from the window to get ready for the writers' conference which is to take place at the newly built Grand Royal Hotel in Sinkor that Friday morning on 20ᵗʰ day of January in 2017.

"Look at what happened to so many of our good friends like Laurence Bropleh and his brother, Matilda Wokie Parker, and even J. Chris Toe that I so admired, and many countless others that worked in government......all of whom were either dismissed or forced to resign from their positions for stealing from this damn impoverished country. Our young people need to learn from the past in order to make a good decision when they are entrusted with public funds or are placed in a decision making position for the nation," Stanley shook his head from side to side in disappointment of the mega dishonesty that pervades the Liberian society.

After spending a few minutes in the shower, he got and and after drying off his skin, he threw on a pair of blue Levi Jeans with a yellow blazer with a Duke Blue Ralph Lauren shirt. He then wore his thin custom-made 24 carat gold chain. Reaching in this watch collection, he took out his expensive Geneva Platinum gold watch on his left hand. After brushing his short hair and taking several looks of himself in the mirror and realizing how good he looks, he grabbed the key to his W205 C-Class 2016 Mercedes-Benz and headed for the door.

Beaten by the sweltering African heat earlier that day, especially in the after math of the worst Ebola virus epidemic ever seen by the modern world, Ernestine stood underneath the huge *"Sensual Writers' Conference"* banner at the entrance of the newly constructed Grand Royal Hotel building in Sinkor, on Tubman Boulevard and took a deep breath. In this culture, most Liberians deceitfully frowned on subjects such as eroticisms, teenage prostitution and pregnancy, sexual gender-based violence against women, while many of them partake in its practices behind closed-door. The fact is that, as soon as she walks through those rotating double glass panel doors, she would officially be entering into her new life. Instead of continuing to write young adult stories, where sex was never allowed to enter into the storyline, no matter what, today she is officially going to make the jump into the dark world of sensual romance and erotica, where the only limit was how far a writer wanted to go. Instead of being lambasted by members of her writers' group for writing, *"Porn"*, she would go where most writers do not dare to go. For the most part, parents in this part of the world forbid openly discussing sex with their children. This lapse in communication between parents and children has contributed significantly to the social breakdown that has permeated our Liberian culture and many African societies. It has led to the proliferation teen pregnancy. Subsequently, the lack of sex education among young children has also led to the increase in the infection rate of HIV/AIDS and sexually transmitted infection, STI epidemics that is destroying the future generation of Liberia and the growing youthful population of Monrovia.

As Ernestine make her sojourn into this overtly but somehow unknown world, she knows that practically nothing is forbidden. The civil wars the Internet revolution in turbulent West Africa had brought some forms of local exposures of people in religiously sex shy Liberia and the neighbor countries. As it is the case with many close-knit society in Africa where everybody knows each other deeds, people live a pretentious life; often shying away from the discussion of sex, sexual gender-based violent and teenage sexual exploitation by society's elite. The long-run Liberian civil conflict enable many of its citizens to have traveled to many countries all over the world. As a result, many of them were now returning home with various levels of skills, knowledge, and sexual exposures. Young women are now piercing the ears in multiple place, tongues, nipples, clitoris, belly button and other parts of their bodies. Our young men are also piercing the penises, scrotums, noses, tongues and their bodies' parts that were once considered a taboo by local cultures and religious mores.

Now, if only Ernestine could just muster up the nerves to walk through those damn double paneled glass doors that lead to the conference room, her life would never be the same. She would not be the soft target for any perverted male sexual exploitation. She would be transformed, she would be hardened by this new venture because of the enmity and disaffection of society's deceitful venoms. She would find a place among romantic gods and legendary Liberian writers like Kiru Taye, K. Moses Nagbe, Emmanuel Clarke, and dozens other who have defied the status quo to become who they are today.

That afternoon, Ernestine tried not to be too hard on herself. After all, anytime anyone made a career change they were bound to have some butterflies in their stomach. She was not the first, neither is she going to be the last Liberian female to switch trade or a professional career. Unfortunately, what Ernestine was feeling went far beyond butterflies or career change shock. She felt more like huge vultures were flying around inside of her, picking at her innards.

This event was the first post Ebola *"Sensual Writers' Conference"* in the seaside capital. It was expectantly crowded. As Ernestine tried to better compose herself, a middle-aged woman brushed past her and hurried inside the conference hall. Ernestine knew it was now or never—time to either bite the bullet and commit to doing the work she loved, or to wimp out by continuing to write the same old stories she'd been pumping out since graduating for the University of Liberia. She needed to live her life without making so many apologies to strangers, not even the President of Liberia who openly ridicules sensual romance writings, but loves reading it behind closed doors. The president has also become a disappointment to many supporters far and near because of the living conditions of the ordinary citizens within Monrovia and other parts of the country, as well as for the manner in which the government's handles corruption.

"If she can do it, so can I," Ernestine told herself firmly. She squared her shoulders, brushed back her braided hair with one hand and set off for the door. Mustering up courage, she pushed the rotating door and stepped inside. Like a scared dragon hunter who has just entered into a dragon's lair, she took a deep Earth shuttering breath with her eyes closed.

Ernestine was so focused on her goal, on making it past the threshold of her current comfort level, she didn't see the attractive, muscular man who was just about to step through the doorway from behind her. They collided as Ernestine bumped into him from the side in a particularly graceless way, the full-body impact knocking them both to the floor. Ernestine tried to catch her breath as she lay in a heap atop the handsome stranger.

Absolutely mortified by her awkwardness, Ernestine scrambled to get up off the man, but not before she became aware of the firm muscles of his butt, back and shoulders rippling beneath her. When she realized what she had done, her heart skipped several beats as she tried to put herself back together again.

Overcome by both embarrassment and a rare jolt of lust,

she blathered on and on without being able to stop herself. "Oh my gosh! Jesus Christ, I'm so sorry! I can't believe I didn't see you and then I walked right into you, and then I fell on top of you and now we're laying on the ground and...and are you okay?"

He pushed himself up on his palms and then spun around so that he was sitting on the tiled floor, the stranger gave her a devastating smile. Brushing the dust off his jeans and his yellow blazer, he stood up and said, *"I'm doing just fine, thank you. I hope you're ok as well. I think it must had been the newly tiled floor."*

Ernestine was bowled over by the dimple in his left cheek and could do little else but gape at the man standing in front of her. She thought she knew him, only her memories could not serve her right at that present moment. *"And besides,"* he added magnanimously with a mischievous glint in his eyes, *"who wouldn't want to have a gorgeous woman like you lying on top of him first thing in the morning?"*

Ernestine felt her cheeks turn purple, and she covered them with her hands, hoping to cool them down. When she turned and bend over to pick up a pen that had dropped out of her bag, Stanley's heart skipped several beats upon seeing her enormous ass that was rubbing against her summer dress. He quick took his eyes off her ass before she could make an eye contact again. He didn't know that is how she was well shaped up when they first met at the We Care Library on Carey Street that night.

Looking slightly repentant, he said, *"I hope I haven't made you uncomfortable. I'm just joking around. You looked like you were heading into a Roman Coliseum to face the lions for a minute. I felt the same way the first time I attended this event 26 years ago at the E.J. Roye Building on Ashmun Street."*

Ernestine dropped her hands from her face and gave him a small smile. *"I just feel like such an idiot for knocking you over like that."*

The handsome eligible bachelor held up his hand to stop her from reprimanding herself any further. *"I can't stand to hear you insult yourself anymore. Especially since I don't even know your real name yet."* Holding out his hand, he said, *"I'm Stanley...Stanley Nimely. I think we met before, haven't we?"*

As the warmth of his skin encircled her beautiful hand, she relaxed for the first time since she'd parked her car outside the hotel's parking lot several minutes earlier. She said, *"Ernestine. I am Ernestine Johnson. It's nice to meet you again, Mr. Stanley Nimely. I never thought I would've seen you since that unfortunate incident at the library that evening. How is your new book coming along? I can't wait to read it."*

She could tell he was trying to put her at ease as he picked up her peach colored leather bag and handed it to her. *"I am having some writer's block here and there, but I am polishing it up for my agent to submit for publication,"* he gave her an easy smile. *"Is this your first conference? I've never seen you here before,"* he asked as he looked the beautiful woman in the eyes.

Ernestine nodded with a beautiful smile. *"Is it that obvious that I'm a newbie? I am soooo....nervous, Mr. Nimely."*

Stanley shook his head and gave her one of his signature deep penetrating looks as he straightened out his blazer of any wrinkle before saying, *"Nope, that's not it. I'm just pretty sure if I'd ever met you here before, besides the meeting at the library last month"*

Ernestine blushed again and silently admonished herself to cut it out. *"I'm sort of new to this genre. I am really going to be needing a whole lot of guidance on my new adventure. The event's promoter said something about a mentoring program for newcomers like myself in the advertisement."*

"To sensual erotica, you mean? Don't worry, there are lots of mentors within this close-knit group you're about to be a part of. We are never short of professionals willing to teach the techniques of the trade to people like you." Stanley replied.

She nodded as if in approval of what Stanley had just said. *"WOW! I'm really excited about making the switch from young adult fiction to sensual romantic fiction, but I guess I'm feeling a little overwhelmed today by it all."*

Stanley smiled. *"I know exactly how you feel. I must admit, I really enjoy your story that night at the library. I hated the way those folks treated you after all. Most Liberians are good at pretending about subjects like the one you had in your storyline, but they are the same people that consume such products in their private lives."*

"You really did!? I just wished people in this part of the world would appreciate our talents and honor us for taken the road less traveled. I wondered what are you doing here being the accomplished romance author you're" Ernestine beamed with excitement followed by a question.

Stanley response was in the affirmative, *"Yes, you're right about that. Some Liberians are very hateful of local talents. Many of them are not supportive of each other. Most of the times, many of these hate-mongers would rather support foreigners than see you and me thrive, Ernestine. I really hated what happened to you that night, but it will make you a better and focused romance writer in the long term. I am here to meet some of the newbies that are willing to be helped. I've been going at sensual romance—"* he stopped and cleared his throat.

"…What I mean is, I've been writing sensual erotica romance for a little over twenty years now. I can honestly say it is the most enjoyable, challenging writing I've ever done. When I first made the switch from general romance to sensual erotica romance, it was pretty daunting. The folks in this country, especially the religious leaders, the lawmakers and even the

government officials, are all hypocrites."

While he talked, Ernestine thought there was something vaguely familiar about Stanley's statement, but she couldn't quite put her finger on it. In any case, although she was greatly enjoying talking with him, she was worried about monopolizing his time.

"Thanks for the pep talk, Mr. Nimely. I don't want you to feel like you have to baby-sit me all morning. I'm a big girl. I'll be all right, this I can promise you." She said followed by a beautiful smile.

Giving her an enigmatic look that set her heart pounding like a drum in her chest, Stanley brushed off her concerns. *"You know what, Ernestine, You can call me Stan or Stanley,"* he said, with her name rolling off his tongue like warm butter on a hot Fante Bread. *"And one more thing, I'd like nothing better than to show you around the conference hall and to introduce you to some of my friends and colleagues that are also in the business."* Leaning in closer to her he added with a wink, *"Not that I don't think you're capable of taking care of yourself, of course. As an old hand in the business, I think you can draw on my strengths to begin with. As a beginner, it is always good to plug into a positive energy, and a worthy fountain of knowledge."*

This time, instead of blushing at his double-entendre, Ernestine laughed. *"Thank God I'm starting to get your sense of humor,"* she said. *"And by the way, if you're going to be my chaperone, why don't you call me Honey? The only people who ever use my full name are either my mother or my elementary school teachers when I really got into trouble for doing something I had no business doing."*

Clearly unable to stop teasing her, in a rough undertone Stanley asked, *"Did you get into trouble a lot, Honey?"*

Ernestine swallowed and stared into Stanley dark brown eyes. The flash of lust she had felt when their bodies had collided jumped inside of her full-force this time. Forcing herself to remember to be cautious, to remember how badly she'd been hurt by Monrovia men. A quick shadow passed over her eyes.

Shrugging, she finally replied, *"More times than I can count."*

If Stanley noticed her swift change of demeanor, he didn't let on. Looping his arm through hers, he said, *"I'm going to take you in now. As a heads up, I'm warning you to be prepared for insanity. We're a naughty little bunch, you know us sensual romance writers. Liberia hates us because of the erotica scenes many of us weave into our books and storylines, but we love what we do so much that we do not give a damn about what they think of us anymore. We just let them worry about what they think of us, as we keep living our lives without apologies. The fact of the matter is, the people that matter to us do not care about us, and the people we care so much about, we do not matter to them. So why worry about who loves or hates you? Take my little advice, live your life without an apology or a regret, Honey."*

Shaking off her painful memories, Ernestine smiled up at Stanley. *"Lead me on, oh mighty wise one,"* she said in a mocked subservience tone. *"Lead me on, and I will gladly follow thee."*

Stanley directed them into a huge crowded room, which had at least a dozen different information booths set up inside the large conference room within the hotel's east room. Ernestine gaped at the displays all around them and started to wonder if it was too late for her to make her escape.

Seeming to sense her growing embarrassment in that incredibly perceptive way of his, Stanley held firm to her hand. *"Now just remember,"* he said, leaning down to whisper in her ear, *"there's nothing to be embarrassed about with these folks. We're all in the business for the same reasons—because we love it, and don't care what others say or think about us. Many Liberians read these books in solitude, but pretend in the open to abhor our work. No one's going to look down upon you or call you a porno writer today, I promise."*

Shivering as his breath gently blew against her ear, she looked up at him, a question in her eyes. *"How did you know people have been giving me a hard time about writing erotica?"*

Stanley gestured to the group of people in the room with them. *"Every one of us has had to deal with misconceptions at one point or another in our careers."* With a grimace he added, *"And I'd be lying to you if I said it's all a bed of roses, even after more than twenty years in the business. I am sure you followed closely the case brought against me by the government of Liberia almost two years ago, right?"* He nodded at her and then continued to speak. *"They hate us when we write about their sexual behaviors. Did you know that some government officials as well as some big shots around here are infecting young girls and boys with HIV and AIDS. The government is not providing the necessary social service program that will get young prostitutes out of the street and give them a future. The elites of this society are sexually exploiting our future generation for as little as five United States Dollars or two hundred fifty Liberian Dollars. If you write about these things and caution people to practice safe sex by using condom or abstain from sex, you're accused of perverting the youth. The President knows about all of these things that are going on, but pretends not to know, or maybe, cares less about the health of the people or the behavior of government's official. Don't listen to these noises, my friend, because they're meant to discourage you or silence you forever."* He quickly pulled her out the way of Gabriel Y. Montgomery who was himself a new writer who had interacted with Stanley and asked him if he could show him how to write a best seller romance novel.

Suddenly, Ernestine was overwhelmed by the clear picture of the two of them, entwined together on a bed of rose petals.

As warm summer heat pooled between her legs, she forced the vision from her head to quickly go away.

Thankfully, he didn't wait for her response and led them up to the first booth by the door, which to Ernestine's dismay had the most comprehensive display of dildos, vibrators, lubricants, and other sex toys she had ever seen amassed in one place—especially in Liberia. *"WOW!"* Was the only word that could come out of her pretty mouth.

Actually, considering she had never even gotten up the nerve to walk into any of the adult novelty stores on Carey Street in Central Monrovia. They were the only dildos she had ever seen outside of a magazine ads or X-Rated adult movies.

"Honey, this is Vernon, aka V. Cap. He's an old-timer around here, and frankly, without him, none of us sensual romance or erotica writers would be worth a dime. He's the owner of Vernon's Playground, a novelty store on McDonald Street." Stanley introduced her to one of his colleagues.

Ernestine managed to muster up a smile for the gray-haired, gray-bearded six-two man, and reached out her hand to shake his.

"Don't be shy missy," Vernon barked at her. *"Feel free to wrap your hands around any one of these babies to find out what they really feel like. I've got rubber. I've got really life-like skin. I've got hard dildos and soft dildos and dildos with vibrators attached. I've got bullet dildos safe and portable for taking on trips. They come in a many different colors, including day-glo green with florescent pink stripes, if you're really looking for something to spice up a scene."*

Ernestine wanted nothing more than for the ground to open up and swallow her whole. She had never been so uncomfortable in her entire life. What made her think she could write erotica, she wondered frantically? For God's sake, she had never even been able to have an orgasm during sex.

And she certainly had never used a vibrator, or any kind of penis-like dildo to get herself off. Considering how naughty she felt when she used her index and middle fingers to bring herself to orgasm, she now had to face just how far over her head she was.

Looking slightly at Ernestine, Stanley remarked, "*Vernon is a walking guru of sex toys. Thank God he's willing to share his knowledge or I'd look like an idiot in more books than I'm willing to mention. This man is a living legend in this business.*"

Ernestine slyly stared at Vernon from the corner of her eyes. "*Really,*" she asked in admiration to the man's reputation.

"*Oh, yes he is. Vernon has a lot of clienteles in higher places—government, the military, local and international NGOs, and even the diplomatic corps. He was the first Liberian to import adult magazines into this country. In fact, he is one of those behind the scene people who run the sex scenes in Monrovia. He has hundreds of escorts that he often places with high-value clients. I heard he was the guy who put Willie Knuckles up to having Ménage à trois with the former Miss Liberia and the other lady that you saw in that infamous picture that was published in one of the local papers and was circulating over the Internet. I know you didn't think that Vernon was the man behind the camera taking the pictures of Old-Man Willie Knuckles. Vernon has a treasure throve of photo of the Vice President of Liberia, the Speaker of the House of Representative, The Nigerian Ambassador, as well as many representatives, senators, and other higher-ups within the country. To be frank with you, I really love this Vernon guy, Honey. He is a real trailblazer in this business,*" Stanley massaged the back of Ernestine's hand as they were about to walk away.

"*Mr. Knuckles never recovered from that incident, even up to his death in 2016. Ever since that time his entire life went up-side-down. The girl… I mean the Miss Liberia you mentioned life became a mess in this damn town. It was a complete wickedness that was done to her reputation. That girl is my first cousin form my mother side of the family. We Liberians are very evil to one another, especially if we want to do something to our fellow citizens as a form of retributive justice. Her image should not have been damaged the way it was. I am not sure where in the world she is right now, but I hope she has recovered from that saga and is going on with her life,"* Ernestine said, almost whisperingly as if she did not want anyone hearing the old new which was an open secret in the small gossiping city by the Atlantic Ocean.

"Believe me honey, I know what you are talking about. I too have felt the way that young woman did, but only on a different level. I think that girl should have defended her reputation by taking to the airwaves and on the different television stations that were operating in the country at that time. Please not that no evil goes unpunished. The person who release that picture will get their pay one day. You know as the saying goes, "Kama is a bitch." Vernon has learned from that mistake of sending picture to his clients' e-mail and through carrier services, I am sure. Life is a master teacher, only the dull ones will refuse to learn lessons she teaches her children," Stanley winked at Vernon and squeezed Ernestine's hands softly.

Ernestine nodded mutely, knowing words were beyond her at that point. She vividly recalled the firestorm that bellowed following the publication of the photograph with Mr. Knuckles in a threesome sex act with the former beauty queen and another local woman who she knew very well. Back then, Willie Knuckles was a government official and a staunched confidant of the President of Liberia at that time. The self-deprecating published photograph forced him to resign his official post within the government. Following the release of the picture, many people believed the publication of the image was politically motivated by one of Mr. Knuckles' political rivals who was a member of the Liberian legislature. As for the fate of the former beauty queen, she went on to found a none profit organization called, Saving Mothers' Femininity. Like Stanley, she has made rescuing young and exploited girls her lifelong mission, but her past has bedeviled her organization's noble quest.

Not letting Ernestine run off, Stanley held fast to her hand. *"We'll talk to you again, Vernon,"* he said as he directed them to another booth.

At first glance, this one looked to be far tamer than Vernon's booth, with a simple display of hardcover books for sale. Ernestine breathed a sigh of relief.

Introducing her, Stanley said, *"This is my friend Ernestine. Ernestine this is Kerkula Joneson. He's pretty much a hero around here."*

Laughing, Kerkula said, *"Only second to you, buddy."* Turning to greet Ernestine, he said, *"Welcome to the wild and wacky world of erotica romance. Buckle your seatbelt and enjoy the wild ride down memory lane. We're a unique group of misunderstood people in this country and elsewhere in Africa, my darling. Do not mind what the critics say about us, we will endure for 10,000 more years, just like the Roman did in time of old. Even the President of Liberia has a dark and freaky erotica side, my darling."*

Ernestine laughed and gave silent thanks that everyone was working so hard to put her at ease. Of course, she knew that meant she was probably walking around with a panic-stricken look on her face. Telling herself she was doing her best in a new situation, she said, *"I'm beginning to sense a theme here."*

When Ernestine caught sight of the cover of one of Kerkula's latest book on display for sales, she almost gasped aloud. Depicted on the cover were a man and a light-skin woman in sixty-nine position along with the title, *Sixty-Nine Kinds of Love Making in Cape Palmas.* Knowing she was trapped in a full-body flush, with Stanley's hand tucked in hers, all she could think about was what it would feel like if his head was buried between her legs, his tongue lapping at her swollen clitoris. No matter how hard she tried to clear the sexy vision from her mind, she just couldn't. He was sexily irresistible to any well-meaning and open-minded female, to say the least.

Fortunately, the two men were busy catching up with each other, and hadn't noticed her reaction to the sexy book cover.

"So, how's the new book going, Stanley? I heard your working title for it is called 'The Black Mamba'? I think a more fitting title would be 'Sex After Dark, A Liberian Erotica.'" Kerkula asked and then suggested.

"Pretty good," Stanley replied, running his free hand over his short jet black hair. *"Although I'm having some trouble with my character's motivations, but I'll figure it out in time. You know us writers, we put too much time in fleshing out our characters. Like me, my main character is having some women's problems such that he cannot find the right one to settle down with."*

Kerkula laughed and said to Ernestine, *"I swear to God, this is the only author I know who wants to know what his characters ate for breakfast in high school. Most of us are contended to be able to do a character sketch for their past couple of years. Our Liberian readers do not care about those fine details in a novel."*

"Wow," Ernestine said to Stanley. *"You sound pretty thorough."*

The look Stanley gave her was so hot she felt seared to the bone. At least to her panties, which were beginning to feel distinctly moist between her legs. *"I am,"* he said hoarsely and then blinked hard a couple of times. For Stanley, it was like being in a twilight zone —especially with the beautiful lady standing by his side as he tried to coax her into stepping into his world filled with limitless sexual adventures.

Clearing his throat, Kerkula said, *"Oh, I almost forgot. There's a woman here from the Inquirer Newspaper and she wants to interview you about your other book, The Scent and Taste of Morning Sex."*

Ernestine gasped. *"You wrote The Scent and Taste of Morning Sex? You're S. Kla Nimely?"*

A faint flush stole across his face. *"That's me, my dear."*

Too stunned to keep the words from falling out of her mouth, she said, *"You're the reason why I wanted to get into sensual romance. You and S. Kla Nimely. I love you both."* Realizing her sentence had come out all wrong, she tried to backpedal, saying, *"What I meant is that I absolutely love and exalt your books. I didn't know you wrote using pseudo names. They move me more than anything else I've ever read! Oh my God, I didn't know it was you all along. I am so sorry. I am your number one fan in the whole world. I am so blessed to be standing next to you, hand-in-hand, Mr. Nimely."* She was now animated as she glowed with excitement.

Stanley looked incredibly pleased. *"Really?"*

Cutting in, Kerkula said, *"You're not the first person who became a convert after reading his stuff. At least half of the people in the room did the very same thing, I included."*

Suddenly, Ernestine felt incredibly foolish. *"And here I am, taking up all of your time, when so many people must be dying to get a word with you. Here I am with my hand tucked in yours, WOW!"*

No matter what she said Stanley refused to relinquish her hand. He saw more in her than the novice she saw herself to be. In Ernestine, Stanley saw a successful writer and a lifetime partner if she was not already taken. In as much as he was attracted to her, one part of him told him to go slow because looks can sometimes be deceiving.

Right then, an attractive, naturally enhanced caramel skin, whose tits were each the size of Ernestine's head, sidled up to Stanley. *"I was just over at the mentoring table and they told me you don't have anyone under you yet."* Licking her lips for impact, having stressed the word *'under'* as if it was a magical spell she could weave around him, she pouted and added, *"They said you had the final word on who you were going to work with."* Walking her long, polished Chinese nails up his arm she said, *"So, are you free for some lessons?"*

Ernestine wasn't sure if her mind was playing tricks on her, considering her gut was teeming with jealous bile, but she thought she saw Stanley flinch and back away from the big-breasted Monrovia-Amazon warrior, as her mother used to referred to a voluptuous woman who aggressively throws herself at a man, even if that man was already married or in some committed relationship.

Turning to her, with a cunning smile on his face, he said, *"Actually, Ernestine has already snatched me up. I am so sorry, darling."*

"I did?" she said questioningly, before she caught the pleading look Stanley was pinning her with. Trying to recover from the shock of being singled out by the man she respected more than any other writer in the country, she smiled and slapped him playfully on the arm with her free hand, trying to look like she was just joking around.

"Of course, I did. I'm just teasing you." Then she turned to the Monrovia-Amazon-bitch and said with false syrupiness, *"Actually, I tackled him the minute I saw him walking through the doors to make sure he'd be all mine."*

Glaring at them both with fire in her eyes, the Amazon spat out *"It's your loss,, buddy"* at Stanley and then went in search of a new prey.

Stanley led Ernestine into a semi-private corner of the room. *"I'm really sorry about that back there. If you don't want me to be your mentor, I understand perfectly."*

Ernestine blinked in confusion. *"I don't even know what my mentor is supposed to do."*

Giving her a reassuring smile, Stanley said, *"All of the established writers sign up to work with a new writer. You know, to show them the ropes. I think God is doing something here.....I think he's trying to make me show you the way to being one of the best around here."*

Ernestine's brain was assailed with visions of Stanley tying her up to golden bedposts, while she writhed underneath him and begged him to make sweet love to her as hard and fast as he could. She shook her head, wondering when the hell she had started to have such incredibly vivid sexual daydreams on one of the most sought after men in the country.

Looking up at him, suddenly shy, she said, *"I can't think of anyone I'd rather work with."*

And just like that, she leapt head first into the unknown, with the most sexually potent man she had ever encountered in the city of Monrovia, the most beautiful city known by Stanley.

That day at the conference, Ernestine waited patiently for Stanley to complete all of his presentations to the more than tree hundred participants in the room. As she watched him give speech after speech at the podium, all she could imagine was seeing herself sitting on Stanley's face as he ate her up from behind she stroked and massaged his manhood with both hands. While forming all these dirty images of she and Stanley, she later cautioned herself to be more careful perhaps Stanley was a married man or he might be in a serious relationship with a woman more beautiful than here. Her caution was for the fact that Stanley is every woman's choice of mate, and it was just impossible for an eligible man like him to be single in a city with so many hungry women and men in search of true love and relationship.

From her fantasy, she then switched her thought to the professional working relationship she was about to go in with one of the country's highly controversial writers. *"If all he will do all that he said, then I have no doubt of becoming one of the best writers in this country,"* Ernestine whispered to herself.

CHAPTER 5

The autumn's sun was beating down hard on the financially recovering and romantically evolving oceanfront city. Schools and colleges were in session and both government and private employees in Monrovia were busy doing their bosses' jobs. On the outskirt of the city and elsewhere in the country, maids and domestic servants were preparing midday meals for their employers and other financial benefactors. Stanley paid the delivery boy from Terravilla Garden Floral Design Shop located in Johnsonville which was about thirty miles outside of Monrovia. He ordered the flower three days earlier to be delivered on this particular day for his first lesson with Ernestine. After paying for the flowers and giving the delivery boy a tip, from the doorway he watched the delivery boy get back into his delivery van and drove away as the watch man opened the gate for the van to leave the premises. He picked up the surprisingly heavy box of red, pink, and purple rose petals, placed them on the floor of his foyer, and closed the front door with a soft click. He leaned his forehead against the back of his front door and closed his eyes.

At least a hundred times in the past week, ever since he had coerced Ernestine into letting him be her mentor, he had told himself not to mess this up. From the first moment he met her at the library, to the moment that she had landed atop him the entrance of the hotel, he knew she was special.

He knew she had a positive vibratory mental energy field around her. The feel of her big round soft ass was something he could not get out of his head. He thought her ass measured at least 40 or 45 inches in diameter. His mind could not conjure up the image of seeing her big and soft mother's gift of an ass without clothing, in its natural state, just like her beloved mother had brought her into this world screaming as a newborn. Stanley was never an ass-man, but lately, he had developed a great appetite for big booty women. In fact, most African men love women with big rear end—Liberian men are more interested in a female's booty than her inner and physical beauties. For some, they are willing to give up or let go of a skinny educated woman that may hold a better promise for tomorrow for an illiterate girl from the ghetto with a big round ass. Many of these men often give sorrowful excuses such as, *"love doesn't ask why and how; or education does not work inside the bedroom"*. Others would argue that they do not care about a female's intellect other than her outer beautiful and her bedroom performance. Many of these contemporary Liberian men aptly believe the acronym for LIBERIA is, '*Love Is Blind Even Relationships In Africa*'.

Talking about women with big booties, since the civil war ended more than twelve years ago, most Liberian women have developed bigger bottoms for some unknown reasons. And the hotter the country has gotten, the lesser and lesser clothes their booties wear—often, they do this so the booty can breathe. No matter which part of Liberia one travels, there are women with killer apple-bottom shapes and amazing asses. Women of all ages in the country can be seen wearing miniskirts and low-cut short dresses way beneath their beautiful butt-lines. The beautiful shapes of Liberian women booties have caused the men within the country to argue among themselves about the county that has women with the biggest and more beautiful cake, as America- Liberian men often referred to the buttock of a female. Based on these gentlemanly booty arguments, Stanley Kla Nimely once wrote a book that solely eulogized Liberian and African women butts. In this book, due to of his many experiences having slept with more women than any man can boast of, he categorized the various booties based on environmental variables, locations, and cultural heritage.

In his book, titled, *Booty-ology* Stanley maintained that Liberian women are not only beautiful superficially, clean on the outside and unique inside, but have the most amazing booty and beautifully astounding shapes in all of Africa. Stanley believed that the Lofa County booty got its killer-shape and renowned buoyancy from its heavy soda torborgee diet that the people of the county are known for. Talking about the Grand Bassa County booty, Stanley said it is the round-shaped and dumboy-like texture of the booty that leaves a lasting sexual-effect on foreigners that visit the country and has made many Indians and Lebanese merchants to take a permanent residence in Liberia without government's permission. While the Grand Kru and Maryland Counties booties, he asserted that the booties firmed shapes are characterized by their booties density, which makes Grebo and Kru women a model of attraction on the shore of Liberia that made early Spanish and Portuguese explorers to make Liberia a rest stop during their exploratory voyages in the 6th Century. As for the Grand Cape Mont County booties, Stanley believed it is a consensus among Liberian and Sierra Leonean men that the women's Sierra Leonean and Lorma genetic contributions have given the booty its jelly mass and fine firm shape that makes a man wants to empty his wallet to the last dime once in the company of a Vai or a Mande woman. And for the Monrovia booty, Stanley asserted that it has been known for centuries that the Monrovia sun and ocean current bakes and sears all the Monrovia booty juices into a slow roast and have given the booty its apple-bottom shape which keeps many of the men living in the Diaspora to keep running home every year to get a good taste of a real homegrown booty. And for the Nimba, Bong, and Grand Gedeh Counties booties, Stanley believed that the elevations in those areas have allowed gravity to transform the booties of women in those counties into a guy's worshiping trophy which often makes men in those regions to commit some of the most unthinkable crimes whenever they catch their spouses in infidelity. In this book, Stanley cited that it is not the warm reception and kindness of the people that makes Liberia foreigners friendly and Diasporas men favorite vacation destination. Rather, he contests that it is the booty that makes Liberia sweet and beautiful—no wonder he nicknamed the country *"LIB"*, short for, *"Liberia Is Bootiful."*

"Don't fuck this up, Stanley," he said aloud and listened to his words bounce off the shiny tiled flooring and the expansive windows that flooded his house with light.

Unfortunately, every time he thought about Ernestine's big ass and queen-size breast, he got lightheaded and his heart would start beating to a heavy-metal rhythm within his chest.

He thought back to their phone call, the Monday after the erotic writers' conference and groaned, remembering how lamed he sounded as he outlined his mentoring plan to her. He banged his forehead against the door several times as his words flooded back into his brain.

"Thanks so much for offering to work with me, Stanley. I am really looking forward to it," she had said.

He had said, *"You know what? I think we're both going to get a lot out of this."* But then, as he realized how creepy he sounded, he backpedaled. *"What I mean is, there's nothing more enlightening than trying to teach another person what you already know. It's a good chance for me to see if I actually know what I'm talking about, or if I've just been faking my way through my last fifteen books."*

Belatedly, Stanley realized he was going on and on about utter nonsense so he added, *"Does that make sense to you?"*

His palms got slick and sweaty on the handset of his cell phone as he waited for her response. Trying to put him at ease, she said, *"I know exactly what you mean, Stanley. And by the way, I've been thinking we should probably be upfront about things when we meet."*

"What things?" Stanley asked, so suddenly nervous his heart was going clickity-click and he could swear he heard Zack Roberts, one of Liberia's legendary musical artists singing "Linda" in his head.

"I want you to know that you don't need to worry about the vocabulary you use when we're talking about work. I know you're a complete gentleman and that everything we do during our lessons is purely professional and not the Liberian professional way. I've read your books and I know your language. Therefore, please feel free to say what you need to say during our mentoring session." She cleared her throat and then added, *"Even if we do happen to deal with things like dildos, anal sex, orgies, and even kinky sex in our profession. I am in for the ride."*

Stanley head was reeling, but he managed to force a chuckle; nevertheless inwardly he felt like the world's biggest scum. Sure, his intentions were honorable. He was going to teach Ernestine how to write great erotica. He really couldn't deny the fact that in the privacy of his heart and imagination he had already devised twenty different ways he wanted to make Ernestine scream with pleasure mixed with a little pain. Stanley was like any typical Liberian man who never render a free favor to a beautiful woman without having a hidden agenda—many of them always want something in return for any gesture that is awarded a female who were not an immediate member of their family. As for Stanley, he wanted to pound her so hard until her squirted sweet juices.

No matter how strongly he felt about her, he had decided to put the lid on his desire until their mentoring sessions were through—jumping into her honeycomb during their lessons would be a complete betrayal of her trust. He only hoped urge for her didn't kill him in the meantime. If God could ask him what he wanted before he died, Ernestine would be the first item on his bucket list of wants he would present to his Heavenly Father.

"Good," he'd said prentiously. *"I'm glad we are being completely upfront about everything right from the start. I knew you were the right person to work with."*

"Frankly, I was afraid that Sheba Queen of the Amazon Hopo Joe wouldn't have left you in one piece by the time she was done with you. I had no choice, but to save you from utter destruction by offering up myself to you, kind sir." She was quite frank with her words.

Stanley let himself savor the vision of Ernestine tied and bound to an altar, naked and gleaming, in sacrifice for him, before he said, *"I appreciate that. More than you know. I come across women like her every time, at least eight or ten times a week."*

"So how do you handle them? How do you deal with those situations?" she asked as she eagerly waited for his response.

"I do just what I did the other day by using diversionary tactic. Sometimes I give them the silence treatment. If they're persistent, I find an 'I am busy' excuse for them," he replied.

"So, what's on the agenda when we meet?" She asked him, and just like that his entire body broke out in a sweat as he unfolded the piece of paper he'd written their lesson plan on.

He tried to keep his voice light, he said, *"I've broken our mentoring sessions into five different lessons. Lesson one will be on how to set a romantic scene."*

"That sounds great. I love the way you paint pictures in

many of your books." Her eyes sparkled with excitement upon hearing the Stanley's plan

"Thanks," he'd said, and then swallowed loudly as he prepared to continue spelling out his list of lessons. Lesson one was the easy one, and he knew things were only going to get harder from here, especially if the rock-hard bulge in his pants was any indication.

"Let's see, for lesson two I thought we'd work on varying positions. Oh shit! What have just said?" He tried hard to back off on lesson two by explaining. *"I mean, we'll take a look at.....uh, you know study the different ways that, ummm..."*

Suddenly he couldn't think of any way to rephrase the sentence that wouldn't sound like he planned on screwing her brains out the minute she walked through his door. Thankfully, she reminded him in a gentle voice, *"Stanley,...... Stanley, please, you've got to stop worrying about offending me."* She tried to put him at ease within his own kingdom.

"Okay," he said, but his trepidation must have been clear in his voice, because she said, *"Say fuck ten times to me. And don't act like you're not a Liberian man. You know guys' sexuality lies in their hands while females' lies deep within their souls."*

He sighed, *"Huh?"*

"Just say it. just say it because it will feel very therapeutic," she demanded.

"Fuck, fuck, fuck, fuck, fuck, fuck, fuck, fuck, fuck, fuck," Stanley repeated as he had been demanded to.

Ernestine laughed and went further to instruct him to. *"Good. Now say, 'I want to lick and fuck your sweet and juicy pussy,'"* she commanded him.

Stanley choked on an intake of breath, but he did as she asked. He repeated, *"I want to lick and fuck your sweet and juicy pussy.*" Even as he imagined how amazing she would taste, he braced himself for her disgust, expecting her to say, *"You're a complete scum and I never want to talk to you again."* Just like Theresa Urey with the big ass and the Nigerian accent did him on their blind date at P.A's Rib House more than two month ago.

"Do you feel better now?" She asked as she looked him deep in the eyes.

He took a moment to gauge his feelings and realized, much to his surprise, that his palms were dry again and his heart rate had returned to near-normal. Ernestine, in her sly way, had forced him over the hump of his anxieties. Yet again, he was impressed by what a clever little piece of work this delectable woman was. He was not sure if she was trying to get into his head or figure him out, whatever her agendas were, she somehow succeeded.

"Thanks for that, Ernestine. You definitely have a knack for dialogue. And now that I've decided to stop being such an idiot, here are the rest of my lesson plans." He spoke quickly and didn't pause between lessons. *"Lesson three–using toys. Lesson four–the joy of sex in exciting locations. Lesson five–how to use role playing to really up the ante."*

He knew if he gave himself even a second to think about her reaction he'd start to make an even bigger ass of himself than he already had, so he barreled ahead. *"So, how about we start next Saturday at my house on Rehab Road in Paynesville? Noon?"*

"Great," she'd said and hung up the phone as soon as he gave her his home address which was located about thirty miles on the other side of a city that was now recovering from the Ebola virus disease and more than a decade and a half of civil unrest.

Now here he was, on the big day he'd long awaited, with

noon quickly approaching. Through great force of will, Stanley stopped banging his head on the door, stopped torturing himself with thoughts of what a jerk Ernestine thought he was, picked up the box of rose petals and walked into his guest's bedroom to finish preparing the classroom.

Stanley had decided the best way to teach Ernestine how to set a romantic scene was to show her one in real life. He knew, however, that using his master bedroom on the second floor for any of these lessons like he had done in the past with other new comers was a very bad idea. As it was, in the past seven days he had beaten off his dick to the picture of her he had burned in his head so many times while lying in his bed and while showering, as soon as he walked into his master bedroom it was practically a reflex for him to reach for his dick and start pumping it in his hand or his vacuum penis enlargement pump Vernon gave him several years back. In fact, he'd wacked off so many times with the image of her he had burned in his brain. From using the penis enlargement pump three time a week to enlarge his dick had caused his manhood to grow beyond his own imagination that he though Ernestine might not be able to handle if she ever agree to make love to him. Again, he knew that any pussy, be it of a girl 18 years old and up, can handle dick of any size and length.

Standing in the doorway of his large guest room, he surveyed the space with a critical eye. He had draped the four-post queen-sized on the velvety-bed with an Indian silk he'd bought from down Walter Street in Monrovia from an Indian merchant. In his writer's mind, he could see two lovers deep within their own world, sheathed in the exotic silk from the East.

He had covered the mattress in red plush velvet, and underneath the luxurious cover, he had put red satin sheets. To top it off, a dozen pillows fought for space near the head of the bed.

Stanley had never been particularly interested in interior design—although he felt like he had done a nice job with making his house as comfortable and cozy reflection of himself—but as he went from store to store on Randall and Walter Streets in search of some of the finest fabrics to spice up his home, he knew he was a man with great taste in material things. As he ran his fingers lightly over the fabrics on the bed, he realized that he was, in fact, greatly enjoying himself in the guest room. Ironically, Stanley did not entertain that many guests in his home because of his busy lifestyle. Due to his busyness, his parents and siblings often complaint about him not being accessible at all. Often, his mother would come to house sit when he was not around. Should had discussed the plight of the orphans that lived behind his six foot fence—she wanted Stanley to care for the two boy, he had informed her that he would thinking about it.

His enjoyment, he thought ruefully, may have sprung from his intense desire to see Ernestine wrapped in the silks, velvets, and satins he purchased several weeks ago.

Or, more to the point, his even more intense desire was to unwrap her from the sheets.

He tried to shake the image of Ernestine naked with her legs spread wide open before him, begging for him to ram his thirteen-inch monster inside her wet and ready vagina. He needed to focus on the task at hand. He had draped the windows with shimmering translucent red fabric, shot through with gold thread. Then he'd brought light back into the room with candles of varying sizes and colors, which he had placed on every possible surface. Stanley was not the typical Liberian man—he seriously had great tastes in clothes and designs, especially homes deco and cars.

On the bare tiled floor in front of the wall mount 50 inch flat-screen television he had laid a chenille rug. It felt so good to the touch in the store he couldn't resist buying it. He wondered if Ernestine lay face down on the rug and rubbed her breasts across it slowly, what would the soft fabric feel like brushing against her hard and ready nipples?

The rose petals were the final touch. Checking his watch and noting it was a quarter to twelve, he bent down, opened the large box and reached into the mass of flower petals.

To his great satisfaction, the scent of the roses wasn't overpowering. As he had hoped, the flowers lent an alluring air of sweetness to the room. *"I see why people choose Terravilla Garden over others. Like me, they know how to take tender loving care of their plants,"* he told himself.

For Stanley, it was just the right scent to mix with the sweet smell of endless, overpowering, passionate sex.

Closing his eyes again for a moment, still squatting on the floor with both hands deep within the box and covered with rose petals, Stanley told himself, *"Get a grip, man! She's just a woman, she's no angel to go mad over. How many men had she gone with? How many innocent souls' heart had she broken?"* He unclenched his teeth, stood up, and began to throw the rose petals onto the floor, on the side tables, on the antique chest, and on the velvet-covered bed.

When the boxes were empty and rose petals beautifully littered the room, he started to play beautiful soul music starting with the number one selling song by Liberia's only Tecumsay Roberts, *'My Susu'* and then painstakingly lit each of the 16 scented candles. Once he had a flame on every candle, he stood in the doorway of the bedroom and smiled. The room had a sensual vibe and fairly glowed with romance, just as he had hoped it would. Stanley thought, the look of the room was something that seemed to come straight out of a Hollywood romance movie.

Thinking Ernestine had been calling his cell phone,

Stanley quickly rant toward the foyer table where he had laid his phone. She grabbed his phone that had gone in sleep mode and awoke it. Realizing she hadn't called him, his heart began to pound

CHAPTER 6

As thousands of thoughts raced through his mind that afternoon, there came a sudden knock on the front door, jolting him out of his pleasant trance. His palms went damp again and he half-laughed, half-groaned at how ridiculous he was being. All he and Ernestine were going to do was look at the room, study its romantic elements, and then do a writing exercise using the room as the setting for a story.

"No big deal," he told himself as he prepared himself to open the door. Normally, the watchman would come in the house to inform him of a guest before letting that person into the premises. That day, he had given Ernestine's description to the watchman and had ordered the watchman to usher her in whenever she arrived. Stanley always does that for his special visitors and his parents.

Knowing it was her, Stanley walked down the hall toward the door and told himself to pretend he was working with Kerkula Jensen. Why should he be nervous? They were just a couple of writers doing research for their craft. Like a good host and teacher, he was going to be at his very best behavior just like his fourth grade teacher, Mr. Humphrey Thomas Redd used to tell him to do when he was still a student at the Monrovia Demonstration Elementary School on Clay Street back in the early 1980s.

He opened the door and all of his God's given, good

upbringing, and good intentions came crashing down upon him like a ton of bricks wall.

The only thing he was cognizant of was her smell, the pulse he saw moving under the soft skin on her neck, and the way the breeze was moving the tips of her black, weaved-in Brazilian hair around on the tops of her luscious breasts. An image of her pubic hair, black and curly and moist with her juices and his saliva, popped into his head and he knew he was in a deep, deep trouble. She was like no other woman he had seen in Liberia, for she was a cutaneous pulchritude that could only be compared to Queen Nefertiti, the most beautiful queen of Egypt and all of Africa. She had the smoothest skin than any woman he'd seen in all of Africa, at least he thought.

By the time he remembered to say, *"Hi! Come inside,"* he had no idea how much time had gone by since he'd opened the door. Thirty seconds? Five minutes? Time was a blur to him. How could he treat her like one of the guys that had been disrespecting her when she was a walking, breathing big orgasm waiting to happen?

Ernestine let out a beautiful wanting smile and then walked into Stanley's foyer and tried not to betray her nervousness by giggling, babbling, or checking to see if her hair was out of place. Instead, she plastered a big smile on her face and squeezed past Stanley and through his front door. He hadn't moved aside very much to let her into his house, but she had to admit she didn't mind rubbing up against him, not one bit. In fact, rubbing on him is something she had dreamed so many times of doing since they last met at the conference.

He was just as gorgeous as he had been at the conference, with the new haircut he was now sporting—his hair was picking up the sunlight that streamed in through the windows. She took in the snug fit of his well-worn jeans and his thick denim short-sleeve white polo shirt. She couldn't keep her eyes from straying to the dark black chest hair that peeked out through his shirt as if they were trying to invite her hands to a hair play. Salivating at the thought of seeing his chest—which she knew she'd never get a glimpse of in this lifetime, but a girl could dream, couldn't she?—Ernestine wished he had left a couple more buttons undone so as to get a better view of his manliness.

Stanley's bare feet were the icing on the cake. Ernestine had never seen any African man with such sexy feet before. She had never even known feet could be sexy until now. His feet were caramel, with well-manicured toenails and a light dusting of black hair a few inches behind the proximal nail fold. Suddenly, she saw herself naked and ready for him, straddling his big toe and...

"No!" Ernestine stopped herself from taking her daydream any further. What was happening to her, she wondered, as she swallowed past her dry tongue. Despite her newfound career, she had never had very many sexual thoughts, let alone ideas of involving a strange man's toes! Now, everything she saw made her think about Stanley's cock and fingers and tongue and then his toes.

Her mind was turning into an X-rated African movie made in Nigeria or South Africa where the women are not bounded by any African tradition or cultural limitation, but pure freaky and slutty thoughts. She was getting turned on by the thoughts of Stanley's anatomy and his gentlemanliness.

Trying to force her naughty thoughts away from the incredibly dirty things she wanted to do to each and every part of Stanley's body, and wishing he would just say something already, she tuned into the details of his house. It was crazy, but Ernestine felt that Stanley was even more potent, even more intoxicating when he was within the walls of his private environment. His home, like the man himself, was luxuriously masculine and yet warm and sexy all at the same time.

"*So,*" she said in a bright voice to break the awkward silence, "*this is your house, huh?*"

As the words left her mouth, Ernestine turned purple and had to fight the urge to run out of his front door, down his steps and back into her car and run for the six feet gate. Could she have sounded any more like an idiot or a sex hungry college girl Stanley had met on Ashmun Street at the United Methodist University?

Stanley's eyes seemed to refocus in on her and he said, "*Yep. Sure is. Glad you could come.*"

"*It was my pleasure.*" She quipped dryly.

He smiled at her and she melted under his gaze. She knew she had a serious case of hero worship, but this was worse than she had bargained for. Don't make a pass at him under any circumstances, she told herself in a firm inner voice. He's your teacher, and you should be grateful that he is taking any time out of his busy and tight schedule for you, she added with a flourish.

She noticed he looked a little uncomfortable as he said, "*I've set up a classroom of sorts for us. It's down the hall.*" When he comfortably added, as if she were a buddy from his College of West Africa, CWA High School basketball team, "*Let me pour you a glass of chardonnay before we get started,*" she decided his discomfort was just a figment of her imagination. How could a guru like him be uncomfortable inside his own castle or classroom, if I may say, she thought as she looked around the living room, moving her eyes from place-to-place, from corner-to-corner as if she was in a museum looking at paintings from Leslie Lumeh and Isaac Doubor two of Liberia's famous artists on display.

Her mind was playing tricks on her. More likely than she

was projecting her own uneasiness onto him.

She followed him into his kitchen. *"You have a beautiful home."*

He turned to smile at her as he uncorked a bottle of white chardonnay. *"Thanks. I love this house. It's a big change from my last one."*

"How is it so?" Ernestine was now being inquisitive. Before she could catch herself, the question had already popped out of her mouth.

Ernestine hoped her question didn't seem like she was prying on him, although she acknowledged that she definitely was. By the time their lessons were through, she wanted to know everything she possibly could about Stanley Kla Nimely. She was already tucking all the little details of his clothes and his furnishings away into her memory for safekeeping and leisurely review on lonely nights. Who knew, she might even buy herself her own personal dildo if she was feeling really brave and name it SKN.

Looking side way, Stanley said, *"I got to design this house from the ground up with the help of my friend Beauclarc Thomas of Innovative Homes, a U.S. based Liberian architectural firm. And I, uh...., didn't have anyone telling me she hated my ideas this time around because I wanted a house that could give me a 360 view of my community from the second floor."*

He handed her the wine glass and said, *"That's probably a whole heck of a lot more than you wanted to know, isn't it?"*

She laughed and patted his hand. *"Trust me, I know exactly how you feel. One more thing, your secrets are very much saved with me, kind sir."*

As she felt a tremor pass through her from simply touching his hand, she immediately pulled back and said, in a shakier voice than she intended, *"Should we get started with things, Mr. Mentor?"*

He nodded. *"I've set things up in the guest room. Follow me."*

She followed him out of the kitchen and down the hallway. When he opened the door to the guest bedroom, she was overwhelmed with the potent scent of roses. Her heart started to beat double time so she joked, *"Are we going to write a story about the florist and—"*

Her words stopped altogether as she rounded the corner and stepped fully into the room.

She gasped. *"Wow, this is amazing!"*

Ernestine wanted to rub herself on all of the luxurious fabrics draped across and above the bed. She wanted to feel the rug under her toes. She wanted to wrap herself up in rose petals.

Turning to Stanley, she said, *"Did you do all this for me? For our lesson? You shouldn't have gone to all the tro —"*

He smiled at her and cut her protest off before she could even think about completing the statement that was about to spew out of her beautiful mouth. *"You know what? I really enjoyed creating this room. And now that I've seen the effects of if myself, I think I'm going to leave it as a nice surprise for my houseguests. Although, I probably won't see much of them 'cause they'll be so busy going at each other. I want to take this time to thank you for your gratitude and sense of flavor and taste. To be honest with you, not that many Liberian women would appreciate this little effort of mine. Thank You!"*

Ernestine could not believe her ears, but she managed to force a laugh and started worrying in earnest as Stanley sat down on the chest at the foot of the bed and motioned for her to sit next to him.

"I think you need to take off your shoes and socks to fully

appreciate this room," he gave has a soft smile and a deep penetrating look gave her a different opinion of him.

She knew he was right and she was certain that he wasn't the least bit interested in her, so she set her wine glass down on the mantle of the bedside nightstand, after removing her shoes and nylon socks, she then slowly walked toward him and sat down next to him.

Playfully she said, "*Should I take anything else off?*"

Stanley's eyes got wide for a moment and then he grinned wolfishly. "*I suppose you'd better, otherwise, how are you going to write about the feel of the material brushing across your heroine's skin?*"

"*Oh, do you really think I should?*" Ernestine said, some panic creeping into her voice. However, as she looked around the room at the candles and the sound of the velvety-voice of David Gweh softly coming out of the powerful speaker, and saw the velvet and silk beneath her, she decided, what the hell. Not giving herself the chance to think, she pulled her v-neck summer blouse over her head, leaving only a skimpy tank top covering her torso.

"*Okay,*" she said impishly, vowing to let herself be carried away by the mood for once in her adult life. "I'm undressed."

Stanley looked her up and down. "*I'm not sure I'd call you undressed, but it's certainly a start. You know the journey of a thousand miles begins with the first few baby steps.*"

Suddenly, something inside Ernestine clicked into place. Or broke down completely. She wasn't sure which. When the new voice inside her was loud and clear, bold without an ounce of fear.

She spoke quickly, before she lost her courage. Before she came to her senses. "*Stanley, you know how we agreed that everything that went on during the mentoring sessions was going to be strictly professional?*"

"Yeah?" he said, drawing out the word as a question.

"Well, it has just occurred to me that it's one thing for me to appreciate this room as a writer." She paused and then said, *"But it's another thing entirely for me to experience it as a woman."*

She saw Stanley's Adam's apple move in his throat and clenched her hands into tight fists at her side. She didn't know how she was going to manage it exactly, but she wasn't going to be a wimp and back down. Not here. Not now.

For the first time in her life, Ernestine was going to go for what she wanted. She reached for the button on her jeans and Stanley's hand shot out to grab hers.

"What are you doing?" He tried to caution her against what she was about to do, but it was what he wanted of her. He wanted her to be the get a firsthand experience on things she would write about, at least to be able to relate to her characters.

She half-grinned at him, but she knew she was far too nervous for it to look like a smile. More like she was baring her teeth at him. *"I'm taking off my clothes."*

He blinked at her in confusion. *"Oh."*

Ernestine tried not to let his utter non-reaction to the idea of her taking off her clothes bother her. She wasn't here because he thought she was a sexy woman. She was here to learn about the art of erotic writing. And if she had to do it on her own, by God's grace, she was doing it.

She stood up and unzipped her pants. As she lowered them to the ground and pulled her legs out of each pants' leg one at a time she looked up at Stanley, who was still sitting in stunned silence on the edge of the chest. *"The fact is, I have never experienced the sensation of silk sliding against my skin. I've never lain naked on a bed filled with rose petals in front of a strange man. I've never rubbed my nipples against satin."* She looked at him imploringly. *"These are all things that I have to do or I'll never be able to write about characters who know what these physical sensations feel like. Can you understand that?"*

Stanley nodded like a troubled child getting an instructional advice from his caring mother.

She stood in front of him in her skimpy tank top, knowing her nipples were jutting out and she forced herself not to flinch, not to run, and not to cover up. She hooked her thumbs into the thin straps of her silk thong panties and said, in a soft, but firm voice, *"I won't pressure you into joining me, Stanley. I'm sure this is all pretty old hat to you, but it's all brand new to me. So I could sure use some help if you were willing to instruct me."* Lowering her eyelashes to *cover her eyes, she licked her lips and then made eye contact with the most sexy man she has seen in Liberia. "In a purely professional way, of course."*

"Whatever happens inside the classroom stays in the classroom?" He asked in a calm, but detached voice. She blinked several times without saying a word. It seemed as if her hope of having a chance with Stanley was being sucked await by her own principles.

A little shiver worked itself up Ernestine's spine. Trying to sound as unaffected by her near-nakedness in an incredibly romantic room with the most potent man she'd ever met, she said, *"You got it."*

In the blink of an eye, Stanley replaced her hands with his on the sides of her thong. She jerked a few time and then bit her lower lip. She had the guts feeling that the lesson might spin out of control due to the crush she had developed for Stanley, the only man who knew how to make a woman feel better, according to many of his books.

With a new gleam in his eyes he pulled her closer to him,

so that her muff was mere inches from his mouth. He relished her mound and the shaped of her womanhood. By this time, Ernestine vagina was dripping wet with her own juices.

"Let the lessons begin." She whispered into Stanley's ears as her need for learning increased.

CHAPTER 7

Stanley hooked his thumbs under her panties and slowly pulled them down to her thighs. Her pussy was pink-ish red with some brown trim around the lips, and so hot he could feel the heat emanating from it, practically scalding his face. Her jet-black public hare had been shaved around the lower left and right edges and trimmed in the center into a Brazilian style—mostly smooth and caramel-like glistening skin with just the barest patch of hair in the middle. Her lips were plump and he was more glad than he could ever say that she had just given him permission to touch her, to taste her, to spread her legs wide open and plunge into her until he had quenched the sexual need that had ridden him hard from the moment he'd met her at the Library and then at the Royal Grand Hotel on Tubman Boulevard, on 15th Street, in Sinkor.

Pushing her panties down around her knees, he pushed her thighs apart and her lips separated slightly, fully revealing her wet pinkish-red slit surrounded by dark caramel skin. He slipped his long middle finger of his right hand into her tight, dripping wet vagina a couple of inches. She moaned and wiggled her pussy against his powerful finger, so he pushed it even further inside her until his palm was cupping her entire vulva and his thumb was covering her swollen clit.

He lifted his thumb and blew softly on the swollen flesh. Her vagina clenched around his finger, and he wondered just how close she was to coming. He blew on her clit again and slid his finger in an out of her slit, juicing up her twat some more. Just as he had suspected, she was a powder keg waiting to explode. Sensitive to each spasm of her slick yet powerful pussy muscles around his middle finger, he bent his head down an inch or two and barely touched the tip of his tongue to her firm, throbbing flesh. It felt good to Ernestine.

She screamed out and pressed her pussy against him, begging for a tongue fuck. Grasping the back of his head with her hands, she ground his face into her pussy, crushing herself against his lips and teeth in a rhythmical motion.

Stanley knew what she wanted, even as she thrashed onto him. Slipping his index finger into her already warmed pussy to join his middle finger, he continued to slide his fingers in and out of her in a slow, steady rhythm—like he was dancing to the sound of a Kpelle cultural drumbeat that the young men of that tribal group usually does after coming of age in a traditional Poro Ritual. He gripped her firm, fat and round ass in his left hand and pointed his tongue so that all she felt against her clit was the hard tip. As if he were typing the same letter over and over on a computer's keyboard, as if she was the page he was making his mark on. He moved his tongue steadily up and down on her clit as she cried out with pleasure from the good sensation. Using his lips, he grabbed her clitoris and gave it a rhythmical suck along with several soft tender bites.

Finally, the pulsing of her muscles around his fingers slowed and Ernestine's body went limp. The muscles in her back and butt cheeks tightened up as she tried to pull away from him, but he wouldn't allow it. She might not have known what she was getting into when she made her *"let's get naked because we're professionals"* comment just minutes earlier, but now, whether she liked it or not, he would decide when they were finished.

After all, he was the teacher.

And she was the very promising new student who had come to learn the tricks of the trade form the master of the trade.

Quickly, he put his arms around her trim and apple bottomed waist and threw her onto the plush bedding, face down. As her body hit the velvet bedding, it was as if flowers rained from the sky. Several rose petals landed on her fat ass, thighs, and calves. As Stanley moved to straddle her on the bed, he blew warm breath up her legs, blowing each of the rose petals off one by one until all that remained before him was her naked, caramel skin, sensitively tendered and ready for what would happen next. With every breath, Ernestine whimpered her pleasure.

She started squirming, but when she tried to turn around, he quickly moved to straddle her, leaning over her back to cup her full breasts in his hands through her tank top. He whispered in her ear, *"I'm going to take off your shirt now so that you can feel the velvet rubbing against your nipples."*

She stopped squirming and in a voice so quiet and so humble, he could barely hear her, she softly whispered, *"Okay."*

Stanley sat back up with a leg on each side of her thighs, the huge bulge in his jeans pressing into the curve of her big and soft ass. He grinned as he slid his fingers underneath the hem of her tank top. He liked to hear her quick agreement. It made him feel like he was running the show, like he was the man. This was a typical sexual behavior of most African men—being in control of situation inside the bedroom. After years of women making him feel like he wasn't worth their time due to his choice of profession, after years of women using him only for his huge bank account, Stanley savored the sensation of being in complete control of a woman's body and soul.

Knowing he had already given her intense pleasure so

quickly only served to up the ante. She was still nineteen orgasms away from matching the number of times he had exploded with her name on his lips in the past week. Before lesson one was through, he wanted her orgasm in the double digits.

Her breath quickened as he slowly rubbed his fingers underneath the hem of her shirt, along her rib cage. With infinite precision he dragged her cotton shirt up her ribs until it caught on her breasts, which were much larger than he had thought a week ago at the conference.

If someone had asked him to guess her cup size he would have confidently said she was a B-cup, given her small frame and big ass. Ernestine is one of those women that are blessed with what many African men referred to as Coco Cola-Shape. Now, having held her globes in his hands, even only for a moment through her thin, damp cotton shirt, he knew himself for the fool he was.

Ernestine was definitely at D cup. At least.

Slipping his hands between the plush velvet coverlet and her shirt, he hooked his thumbs up under the hem of her shirt and tugged it up over her perfectly proportioned tits. As he pushed the shirt past her nipples and the tips of his fingers covered her tits, he heard her rapid intake of breath and almost came in his jeans. He was already breathing like he had run a marathon from the Samuel Kanyon Doe Sports Complex through Paynesville Red Light all the way to the Monrovia City Hall.

"Put your arms up," he whispered into her ear, and she obeyed him as he slid the tank top off her body and threw it onto the floor.

Ernestine turned her head to face him, but he already had a plan of action and was not going to let her deter him.

Putting his hands on her rib cage, he lifted her torso slightly off the bed so that her nipples were just barely touching the velvet.

"I'm going to rub your tits against the cover, slowly, focusing all of your attention on how good it feels." Stanley said in a deep voice.

She nodded, just barely, showing him she understood. He pressed his groin into her ass, which pressed her mound into the velvet. He separated her legs with one of his and her juices soaked through the denim covering his legs. Roughly, so she could feel the coarse fabric pull and tug against her tender lips, he moved his thigh up and down against her.

Tightening his hold on her rib cage, he lifted her torso up just high enough that her nipples floated just above the velvet cover. *"I want you to concentrate on your nipples right now. Your breasts are the only things in the world that matter. Forget about my thigh rubbing against your lips and clit."* She groaned and tried to protest, so he squeezed her ribs tighter in his strong hands. Like an innocent Liberian eighteen year-old under the spell of her manipulating godfather, she concurred with his every command.

"Do as I say," he said forcefully. *"It's for your own good."*

Ernestine's body tensed underneath him for a split second before her hips started to buck wildly against his leg. She was coming again, convulsing helplessly against his leg. His mouth curved up into a steamy look of satisfaction as he drove his thigh against her pussy and gave her what she wanted.

The fierce rocking of her lower body blew dozens of rose petals off the bed, into the air and onto the floor. The mingled scents of her pussy, her pleasure, and the rose petals were a fragrance he knew he would never be able to forget.

When Stanley still hadn't forgotten his goal. Before they

left the room, before lesson one had come to its incredible, unforgettable end, he wanted her to realize just how sensitive a woman's breasts were, so that she could write powerful sex scenes in her books that left no part of the female body unexplored.

He almost laughed aloud as he realized what a poor job he was doing of fooling himself that he cared one whit about her writing skills at this moment as he lay over her, his fingers mere inches from her tits, his leg practically jammed up inside her dripping-wet penis purse.

Even if the President of Liberia could offer him the fucking 'Presidential Medal of Honor' right now he wouldn't care. Frankly, what he was doing in his guest bedroom—what he and Ernestine were doing together—had nothing to do with writing and everything to do with sex. And he wanted Ernestine to experience sex in its most heightened form. With him and only him. Besides writing sexually explicit books, Stanley knew how to pleasure a woman better than any man in the small West African city. It was something he'd prayed to his maker to be a master of, and it was something he had practiced and perfected over the years.

Still holding her rib cage in his large hands, he began to slide her torso ever so slightly back and forth, so just the tips of her breasts were rubbing up against the velvet fabric on the bed. He thought about turning her over and taking her tits into his mouth and sucking them, nipping them until she was crying out again, and he barely kept his own needs reined in. He was wondering what kind of teacher she would take him to be if he changed the lesson plan mid-way just because his dick was about to explode in his pants? He didn't want to rush for sex like many of the men in the country do whenever they're in a similar situation with a strange and sexy woman. He had to exercise restraint to maintain his credibility and the value his cooperative saw in him.

He heard her whimper again and he knew she had fallen ever so slightly back down to earth from her explosive orgasm, so he leaned forward and whispered again in her ear, *"You're going to come again, sweetheart. Any minute now, you're going to feel the way the velvet caresses your rock-hard nipples. You're going to realize that your breasts are the center of your body and a doorway to your sexual soul. Whenever you're doing a character sketch with your female characters, you need to reflect on this feeling you are experiencing right now."*

She started to say, *"Stanley, I—"* but he cut her off saying, *"Shhhhh. I don't want you to talk to me. I want you to feel. Allow your feeling to do the talking and not you, sweetie."* Then he wrapped his left forearm around her waist, while still rocking her breasts gently from side to side on the velvet comforter, and ran the fingers of his right hand down from the bottom of her rib cage, down along her flat stomach, which convulsed as he lightly touched her skin, to the top of her mound.

"Uhm, uhm, uhm, Honey," he admonished her when she strained to move her clit closer to his fat and long finger. *"What did I tell you?"*

"My breasts," she gasped.

He smiled and moved his fingers down a millimeter. *"That's right. If you keep doing what I want, I'll keep doing what you want."*

A small female betrayal sob left her throat, and he knew she was close, so close that if he so much as touched the tip of her clitoris with his fingertip she'd explode against his hand. He moved his left arm slightly toward her sensitive breast. He was still holding her torso suspended from the bed, but now every time he slid her body to the left side on the velvet, her breast slipped into his palm.

"Stanley, Stanley, Stanley, Stan, Stannnnnnn!" she moaned and again he had to fight the urge to rip his jeans off and split

her wide open with his massive thirteen-inch dick.

He kept his palm open at first, so that all she felt on her nipple was the callused skin of his open palm. *"Are you focusing on your breasts and only your breasts right now?"* he asked her in a low soft voice.

He saw her nod her head and rewarded her by moving his right hand another millimeter toward her already swollen clitoris. Even though he was no further than the top of her slit, her juices were soaking his hand, so he rubbed his fingers around in circles on the slick skin of her well-shaved mound.

Then as he slid her left breast into his palm again, he held her still and pinched her nipple between his fingers, rubbing it between his thumb and middle finger. At the same time he plunged his index finger down into her wet, hot pussy and ground one finger and then two and then the tip of a third finger into her.

She screamed *"Stanley!"* and the muscles of her pussy clenched as they tried to hold his fingers hostage inside her sweet and moist honeycomb.

When she was still so far gone, still so entranced by the waves of pleasure washing over her, he took advantage of her pliability and effortlessly rolled her over onto her back. *She's an angel on Earth,* he thought after looking at her beautiful face.

Looking at her luscious breasts for the first time, he gasped at her perfection, at her beauty in the candle-light, surrounded by the deep hues of the silk, satins, and velvet furnishings all around them.

Her breasts were lush melons and he knew immediately that they were entirely and naturally endowed on her by the creator of Eve, the mother of all of humanity. Having felt one of them in the palm of his hand, he knew how deliciously heavy they were. His mouth watered like a hungry child greedy for a long overdue food as he anticipated tasting them.

Don't get ahead of yourself, Stanley, he warned himself. He had to stay on track with his lesson plan. *All in good time,* he told himself. All in good time.

Ernestine's eyes were just starting to open and she was trying to refocus them on his face, when he slipped a length of richly patterned silk fabric off the bedpost. He quickly grabbed her right wrist and tied one end of the cloth around it and the other end about the bedpost. He slid yet another length of fabric around her left wrist and tied that one up as well.

Looking deep in her eyes, he moaned in a deep voice, *"You're such a good student we're moving straight to lesson two."*

Her eyebrows scrunched down in an unspoken question as he splayed her legs and tied up both her ankles to the nearest bedpost.

"Varying positions is lesson two," he whispered. His voice was deep with passion and needs.

He tied the final bow on her left ankle, then lapped once at her very wet, well worked vagina, with his tongue. She tried to buck up into his mouth, but he had tied her just tight enough that she couldn't move more than an inch or two off the bed. She was in the perfect position he wanted her in.

He took one of the thin pillows from the headboard and slid it underneath her big, juicy, and perfect cake of an ass.

Breathing hard, he said in a low voice, *"I just want to look at you for a few moments before we take this any further."*

Ernestine's head was spinning. She had definitely surprised herself when she decided to take off her clothes during the lesson. After coming three times in rapid succession with a virtual stranger, in his guest bedroom, during her mentoring session, she was more than surprised.

She was stupefied!

She was flabbergasted!

And damn it, she was still horny as hell. Hornier than she'd ever been her entire life. And this was how she felt after three, counted three, mind-blowing, soul-shaking orgasms with the master of sex and relationship in Liberia.

Ernestine could hardly believe it when the first *"Big O"* had rocked through her. During a decade of dull sex, she had never, ever had an orgasm with a man in the room. Most of her sex partners were complete disappointments in the small city. Like her last cheating boyfriend, many of her lovers were one minute men—many of them never engaged in foreplay for more that would last for five minutes, and when they entered her sweet love tunnel, off they came without given her the chance to have one. This is a typical behavior of some Monrovian and African men when it come to satisfying their partners inside the bedrooms—they usually satisfied themselves while the woman is left dry and horny. Many of these men really do not know how to satisfy a female beyond the fulfilment of their own sexual desires. Often, this caused their partners to go out and have that unmet desire fulfilled by some other person, be it the opposite sex or the same sex. Whenever this happened, these men result to domestic violence and other gender based violence. The only paltry orgasms Ernestine had ever managed to bring upon herself were with the tip of her middle finger swirling her swollen clitoris—usually after reading one of Stanley's books.

However, that was neither here nor there, so she left that thought to dissect later when the man himself wasn't looming over her with an unholy gleam in his eyes and her come all over his hands and clothes. She couldn't believe how quickly she responded to the barest touch from Stanley's tongue, from his finger inside her swollen labia.

And then again with his muscular thigh between her legs.

And then again with one of his hands on her breasts and one between her legs.

Oh God Almighty, she thought to herself, he must think I am a total slut. Just like that other woman with the huge tits who wanted him to be her mentor.

She looked down at herself and realized he had tied her to his bed. I'm no better than that damn Bassa bitch from the conference. And now he knows that I am a damn hoe. Worse than having her hero know what a slut she was, she internalized that she now knew what a slut she is.

Suddenly wanting to be as far away from her embarrassment as possible, far away from Stanley's probing fingers, from his tongue and his all-seeing, all-knowing eyes, she laughed nervously and said, *"Stanley, I feel like I'm all spread out for you like you're Jesus and I'm The Last Supper. I just want you to have me, eat me and full me while you're at it. No man has ever made me feel this way, and I don't want you to stop or hold yourself back."*

He was still kneeling between her legs, clothed in his jeans and short-sleeve Polo T-shirt, and she could see where her come had stained the fabric over his knee and along his right thigh.

She was so embarrassed she wanted to die. Right there, right now and she said to herself, *God, you can take me now. Please!* What she didn't add to her plea, although she wanted to, was, *"that now I've experienced pleasure like this, it's all right for me to come home to you and find a place among the angels in your kingdom. At least, I know I've truly lived in this man's romantic arms."*

He didn't laugh at her lame joke about the Last Supper. Instead he leaned over and lapped at her dripping wet pussy once more. She felt all of the remaining blood from her head and the rest of her body rush between her legs, straight to her clit. If she weren't so damn embarrassed, she would have begged him to lap at her pussy and anal just a couple more times.

One more touch and she'd be over the edge into oblivion.

For the fourth time in the past hour.

She was Ernestine Connie Johnson, for God's sake. A girl who had gone to the St. Theresa Convent High School with rules-enforcing teachers and an overbearing principal who told them abstinence was the best and safest sex before marriage. A girl who still turned purple every time she thought about the astonishing array of dildos on display at the erotic writer's conference she attended at the Grand Royal Hotel in Sinkor, on Tubman Boulevard.

Before she could make any more feeble protests about how ridiculous it was for him to have her splayed open and tied up like some sort of sex slave on his four-poster bed, surrounded by rose petals and a hundred candles, Stanley slid another length of silk fabric off the four-poster bed frame. Slowly, as if he knew how much his every move tortured her inflamed libido, he twisted the thin fabric into a tight cord.

Then he stood up and began to walk around the side of the bed. She wondered, somewhat wildly—hopefully too, much to her ongoing chagrin over what an utter and complete slut she was turning out to be—if he was going to whip her with the tip of the fabric. She knew it would hurt. At the same token, she knew Stanley would make it feel good too. And then he could kiss it all better.

Instead, he took the fabric and covered her eyes with it,

lifting her head slightly so that he could tie the fabric in a knot behind her head.

Ernestine had never felt more powerless as she did.

And she had never been so full of anticipation in her whole life.

Firmly tamping down on the logical part of her brain that said their lesson had gone too far, way too far, she let her senses take over. She listened to the voice of Luther Vandross coming out of the speakers, the sound of Stanley's footsteps on the floor and then the carpet. She smelled the potent scent of rose petals mixed with her own come and the faint scent of vanilla from the Yankee scented candles. She tasted her own musky desire on her lips.

Feeling silk slide around her ankles and wrists, holding her hostage, for the second time in her life, for the second time in one short, afternoon in quiet suburban Paynesville City, Ernestine gave herself up to a greater power.

For Ernestine, the power of a good late afternoon fuck that left her pussy craving for more long after it was over was what she was experiencing the Stanley's guest room. Being a man true to the legend around him, Stanley never disappoints any female that encountered him. There is never a dull moment with Stanley and his sex partner. Having made her come so many times just by his mere touch, Stanley wanted nothing more than plunging his thick—meaty thirteen inches dick into Ernestine's already heated poonanie until she can come some more.

After coming so many times under Stanley's power, Ernestine wondered why she had never let herself experience sex like this before. Perhaps it was because of the negative love vibertory energy that radiated from the selfish Liberian men who only thoughts and missions in the bedrooms were satisfying their own sexual desire. Friends of hers from the United States that have experienced love with a non-Liberian often tell her of the short comings of Liberian men within the bed. Though Liberian men are dead good-looking and sometimes kind at heart, but most of them do not know how to make their women happy. Like Ernestine, the secrets to winning Liberia women's heart and love are as follow, show her respect, show her love and affection, wear the look of a God fearing person even if you're not, put a few dollars in her purse or bank account, and make here come as many times as possible. Without meeting at least 60% of these needs, the Liberian men with keep running after their own tails like kay—kay dogs for the next 1,000 years.

CHAPTER 8

For the past 20 minutes in the guest room, Stanley had watched the play of emotions work their way across Ernestine's face as he'd turned her over on her back. Feelings of self-doubt and self-consciousness were the reasons why he had wanted her face down for his initial sexual onslaught. It was so much easier for her to let herself go if she forgot anyone was watching. Whatever that case was, what did she care—he was the mentor and she was there to learn from him. A typical class act which is often perpetrated by many sexually unscrupulous school teachers and college professors in the various institutions in Liberia and many parts of Africa—Guinea, Nigeria, Sierra Leon and Ghana that are very notorious for this practice of sexual exploitation.

From what she had already said to him, from all of the nervous signs she tried to conceal from him, he knew how badly Ernestine wanted to experience incredible heights of lust and passion. One thing he was aware of was the fact that love cannot hide no matter what; even if a person tries to use self-indulgence and moral-sanity as weapons of suppressing their feelings for another soul. He knew she wanted to learn what it was like to fuck and be fucked so hard and so long by a thirteen-inch long and a three-inch girth dick that the tender, slick skin between her legs was raw and bruise from it. And to still want more, even when pain was beginning to get all mixed up in with pleasure.

Knowing she was a beginner in the sensual arts, he was going as slow as he could with her. Putting her face down. Showing her how strongly she could react to the simplest, lightest touch. Letting her hide from her embarrassment, he wondered who had taught her that sex was dirty, but knew it was a conversation they would have later, down the line, when she had accepted what her body wanted from him.

Oddly enough, while Stanley was no Monrovia sexual novice—he'd had his fair share of hot one night stands and had been sandwiched between more than one woman during the past five years since his divorce—he had never wanted to juke anyone this badly. Ever!

Not even when he was a fourteen-year-old virgin who used to jerk off to Playboy and Penthouse Magazines, and was finally ready to sink himself into the pussy of one of his mother's friends' daughter, Connie Porte, who he had gone on to one afternoon in September of 1985, but he did not feel this out of control. It was taking every ounce of restraint within him, and then some, to keep from thrusting his monster deep into Ernestine warm and moist twat and yelling her name out until the little orphan boys and other people in his Rehab Road neighborhood could shamefully hear him.

At the same time, he had never wanted to give anyone as much pleasure as he wanted to give Ernestine. He felt like he could make her come a hundred times and then a hundred more, and though his manhood would surely be turning purple-blue by then, he would gladly give up his own sexual release just to see her achieve hers.

Without knowing just how or when it had happened—was it the minute she walked through his door, or was it when they spoke on the phone, or maybe it was when she had accidentally tackled him at the conference—inadvertently, the teacher had become the student.

Stanley would have been amused by this realization was it not for how painfully she aroused him. She was innocent, she was confused, she was unknowledgeable, yet her body had the answers from all the way back to Eve—the mother of all procreation and the gene pool from which all beautiful Liberian women got their inheritance.

One fact was that they weren't done with her lessons yet and he knew the only way to keep her imprisoned in her own sexuality, the only way to show her how many ways she could feel good, was to take control away from her. Just the way many controlling Liberia government officials and corporate lawyers use their positions to exploit young women and men of their sexualities and their correct sense of decision making. So he tied her up and blindfolded her, praying all the while that he was doing the right thing. Hoping that he wasn't pushing her too far. In the land of the poor, the man or woman in the air-conditioned car and big house get his or her way.

As he tied the knot around the back of her head and felt her soft black hair caressing the backs of his arms, he noted with satisfaction that the tension was leaving her body, almost as if she had made the decision to give in to everything he was offering her.

He stood up and picked up one of the candles from the dark-pine bedside table.

"I want you to tell me if I'm hurting you, Honey," he said.

She swallowed once, then twice, then licked her delicious lips, nodding her agreement.

He blew out the candle and then kneeled at the side of the bed. With infinite precision he poised the candle over one of her thighs and tilted it so that the barest amount of hot wax dripped onto her skin.

Like actors do in a western adult sex movie, Ernestine hissed out a stream of air between her teeth as the wax made contact with her skin.

Immediately concerned, Stanley covered the patch of skin with his hand and said, *"Did I hurt you?"* If he had, he knew he would never forgive himself.

"No," she whispered. Her voice sounded heavy. Drugged with sexual pleasures and needs.

Stanley breathed out an enormous sigh of relief, but he couldn't help but worry that he had crossed a dangerous line.

Instead, she had surprised him. *"Do it again,"* she whispered her request.

Stanley's heart flip-flopped in his chest and swelled with something he couldn't quite name. He replaced his hand with his lips as he kissed her softly on her thigh, right above the now-dry vanilla Yankee Candle's wax. Reaching for another candle, he blew out the flame and slowly dripped a trail of hot wax up the inside of her left thigh, enjoying the sound of her moaning as the wax came closer still to her wet, hot vagina, enjoying watching her try, futilely, to move her sopping mound closer to his hand.

Again he followed the line of quickly drying wax with his tongue and his teeth as he nipped at her skin.

"Stanley, Stanley, Stanley, Stan, Stan, Stannnnnnnn. Oh my, Goddddddddd," she whimpered with every touch of his lips to her skin, and Stanley wondered what the hell he was doing still fully clothed while a sex goddess was tied to his bed in his guest room within the quiet neighborhood.

He reached for another candle and told himself to chill out. There would be time enough for him to pump into her wet, tight hole, but not before he gave her more of what she so desperately needed.

So he dripped wax along her stomach, and kissed his way along her rib cage, until his face was so close to her breasts he couldn't hold off needs of her any longer.

When he gently touched the tip of his tongue to one of her nipples, she nearly broke the silk binds off her wrists.

"More!" she urged him.

"Please do it again!" she begged him like a child wanted more of a play she had just experienced.

Obeying her wishes, he took her nipple into his mouth and sucked her dark caramel areola in as well. He wanted to be gentle, but he was too far gone himself to hold anything back. In the back of his mind he hoped he didn't bruise her, but he knew she wouldn't care even if he did, because she was moaning, *"Yes! Just like that! Yes! Oh! Oooooooohhhhhhhh. Shit! Yes, yesssss!"*

As if he had a timer in his head, Stanley knew her fourth orgasm was long past due. And if he played his cards right, he thought he could move her from four to five in rapid successions.

Moving his tongue back and forth over the hard nub of her nipple, he moved his index finger into the cleft of her vagina and just as he touched her incredibly swollen clitoris he bit down slightly on her left nipple.

She screamed again and Stanley sucked as hard as he could on her breast while ramming his finger in and out of her wet honeycomb feverishly.

"Your pussy is so wet and hot, Honey," he said, unbelievingly, and knew that by the time he stuck his dick in, it would be scalding.

Thinking of all the heat pooling in her juicy poonanie gave Stanley an idea. He took the long, slim pillar candle and slid it into her vagina, just a little at a time. By the sound of her moans, he knew she was still coming, and easily turned on enough for whatever he wanted to slip between her legs.

In the midst of her orgasm, Stanley removed his lips from her breast and joined the candle in her pussy with his tongue on her clit. Even as she was resurfacing from her explosion, he felt her clit twitching again beneath his tongue. He could feel the candle jerk as the muscles of her vagina wall clenched together.

She screamed out, *"Oh my God! Jesus Christ! Stanley. I'm coming again! Damn, fuuuuuccccckkkk, shhhhiiiiiit!"*

When the spasms that rocked her had subsided, Stanley untied the silk bindings around her arms and legs. Leaving the blindfold on, he picked her up in his arms. Her body was completely limp from her five intense detonations and slick with a faint sheen of sweat. Thank God Stanley house was fully air-conditioned. Hadn't it been, she would have been drenched in a river of sweet.

Gently, he carried her over to the chenille rug in front of the wall-mount television.

She wrapped her slim arms around his neck and as she sank into the deep rug, softly pressed her lips to his.

Stanley was unprepared for their first kiss, and even the merest touch of her lips on his was more than he could handle. Roughly he pulled the silk fabric away from her eyes and stood up, pulling off his jeans and shirt as he did so.

In a few seconds, he was completely naked and kneeling on the rug between Ernestine's legs. He paused briefly, knowing it was longer than he could stand to wait, but he'd kill himself later if he didn't have this image of Ernestine burned into his brain forever. He memorized every gleaming, creamy, perfect inch of her incredible body, her luscious breasts, and wet, soft vagina in the flickering light of the candles and nightstand. He pushed her legs open wide, bent her knees so that she could take him into her and reached for one of the condoms he had placed at random in the room, just in case he should get as incredibly lucky as he was right now. One good thing about Stanley is his aversion to unsafe sex. Unlike many Liberian men that do not practice safe sex, Stanley is a very big fan of condoms. He often conducts public health awareness program in local schools and colleges on the danger of having unsafe sex. No wonder he had a fan of over a million men and women nationally and internationally.

Her eyes followed his movement, and she shook her head.

"No. I want you like this." She reached out tentatively to touch the skin on his penis with the tips of her fingers. *"I want to suck you first and feel you inside of me. Skin to skin...flesh to flesh."*

Stanley wanted it too, more than anything in the whole world, but he was torn between her wish and his sense of safety. Ernestine broke into his confusion and said, *"I haven't been with anyone in over a year. So you don't have to worry about me. I am very much safe. I just did my HIV test at Dr. Kpoto's Med Link Clinic on Randall Street."*

He shook his head and grinned ruefully, *"Me either, but safety comes first, Honey. What was the result? Because there is only one life to live and I am too young to die at age 45."*

"Negative, of course. I want you to trust me for once. I can show you the result tomorrow if you do not believe me. I don't want to contract anything and die a premature death, myself. I trust you and I want you to trust me too," she exclaimed in an honest tone.

Stanley interjected, *"Me either, but I will take this once in a lifetime risk. However, I need to see your result tomorrow."*

"Thank God!" She exhaled and then laughed as she reached for him and pulled his head back down. As their lips

touched, her laughter died in her throat. She maneuver her way between Stanley's legs until she was mere inches from his erected penis while in a sixty-nine position. She then wrapped her right hand around his rock-hard meat and brought it down to her wet lips. After lapping his glans which is the head of the male's penis, she slowly opened her mouth and let the huge meat drop in her mouth and then down her throat. She worked his dick for about fifteen minutes using several deep-throat rythmical movements until the muscles in her jaw were tired. All the while she was performing, Stanley had to restrain himself from coming.

"Fuck me, Stanley. I need to feel your huge dick all the way inside me." Her words were punctuated by a firm squeeze of her fist on his throbbing trunk. For a moment, he was afraid he was going to spurt all over the skin of her belly.

Reluctantly, Stanley took a final kiss from her, sucking her lower lip between his, and he then reared back up, spinning her in the opposite direction before kneeling between her legs. More than anything, he wanted to watch as his dick slid into her pussy, just like the candle, but this time it would be his own throbbing flesh and blood pumping into her like a NASA space rocket piercing through the hostile sky on a mission to discovery deep space where no man has gone before. His big hard, thirteen-inch thick trunk was about to make her scream with pain and pleasure.

Spreading her lips with his fingers, he angled the tip of his dick into her soaked labia and probed her entry with the very top of his head.

She was not the only one wet with come. The head of his bazooka was slick with his sperm, slick with his intense desire to explode inside her womb.

He slid his dick up and down from her clit to the opening of her anus and back again. He knew she was going to come again, and he wanted her to do it before he got inside her, lest the convulsing of her muscles send him could end his own too fast before he could even start.

Reaching his hands up to her breasts, he fondled the huge globes, rolling her nipples between his fingers, cupping her breasts. His dick was his weapon of delight on her pussy and within moments her eyes drifted shut and her neck arched. Her hands held fast onto his ass as she came against him.

Taking a deep breath, he slid his dick into her an inch. She was so tight, which he already knew from how snugly she held onto his fingers when he pushed them inside of her, he wondered how he was going to make it one more inch, let alone the next eleven inches.

"Wow, your prick is so big! I want you to go easy on me, Stanley," she pleaded with a soft throaty moaned.

He grasped for control, not wanting to blow his wad before he had sheathed his entire trunk inside her vagina walls. More than he had ever wanted anything his whole life, he wanted to feel Ernestine's slick heat wrap around his manhood, her tight muscles milking him dry with every thrust.

Gritting his teeth, he slid his hands underneath her hips to cup her big ass cheeks in his hands, and he slid in another couple of inches. She began to buck into him while using her own strength to pull his dick into her.

"Damn, Stanley, you feel so good inside of me. Damn, I didn't know sex could be this good," she moaned.

Stanley began to say, *"Honey, you've got to let me move slowly here. Or else..."* he later let his words drift off as she smiled a teeny smile at him.

She lay back against the rug, rubbing her hands up and down his thighs. *"I wouldn't want to disobey the teacher because there are many women in this city that are earnestly praying for this moment with you," she said, her voice a husky whisper of need. "You might have to bend me over your knee so that you can spank me," she added,* her voice thick with desire.

A vision of himself spanking Ernestine's sweet cake as she cried out on his lap gave Stanley no choice but to plunge as deeply into her pussy as he could go. Mindless with the need to ravage her, to blow his seed as deep within her as he possibly could, he dragged her legs over his shoulders and rammed the full length of his thirteen-inch weapon into her again and again until her pussy began to queef from the powerful thrusting.

Joined to him in the most elemental way, Ernestine's hips bucked wildly, taking him all the way inside of her and then forcing him back out along her slick canal. She cried out his name, begging him to send her over the edge, but the roaring in his ears was so loud, he could hardly make out her words. He thought he tasted blood in his mouth, so he knew he must have bitten his tongue in his crazy rush to ravage her.

Breaking through his fog, he heard Ernestine's impassioned sob, *"Oh Stanley, oh my God, yes, yes, there, right there, now! Oh shit, yes! Oh, dammmnnnnn!"*

As her vagina clenched and sucked around his dick, he crashed into her tight pussy one last time. Gripping her hips against his, they pounded back and forth in perfect rhythmical motions. The muscles in his penis released and he emptied out all of his penis juices into her warm and juicy womb.

And as he collapsed on to her, with his heartbeat sounding louder than a bass drum during an Armed Forces of Liberia, AFL parade, he said, *"Sweetheart, you are definitely an A+ student."*

CHAPTER 9

Monrovia has its own way of enticing and keeping people grounded, especially those that are hopelessly in love. The city though great, is not living its true potentials because of the attitudes of some of her leaders. Everyday people of the city watch buildings being erected by foreign developers anywhere there is an empty space available without adhering to the city's building codes and other city's ordinances. Just as the City of Monrovia is being taken advantage of by the wealthy political class, so is her sons and daughters—they are being used and abused by the capable and powerful people. On the good side of things, it is women and men like Ernestine and Stanley that are keeping the city's hope alive through their literary renaissance and their search for true love.

On this Sunday morning, less than twenty-four hours after the most mind-blowing sex of her life, Ernestine had just returned from Mass and was sitting in her cozy home office at her little computer desk with her laptop open to a blank Microsoft Word file. Not know where to begin, she stared blindly at the cursor as it blinked at her. Since Monday was going to be a national holiday in the country, she had decided to spend the rest of the day fleshing out ideas she had gained from her mentoring session with Stanley. One thing was evident here—she could not believe that she actually had sex with one of the most eligible bachelors in the Monrovia, S.K. Nimely. He was every married and single female's secret fantasy—though hated by men that were lacking in the penis department, but beloved by females of all tribes, races and nationalities. Because of his fear of commitment, women often cautioned each other about him. He was one of those men that women found easy to love, but quite difficult to hate or keep as their own.

"What happened to me yesterday?" She asked herself for the hundredth time since her lessons with Stanley had come to an end the previous day. Her breath fogged up her computer's screen, but she didn't notice it. She couldn't see anything beyond the images burned in her head of her writhing beneath Stanley, of Stanley plunging hard and fast into her, of his fingers wet with her juices, touching her, making her scream out his name again and again like a woman in want.

She couldn't for once in her life figure out how she had managed to put her clothes on, find her way to the front door, get in her car and drove off from Rehab Road to her home. Less than twenty-four hours later, she looked back on the entire experience and could barely make out the details of the scene through the thick sensual haze that blanketed her memories.

"Lucky me," she whispered to herself in a victorious voice.

It was as if she was looking into a forbidden realm of pleasure, where only the privileged, where only the elite were allowed to participate. And since Ernestine knew she had never been one of those elites, her brain was bewildered by the entire experience. And she was struggling to come out of that utopia her mind had placed her in. While she might have come from a middle class background and shared her name with people from the elite class of her society, she was by no means privileged to enjoy the benefits that circulated among those in that upper echelon.

She had hardly slept the night before. Every time she closed her eyes she could swear she felt the imprint of Stanley's tongue between her legs, and when she gingerly touched herself she was dripping wet. So wet that she couldn't resist touching herself some more. She couldn't resist thinking about everything he had done to her body. Everything he had done that made her feel so damn good like a natural woman. For a second, Ernestine could not believe that the aftermath of a love making episode could last this long. It was surreal, and she love the feeling. It made her feel like she was flying without wings. *"No wonder women flock on him like bees on honey, no wonder he's called the master of love, sex, and relationship,"* she said out loud.

"No wonder women warn each other about him. One can never get enough of this love genius, his kisses, his touching, his sense of female sexual physiology, and the full penetrating effect of his hurricane-size dick," she sighed and stared some more at the blinking cursor on the computer's screen.

She didn't know exactly how many times she had masturbated during the night. Five times? Six? Maybe a dozen times, she thought.

As soon as Sunday morning had arrived, bright and shiny through her windows, she dragged herself out of bed. She put on her summer robe, made herself a hot cup of strong coffee and got ready for Mass where she spend the next one hour praying to God and confessing her intentional sins to the Heavenly Father who is faithful and just, as she reminisced her encounter with Stanley and getting wet while at it. Stanley's love was contagious, not even being in the presence of God could stop Ernestine from thinking about their explosive encounter.

Ernestine had never allowed another human being to control her before. Always, even when she thought she was in love, she held a part of herself back. Kept a part of her soul safe from the pains and heartache that love brought to its innocent victims. Women in Africa and the world over have developed this protectionist mentality whenever they are in a romantic relationship with a guy who they consider a heartbreaker. Many of them hold back their love from the men in their lives—often, to protect their soft hearts from being broken due to the lies and deceits meted on them daily by their unfaithful partners who often engage in multiple synchronized sexual relationships with other women and sometimes men. This was exactly what was wrong with 25% of the educated Liberian and African women, especially when a guy thinks the woman of his dream has fallen in love with him, she sometimes gave him a quarter of her heart. 75% of Monrovian and Liberian women were once hopeless romantics, but certain environmental variables have transformed them into women of second thoughts. At a point in time in their lives, they fell in love unconditionally—unlike Ernestine, they did not keep a part of their souls safe from the individual they were involved with. Rather, they gave all to that man who did not give a shit about them besides their vagina and sometimes, their money. For now, she was head over heels for him at that moment.

With Stanley surrounded by rose petals, candles, and sumptuous fabrics, she had given in to his every touch. If he had stopped touching her, stopped tasting her at any point, she would have begged him for more.

Disbelieving still, she shook her head and tried to make sense of her feelings. After she caught her last boyfriend cheating on her, after he had made it perfectly clear that it was her fault for being a prude, for being cold and lifeless in bed, she accepted that she was never going to know true passion. Even worse, she believed she wasn't good enough for the bastard and all the men who had come before him. They all wanted to bend her over and fuck her doggy style, but didn't give a shit about her heart. Like her ex-boyfriend,

Samuel T. Coleson who told her she was a cold fish, she hated herself and every man who she came across. For this reason her writings did not click because she could not relate her experience to those characters in her writings.

Now that Stanley had pleasured her more ways in one afternoon than she had ever felt in the first twenty-nine years of her life, she wondered if it was because they had a deeper connection than just bodies.

"I'm in love with him," she whispered to herself, stunned by the discovery. The question now is, how could she not be in love with him, she asked herself. He was the perfect man in every way—rich, handsome, smart, and above all, knows how to make a woman feel good. Not that many men in Liberia or in the west she could say that about—many of Liberian men were sexually and romantically unexposed. They were urge fulfilling brats that didn't learn good manners from their mostly over controlling fathers. As a result, they did not know how to treat a good woman like a queen. On the other hand, many of the women in country were becoming very dishonest and where prostituting themselves with multiple men due to the hardship in the country. For this reason, many of the men have become distrusting of them. But Ernestine had the heart of gold because she had been raise right and been taught to do the right thing.

She sighed and told herself to get over it. Just because their mentoring lessons had spiraled way out of control—Ernestine hadn't forgotten that it was entirely her own idea to take off her clothes—he was probably thinking how she was just another fan, another wannabe writer who wanted to get into his pants and later lie to him like the other women had done to him before

"I'm not in love," she said aloud. *"I'm in lust. A big difference."*

Feeling a little better, a little saner, Ernestine took a sip from her hot cup of Nescafe and suddenly, words began to dance through her mind. She shook her head, but they refused to go away.

"*No,*" she suddenly said aloud. "*I can't write this. I won't write this. I promised!*"

When the words continued to appear in her mind, one after the other in beautiful rhythmical succession, she accepted she had no choice but to type them into her waiting computer.

……Mardea was a good girl. She was the kind of girl boys took home to their mothers and said, "I'm going to marry her, Mom." They took one look at her angelic brown eyes and smooth black hair and knew she was pure as white swamp rice from the fertile valleys of Zorzor in Lofa County.

Mardea had spent her entire life with nuns down Randall Street South Beach. In Catholic school uniforms. When she was a little girl, she thought every other little girl got ready to go to school in the exact same way she did, automatically reaching into their closet for the green pleated jumper and white cotton shirt. She thought the only clothes in the world were white cotton knee socks and black patent leather shoes.

Mercy Johnetta Moore, Mardea's mother, was pleased with how well-behaved her daughter was at home. They were more like sisters than mother and daughter, and Mercy thought Mardea told her everything. If Mardea ever had secret thoughts in her pink and white ruffled bedroom late at night, was when she was in bed under the covers with a flashlight, reading the latest Emmanuel Clarke thriller about a mysterious man named Robert Darkly who kidnapped her and gave her forbidden kisses, she never told her mother about them.

The day Madea turned twenty-one, she was offered a full-time position as a secretary for a local law firm on Cheeseman Avenue in Sinkor. For the first time in her life she was torn.

She loved the nuns with all her heart. Growing up in the safe environment of her private school had brought her nothing but happiness, but lately, she had begun to feel a yearning inside of her that grew stronger every day. She knew that Monrovia had lots of things to offer beyond the innocence that clothed a young Catholic girl.

Unbeknown to her teachers, to her parents, and to her few chaste and respectful boyfriends, Mardea had been sneaking off to Vernon Playground as well as various used bookstores downtown Broad Street, under the old Ministry of Education and spending her allowance on worldly books.

Mardea had long ago outgrown Emmanuel Clarke's historical fictional thrillers or K Moses Nagbe Romance. With her fingers trembled as she read Eric Jerome Dickey's new romance novel, if her parents had paid attention to their only daughter, they would have sensed something odd about here behavior. Mardea had also begun reading romantic books from Alissa Baxter of South Africa. And then Blanche Richardson. And then Samiya Bashir and other love odysseys that she could find under the crumbling King's Building.

Mardea would have sworn that no one liked sex, that her parents had copulated only to create her and then settled back in their separate bedrooms as soon as her father's sperm sunk into her mother's egg.

In these books she saw a far different reality and knew it was something she had to experience for herself. Before she agreed to marry one of the stupid Catholic boys who wanted her only as a wife and mother of the children she would bear. Before she agreed to spend the rest of her days shoving papers in and out of male lawyers' offices in the law firm while they voyeuristically would stare at her queen-size fat buttock when she turns around to walk away—just like they now do her would be female boss in the big office upstairs whom usually have sex with the big lawyer in the big office who suffers from a terrible back aches, but wears a metal back brace to support his bad back. Though Mardea did not want to accept the offer to work with the young lady whom she considers a cheap hoe, she was having a second thought of accepting the job just to please her commanding parents who were friends of the big lawyer turned politician. They had asked him to let her gain some real-world work experience before she can start college at the Cuttington Unversity in Bong County. At this law firm, rumor has it that the big lawyer keeps most of the females that work for him. As for Mardea's would be supervisor, it is believed that he has her wrapped around his fingers so much that she's afraid to have a relationship of her own or commit to any man who dearly loves her. A stinking shame for a purported sound—minded woman to allow herself to be exploited and manipulated by someone who could be her father, especially where you and others are seen by the exploiter as objects of sex without any gleam of hope as being a part of his world beyond the dark bedroom.

Bravely Mardea told her parents and the nuns at the convent on UN Drive that she was going to spend some time in the city once school closes. She told them she was going to work with a progressive local Catholic youth group on Ashmun Street—which in fact, she worked part time for—and they were all so proud of her. Her parents found her an apartment in the Mamba Point neighborhood, the diplomatic district of the city and paid for sone year rent and didn't worry about their precious little daughter going astray. Why would they, when she had never given them even the slightest bit of trouble as a teenager.

Mardea Moore was a good girl. She dressed like a lady—no mini skirt or dress, no low-rise jeans to show her ass crack, no Brazilian wig or Mohawk haircut to make her look street-like. She had been raised to behave like a lady at all time. For the most part, she spoke eloquently to her teachers, her parents and everyone she met.

On the other side of downtown, Wilmot stood behind the bar and wiped another glass dry, sliding it beneath the counter in preparation for opening the bar. His bar. He had been through so many legal battle to retake control of something he owns. His situation was not unique—many property owners are forced to go through a similar situation due to the thievery mentalities of some of the residents of Monrovia and in other places in the country and Africa.

He still couldn't believe "The Candlelight Bar and Restaurant" was finally his after a bitter fight with his ex-wife Jewel B.T. Parker, who nine months ago ran off with another man in the United States, but came back to claim some of his properties he owned before they married. Every time he pulled up underneath the neon sign in his dark-blue BMW, he got a rush. As he wiped down the vinyl counter one more time, he frowned at his reflection. If he didn't find a great manager, and fast, "The Candlelight Bar and Restaurant" would be a laughingstock among restaurants in the thriving city. Unfortunately, the last five people he had interviewed stunk. Most of them could barely write a simple report, though they all claimed to have BScs, and MScs as well as MBAs from local colleges and universities in the country.

Hell, he could manage the business better than the last manager who happened to be his ex-wife's fuck-mate. In fact, he did not have a patient for a lot of his patrons, but was forced to put up with them for the sake of remaining in business. Wilmot was a type 'A' personality and hot tempered at it. He spoke his mind freely and was not afraid to tell any female if her perfume smell was overpowering. He once told the son of the President of Liberia how corrupt the president was. His candidness landed him behind bars for weeks without being charges with a crime. When he was finally released, he was warned to stay out of government's way and to reframe from bashing the president.

Someone from outside pushed the door open slightly and a

shaft of blinding light hit Wilmot across the forehead. "Excuse me," he heard a timid little voice say.

"We're closed," he said gruffly. "Come back at five."

The beautiful young girl disobeyed him and walked right through the door.

Wilmot looked at her in disbelief. The last time he'd seen someone as prim and proper as the young girl standing before him, was when he was in church looking at a nun. And only the Lord of Heaven knew he hadn't set a foot in a church for well over a decade. Maybe two. He often told his church going and Holy Ghost filled siblings, that Heaven and Hell are found right here on Earth. His now deceased mother, a Baptist minister, once kicked him out of the family home for blaspheming against God when he told her that, Hell is not somewhere under the ground as most people claimed, rather, it is right here on Earth where we live. Since the divorce, he turned to Eastern Philosophy and Mysticism as a form of enlightenment.

On second thought, no nun ever had such gorgeous brown eyes and a mouth he could imagine wrapped around his long and rock-hard penis giving him pleasure.

"I said we're closed," he said, glaring at her. It was pissing him off knowing that she had ignored his words just the way his dick was perking up just because some meek, glossy dark-skin girl, barely out of pigtails, was walking across the floor toward him.

"Are you the owner?" she asked him, as if she hadn't heard him tell her to leave twice already.

He glared at her, trying to scare her away, but when she kept staring at him with her huge, brown eyes, and held her ground, he nodded. "What's up with you?"

She held up the 'Help Wanted' ads. "I'm here to apply for a job. I was told that you're in search for someone to manage your restaurant"

He snorted. "You? Shuuuuuu. I don't think so!" He shook his head from side-to-side and laughed in her face to drive the point home. "Honey, this ain't no church, and you certainly ain't no manager."

Her face set in a mulish expression. She turned away from him, but instead of walking back out the door, she walked toward the small table and sat down.

"I'm interviewing. You will interview me before I leave this place today, sir," she said, and he knew she was trying to be brave, but even in the dim light of the bar he could see her hands shaking at her side.

He looked down at his jeans and cursed the huge bulge in the front of his pants before taking several menacing steps toward her. Before he could forcibly grab her by her skinny little shoulders and throw her out onto the sidewalk, she began to tell him about the advertisement campaigns she would run to attract more young people to his restaurant and bar.

He stopped in his tracks. She spoke for about thirty seconds about auto drop, social median outreach, radio promotion and food and wine tasting—this was something she had read in one of Emmanuel Clarke's books. For three minutes she schooled him on customer relationship management and sales promotion. Wilmot sunk down into the nearest chair. This was something straight out of a business school from the United States and not any of the substandard local colleges or universities that were rubbing students of the hard earned cash and were kicking their butts out of their doors with cheap degrees that a street smart kid can earn for $1 at a local library in Monrovia.

The little choirgirl was incredible. She was the manager of his dreams. Shit! He couldn't have her in the bar. Every man in Monrovia that would come in the place was going to start having dreams about laying her sweet little body over the front *of his thighs, pulling up her pleated skirt and...*

"Stop!" Wilmot said loudly, almost more to himself than to her, but this time she obeyed him. "I want the job, sir," she said in a calm but firm voice.

"No. This place is called The Candlelight Bar and Restaurant, Not School or College Girl Bar and Restaurant." He looked hard at her before spitting out another question, "In fact, how old are you?"

"I am old enough to perfectly manage this place. In fact, what you just said is sexism and a sexual discrimination. You know what the president said about equal employment opportunity for us female minorities in the workplace, right," she reminded him.

Wilmot rolled his eyes, almost disgustingly. "Damn, I hate the way this president has spoiled this damn country with all these women's rights shit. I am sorry, pretty girl, you're not good enough for The Candlelight Bar and Restaurant, period!"

Her eyes shot fire at him. "Yes I am!"

Suddenly Wilmot had a thought. "How badly do you want this job?"

She lowered her long eyelashes and then looked back up at him. "I want it. I really do. I need some kind of real world work experience."

Slowly, Wilmot got up from the chair and sauntered over to her. Sitting down next to her on the adjacent chair, he said, "I'm willing to make you a deal. This is a deal many girls of your age in this hungry and broke city looking for a job will never refuse" He saw her swallow and then she licked her lips.

"I'm listening," she said as she removed her slender fingers from the middle of the folder she was holding in her hand that had her sheets of presentation and clasped them primly in her lap.

He pulled the chair directly in front of her and leaned

forward until their lips were touching and then he slipped his tongue into her mouth, dying to taste her. "This is what I want. You know how things work here in Liberia. Are you willing to give it to me?"

Her eyes grew even wider, but she nodded innocently.

"Whenever and wherever I want it?"

She nodded again.

"However I want it?"

"Yes, I will try my best to make you happy, sir," she said, almost inaudibly.

As it was an open secret in the country, most bosses exchanged sex for jobs. A country of 4.3 million people with unemployment in the double digits—more than 80%, doing what your boss demands was a norm. Self-reliance was a divergence and a self-inflicted wound that could cost a person his or her job. Many of the unscrupulous bosses took advantage of the high unemployment rate in the country and exploited those they hired. For that poor and destitute boy or girl of the society without the right social connections, going to college and earning a degree was just an act of self-fulfilment and not a bridge to getting ahead or getting a job. Often, a college graduate would tramp the streets and various government's offices and businesses in search for a job without one shred of luck. Every year, the more than 10 colleges and universities in the country graduates tens of thousands of students under poor academic conditions without any sound employment prospect for these graduates. Many young men seeking jobs without luck have turned to being homosexual or bisexual in a bid of satisfying a would be sexual demand. In some cases, some bosses are in the practice of pay to play—where the newly hired employee gives a percentage of his or her monthly salary to the person who hires them or their inside connection who made the employment possible. This is a very sad practice in our country.

This time, Mardea smiled at him and reached out her hand to shake on the agreement. "I'm Mardea," she said in a voice as sweet as honey. "What's your name?" Wilmot did not respond to her gesture. Instead, he told her the day to report for work.

That first day, Mardea came to the restaurant seemed as if she had been working there for the longest. The staff respected and admired the manner in which she handled problems. She knew she was still walking on shaky grounds. Besides, she was so excited and nervous about the terms of her contract with Wilmot, she needed to blow off her energy at the restaurant and the bar or she'd go crazy if her boss wasn't impressed with her performance.

All day and all evening she had watched him out of the corner of her eye. In her fantasies, she had never created any man as incredible as this one who was three times her age. Six foot five inches tall, and all muscle beneath his worn jeans and tight black t-shirt, his teeth gleamed white against the dark skin. Stubble covered his jaw line and his low-cut-length jet black hair and piercing brown eyes made him look so much like a 16th Century African sea rover that Mardea felt as if he was living in the wrong century, and on the wrong part of the African continent.

At the end of the evening as the last customer walked out and the rest of the staff left, he locked the door and then joined her in the back office to go over the day's transactions.

"Sit down," he said as he sat down on an empty chair.

She did as he asked and tried to get her knees to stop shaking. He slowly stood up and Pulled up to get her stand on her feet so that she was standing between his knees, he reached around the back of her skirt and popped open the top button, then slid the zipper down until her skirt fell into a heap at her heels.

She looked around the room at the pile of papers stack on

the office desk and at the hundred tea-light candles glowing, at the overhead speaker with soft soulful music blaring out of it, and knew that all of her fantasies were about to be made real.

He hooked his fingers into the edges of her cotton panties and slowly slid them off, over her round ass and down her smooth, untouched thighs. Mardea had to fight the urge to cover herself from him, and she barely managed to keep her hands clenched at her sides. She weighed about 130 pounds, small in the middle and buff in the hip with a firmed soft queen-size ass.

Before she knew it he had moved his hand between her legs and slipped the index finger of his right hand deep into her wet vagina. She gasped even as she felt her muscles convulse around his thick, long finger.

Mardea was scared. She had barely even touched herself there in the shower! She was so excited her fear hardly seemed to matter. She strained against his finger and he pushed it so far inside her, his palm covered her doorway, and his thumb was pressing on the sensitive flesh at the top of her vagina mound.

She knew from her books that it was called the clitoris, but she could hardly think the word to herself. Her innocence of sex and relationship made her behave like a new virgin who had just come out of the Sande Society in Grand Cape Mount County.

"Your clit is so swollen," he murmured, his mouth less than an inch from the cleft between her legs.

She liked the way clit sounded coming from Wilmot's mouth and she forced herself to say the word out loud. "My clit has been swollen all night," she murmured.

He groaned, then lifted his thumb off her clit and blew softly on the engorged flesh. Her tight vagina clenched around his finger and as he blew on her tender clitoris again and slid his finger in and out of her vagina, she closed her eyes and started to see a rainbow of colors. Her legs were shaking uncontrollably *now, but not from fear. She was trying to crest Mont Nimba or the tallest hill she had ever encountered, and she needed Wilmot to help her over it.*

She put her hands on the back of his head and pressed his mouth to her. "WOW! Is the way I am feeling right now really normal," she asked while still pressing his mouth into wet pussy.

"Yes, sweetheart, it is a normal feeling every female gets during sexual intercourse. I hope you like it," Wilmot replied as he worked his tongue around the swollen clitoris and vertically on her enormous labia surrounding her sweet virginal canal. Her juices were all over his mustache down to his beard.

"Thank God! Yes, it feels so good and I don't want you to stop doing what you're doing," she cried as he worked his tongue and his teeth over her inflamed flesh and clasped her big ass with his strong hands.

Wasting no time, Wilmot almost ripped the clothes off his skin as he could no longer hold back his urge for her. Wedging out his already hard and large dick from his boxer, he wasted no time in plunging it into Mardea's young and untouched pussy. With a soft, "Oh Wilmot take your time," he let her sink on his angry monster that had been in an ambush of her for most of the night. The massive penis broke her hymen, but Mardea didn't squeak as the pains were mixed with the pleasure that came with it.

Mardea's world exploded in a blaze of fireworks. Now that she knew what awaited her on the other side of life, she knew she would never be able to go back to the perfect world she had come from. She knew there and then that she was never going to be the innocent Catholic school bred girl everyone in St. Theresa Convent Catholic School knew her to be. She had finally tasted the Forbidden Fruit she was warned never to eat until marriage.

Mardea Moore wasn't a good girl anymore….

…..Ernestine looked up from her computer screen and realized she had been writing all morning. She reread the beginning of her new story and smiled.

Evidently, Stanley's lessons had inspired more than her underutilized silver vibrator. His incredible lessons had stimulated her mind and imagination as well. Her writing clicked and she knew her life would never be the same with the master of love, sex, romance, and relationship mentoring her. One thing Ernestine hadn't forgotten was the fact that she was not the first person to be mentored by Stanley and she will not be the last woman to be mentored by this master crafter of every love, lies, relationship and all those positive vibes that put back park and spice into any dying relationiship as well as keep any cold bedroom warm and cozy for love making.

However, she remembered their promise to each other to keep whatever happened in Stanley's "classroom" stays inside the classroom, she was assailed by guilt, but remember a stark reality that bedevils every human—keeping one's promise. As it is a dark fact, most Liberians will never keep their words to their own brother and sister, let alone keeping their word to a stranger who may not even keep their words to them in return.

A bad little voice inside Ernestine's head said, "Don't worry, honey. He'll never read your book. He's too busy with his own career and getting a lot of attentions from better eligible women in Liberia and he'll never find out that you and he are the live action figures playing out your sex scenes." No matter how she tried to frame the situation, she was guilty as hell for betraying Stanley's confidence.

Ernestine had never written so fluidly before. What's more, she had never been so inspired to continue with her story, to find out what was going to happen with Mardea and Wilmot, and with Fatu and Melvin and the host of other characters and stories she had created, but had not been able to complete. She was sure, pretty sure that with more mentoring session with Stanley, she would be on her way to the top as one of the best female sensual romance writers who had ever lived on the other side of the world, especially Western Africa.

CHAPTER 10

Stanley stood up from his desk and walked into the guest bedroom of his house. He hadn't been able to work since Saturday, since the day his whole life had been turned upside down by a hot vixen who didn't even know the power she wielded. He needed to call her, but as it was, he was still too chicken to dial her entire number without hanging up. Instead, he walked to his window to watch the orphan boy and his brother prepare for school that early morning. After watching the 12 year-old feed his little brother with a leftover rice only mixed with palm oil from the previous day, the two boys went off to school without Stanley reaching out to them as he had promised his mother that he would.

As his mind went back to Ernestine, he hoped she would still talk to him. After the way they had parted on Saturday, after she stood up, put her clothes on mechanically, and then turned to him with a plastered smile and shook his hand, saying *"Thank you very much for the lessons, Mr. Nimely,"* he wasn't sure if he had done the right thing with her at all.

His conscience was bothering him more than he wanted to admit. Above and beyond the fact that he was worrying he might have taken advantage of her, was the undisputable truth that if he were with her again, he knew he wouldn't have one single qualm about making her scream his name out, over and over again. Again, it was a choice both of them had made to allow things to have spiraled out of control.

He was still upset that she had left after only seven orgasms, when he had planned to give her at least ten. He supposed, somewhat ruefully, the three times he took care of himself that night after she had left practically made up the difference. Nonetheless, he would rather have Ernestine coming in his arms or on the tip of his tongue, than his hand and his memory making him shoot all over the shower's walls.

The phone rang and Stanley picked up the mobile phone from his home office desk. It seemed as though this was the phone call he had been awaiting all morning.

"Stanley Nimely." He said in the mouthpiece of the mobile device. Oddly, Stanley had not saved Ernestine's phone number in his phone. Instead, he had memorized the number like his ABC.

The was familiar and it send bolt of lightning through Through Stanley's being. *"Hi Stanley. It's Ernestine. How are you doing this morning?"*

Stanley nearly dropped the phone, he was so surprised by her phone call. *"Um, uh, I'm fine. Great. Super."* He thwacked his forehead with the back of his hand for sounding like such a big jerk. *"How are you doing as well?"*

He heard her laugh across the wireless network and the choking sensation around his heart eased up a bit.

"I'm great Stanley. Really, really great. I wanted to thank you for your excellent lessons on Saturday. It made all the difference in my life." Her replied was relieving. Stanley rubbed the back of his neck to relieve the pressure in his neck. This often happens whenever he's stressed.

"You do?" he asked and then tried to cover his gaffe by saying, *"What I mean to say is, I wasn't sure if—"*

Thankfully Ernestine cut him off before he could make an even bigger ass of himself. *"—I loved every second of it,*

Stanley. And you know what, I've been writing better than ever."

"WOW! That's great," he said to her, and meant it. He hadn't written anything worth a shit since Saturday, but he didn't care at all. All he wanted was to see her again, but he was afraid he'd be coming on too strong, that he'd be too obviously sniffing after her, if he suggested moving onto lessons three so quickly.

"Anyway," she said, *"I was wondering if you'd be up for lesson three?"*

Her matter of fact, professional tone confused him, again. Didn't she know what was bound to happen again when they got in a room together? The one good thing is that, he was so glad she wanted to see him again, he pushed the thought aside. He knew that if she came around, he would eat her up like boiled peanut, as many of the young boys refer to having wild sex with a new girl and then dumping her, but Stanley was in noway going to dump Ernestine. He had a deep feeling for her.

"I certainly am," he said, trying to sound as detached as she did.

"Should we meet at your house again? Or mine perhaps?" Her question caught Stanley by surprise.

"Actually, this time I was thinking we would meet at a restaurant." His replied was not what Ernestine was expecting. There was a brief pause on the phone before she could utter another word.

"A restaurant?" She said, her misgivings sounding clearly in her voice. *"To learn about sex toys?"*

He chuckled softly into the phone. *"Don't you trust your mentor, Ernestine Johnson?"*

She was silent across the line again for a couple of seconds and he knew she was thinking it over. Say yes, his brain urged her telepathically.

"Yes I do, Stanley," she said. She liked the way he called her by her full name, *'Ernestine Johnson'.* Her name rolled smoothly off his tongue like warmed honey syrup on a homemade buttery pancake.

"Great," he said. *"Do you know where Krystal Ocean View Restaurant is in Mamba Point? We can meet there on the Deck Terrace overlooking the Atlantic Ocean or within the restaurant."*

Ernestine was shocked by Stanley's suggestion. She had been shocked ever since she and Stanley had hung up the phone that morning. She was taken aback by his question, *"Do you know where Krystal Ocean View Restaurant is on Mamba Point?"* For God's sake, she was born and raised in Monrovia, the renamed capital of Liberia. She was not one of those people that migrated to the city during the 1990 to 2003 civil war and have refused to go back to their village of origin. The 1990 war—migration is the main cause of the overcrowdedness of the small city that was now beginning to expand outward.

When she had boldly called him, she was completely sure she was going to have no problem rolling with whatever Stanley was going to throw at her. In spite of her misgivings after their first two lessons, she couldn't suppress a shiver of delight as she imagined him using a dildo, or something even more creative, on her during this lesson.

She couldn't help the flicker of disappointment when it didn't look like that was going to happen. There was no way he could stimulate her with a dildo in a crowded restaurant, was there?

Besides, wasn't learning about having sex in new locations lesson four, not lesson three? There wasn't much she could do. He was the teacher, and she was his student ready and curious to learn from the guru of love, sex, and relationship.

That early evening, she drove carefully through congested traffic on United Nations Drive in the Vai Town corridor through the noisy Waterside Market on her way up the Hill toward Krystal Ocean View Hotel and Restaurant. Even though the government was just beginning to install hydro powered along with some solar powered traffic lights in the city that was recovering from economic downturn due to virus outbreak more than two years ago, many of the citizens had a glimmer of hope in a better tomorrow that their government had promised more than 10 years ago. When she finally found a parking spot in the parking lot, she neatly parked her car in one of the available spaces. She checked her makeup and outfit one last time before stepping out of the car. She didn't want to look as if she was trying to seduce him, but then again, she wanted to look as sexy as possible. Walking into the restaurant, she helloed several people she knew that were out in the parking lot. *"I hate these nosy people in this damn town. These men in this place can't keep their freaking eyes off females' asses. I hate when they greet and rudely stare at my damn butt."* The attractively beautiful woman complained to herself. She adjusted her skirt a second time before walking any further out on the parking lot.

That Saturday at his house, he had seen her under forgiving candlelights and fire glow. As the sun hadn't set yet and he was going to see her in full daylight, she wanted him to think she was pretty—prettier than any woman he'd been with. She had the full package most Monrovian females yearned for—pretty face, above average breast, and a big ass to go with them.

She had dressed a little more risqué tonight than she usually would have for a date. She shook her head to clear it of any self-deprecating thought as she made her way toward the entrance of the building. This is not a date, she reminded herself again. He was her mentor and she was his apprentice learning all the tricks of the trade. Thought their student and teacher relationship went out of control the other day, she had to keep thing professional or else she would let her guard down. One thing that was evident here was the fact that Stanley had reignited the romantic spark in her—he had reawakened her dead passion. It was a typical case of the Lazarus Syndrome where sometimes a patient in a hospital is pronounced dead only to be brought back to life by some unknown phenomenon. In this case, Stanley was that invisible force that had brought Ernestine back to life and given her a reason to live and love again.

If she read anything more into it than professional education, she was going to end up with a broken heart. Ernestine figured out she already had enough of those as it was. Besides, Stanley was a heartbreaker himself—he was highly picky and every woman's secret fantasy. And she was not ready to become one of his victims.

Nonetheless, she had dug out a gold-sequined tank top from the bottom drawer of her dresser and paired it with a flirty black skirt, which brushed the tops of her kneecaps when she walked. She had swept her hair into a ponytail that neatly went up onto the top of her head with a gold clip and wore small gold-hoop earrings on her lobes. The final touch to her outfit was a pair of frivolous spike-heeled black and gold sandals that she had bought at a Boutique on Randall Street and never had the nerve to wear before.

When she finally left the parking lot, she walked up the pathway through the crowded bar onto the Deck Terrace which had an amazing view of the Atlantic Ocean as a backdrop. Stanley was waiting for her at the doorway to the terrace overlooking the street below and the open ocean, looking at busy ships plying local and international waters. She noticed he had a plastic shopping bag in his hand and shivered, wondering what was inside of it.

She put her hand on his arm and he turned around to face her with a huge smile plastered on his gorgeous face.

"Honey," he said, "You look amazing, wow! You are so beautiful."

She blushed. *"Thank you. So do you."*

He looked better than ever, which was really quite a feat considering how incredible he had looked the two other times she had been with him. He had dressed up slightly, wearing a navy blue light-wool slacks and a beautiful pink pin-striped long-sleeved Ralph Lauren shirt.

He slipped her hand into his and was moving toward the front door of the restaurant terrace. She pulled back slightly, saying *"I'm curious about what you've got in the plastic bag."*

Stanley turned and smiled at her. *"I was going to wait to give it to you until we went inside, but now's as good a time as any, I suppose."* He opened the bag so that she could look into it.

"A pair of panties?" She said and looked up at him in confusion.

He nodded. *"I want you to put them on."*

Somehow confused, she asked, "Now?"

"Once we get inside, go to the restroom and change out of the panties you're wearing into this one. And I don't want you to worried about sanitation because I have already washed it clean." His instruction was followed by a sweet little mischievous smile.

Ernestine felt her face turn dark purple. *"And then what?"*

He shrugged. *"And then we'll eat and enjoy each other's company."* He handed her the bag, then pulled her back on the path toward the restaurant terrace.

"Let's go out on the terrace where we can get a better view of this beautiful place and the incredible Atlantic Ocean view.

I'm really starved," he said, and she had no other choice but to follow him.

Ernestine wondered how it was possible for her pussy to already be soaking wet when all she had done was say a few sentences to a guy whom love was so intoxicating. He was turning her into a walking orgasmic machine, for God's sake.

They walked past the bar of the beautiful restaurant and he whispered in her ear, *"I think the bathroom is just down the hall to the left."* A shiver ran down her spine as his breath stroked her cheek and she obediently headed off to the ladies' room, plastic bag in hand.

Once in a stall, she took a deep breath and wondered if she should cut bait and run before she got in any deeper than she could handle.

Then she thought about the hundred pages she had already written of her new book and how well it was going, and she knew that a true professional woman should be willing to give everything to her work, to try anything if it had the potential of enhancing her art. So after listening carefully to make sure no one else was in the bathroom, she slid her red silk panties off her bare legs, folded them neatly, and slid them into her gold hand-purse. Gingerly opening the plastic bag, she pulled out a black thong.

"Is this it?" She whispered to herself in the bathroom's stall, as she turned it this way and that way, poking her hand back into the bag to see if there was something else inside.

Wondering what the big deal was about the thong, and knowing it was bound to be something good if Stanley was behind it, with her heart racing, Ernestine slipped her feet into the thong. Settling the panties up on her hips she let her skirt fall back down over her hips to her knees. What she didn't know was that Stanley had bought this special vibrator thong from one of Vernon's Playground on McDonald Street. Vernon imported these panties and other sex toys from the United States and China for his high-value clients, many of whom were well placed in high positions in government, NGOs, and other private corporations.

Wadding up the plastic bag into a ball, she stuffed it into the garbage can in her stall and stepped back out under the fluorescent lighting above the sink. Taking one last look at herself in the mirror, she thought she looked pretty confident considering how jumpy she felt. She grabbed her purse from the counter in front of the mirror and pushed the bathroom's door open.

She rounded the corner and headed back into the entryway, careful to walk slowly so she wouldn't trip in her nine-inch pump heels shoes and make a fool of herself. She looked up and saw Stanley watching her carefully and she gave him a little sweet grin as if to announce her presence. He reached into his right pocket with right his hand and suddenly she felt her vagina tingling and nipping under the thong between her legs.

She stopped dead in her tracks, propped herself up against a nearby wall with her left hand and closed her eyes, trying to determine what had just happened to her.

She felt as if she had just sat down on a bullet vibrator! Not that she would know firsthand what that would feel like, since she didn't own any self-stimulants bullet vibrator, but she couldn't disregard the quivering sensation between her legs.

"How could that be," she asked herself. Comprehension dawned on her and she opened her eyes to meet Stanley's gaze.

He looked like a predator in the Sapo National Park who had just captured a delicious prey and was about to consume it, and would savor every single bite of it.

He held his hand out to her as he met her halfway down the hallway and said, *"Good. I'm glad you did what I asked you to do. Now let's go eat."*

"Eat?" Ernestine asked him, her voice squeaky, off its normal pitch. *"We're really going to eat real food?"*

The next thing she knew, the hostess was seating them at a table at the edge of the terrace overlook the street below and the open Atlantic Ocean, as Stanley ordered drinks for them.

"This is a joke, right?" She asked him, half-hoping he'd say, Yes, go put your regular panties on and then we'll head back to my place so I can fuck your brains out, but mostly hoping he'd press the button on his little remote control again to send her into orbit so she could boldly go where no Liberian woman had gone before.

"There are lots of strangers in the room with us, aren't there?" He said rather wickedly.

Her mouth fell open. She quickly moved to shut it, intent on keeping her cool even though this third lesson of theirs was already moving far beyond their last lesson, far beyond her realm of comfort, far beyond anything she ever thought to encounter in her lifetime. It was something she thought came straight out of a Hollywood movie and not any of the low quality and low budget movies produced in Nigeria and sometimes Liberia.

"And here I thought I had experienced everything with him on Saturday," she mused silently as she pretended to study the menu. The words were a blur, and when the waiter came to take their order she couldn't seem to open her mouth. Thankfully, Stanley ordered for them both.

Ernestine was on pins and needles as she waited for the next surge of energy on her pussy lips, as she waited for Stanley to gratify and simultaneously embarrass her across the table. Her vagina was already incredibly wet, just from seeing

Stanley, from the one jolt he had already given her, and from the sensual promise she read in his eyes. If he was a trophy, she would have enshrined and worshiped him like God—for he was one fine man to behold.

"So, how was the rest of your day," he asked her innocently, as if he didn't hold the control to her entire world in the pocket of his wool slacks.

She opened her mouth to reply, but her mouth was as dry as her pussy was wet. She reached for her water glass and as she lifted the cool rim to her lips, Stanley put his weapon of pleasure to use again.

The sensations that washed through her vagina were so intense she nearly dropped her glass. Suavely, Stanley reached for the glass and slid it from her fingers back to the table without spilling a drop. She gripped the edge of the table and rode the waves of pleasure her panties were giving her under her skirt.

Stanley let off his pussy controller—as she was beginning to think of it now that she knew the absolute power he wielded over her—a second later when the waiter dropped off two glasses of champagne and two small salads. Ernestine looked around at the other diners in the posh restaurant and wondered if any of them had noticed her writhing in her seat. From the expressions on their faces, she didn't think anyone had taken notice, thank God.

Stanley speared a crisp slice of fresh locally farmed tomato and held it out for her across the table. "Taste this," he said, and she noted he was holding the fork with his left hand, so she shook her head.

"No thank you," she said as formally as she could under the prevailing circumstances.

He took his right hand out of his pocket and put it on the table. *"Look, both hands are free now."* He held out the tomato slice again. *"I want to watch your teeth and lips take in this plump, juicy tomato,"* he urged her and this time she acquiesced.

As she began to open her mouth to slide the sweet fruit off his fork, the buzzing on her clit began in earnest. This time, she was too close to the edge to fight off the explosion.

A low sound came from her throat, and she clenched the edge of the table so tightly the skin on her knuckles turned dark purple.

"Let it go," Stanley implored her softly across the table.

Ernestine closed her eyes and let the waves of intense pleasure suck her into the abyss of joy once again. Little whimpers escaped from her mouth, no matter how hard she tried to hold them back. She was dimly aware of Stanley's intense gaze as he watched her come in her seat.

Just as her orgasm had rocked all the way through her, turning her completely inside-out, their waiter approached their table with a concerned look on his face.

Noticing Ernestine's strange behavior, the wait staff came by and said, *"Is everything all right here?"*

Stanley let off the controls and looked expectantly at her, waiting for her answer. She smiled tremulously at the waiter. *"Yes. Thank you. Everything's fine,"* hoping he would just get the hell away from the table and leave them alone. Ernestine was afraid to show any sign of her just ended orgasm to the wait staff, knowing how people in the tiny city spread petite gossips like wildfire. It would start with a *"You girl or my man guess what happened today at Krystal Ocean View Restaurant,"* and before the real facts are known, everything is blown out of proportion. The itchy ears of residents of this city fed on gossips and lies as food for their hungry souls. After forcing a fake smile at the nosy waiter, she locked eyes with Stanley who concurred with what she had told the nosy man who seemed not to be convinced as though he was their class teacher who was ready to reprimand the two lovebirds.

Instead the waiter said, much to her ongoing chagrin, *"I was afraid that something was wrong with your salad. The look on your face while you were eating was—"*

Their young waiter seemed stuck on searching for just the right word to describe the public agony of her sexual release, so she jumped in and said, *"—It's just that the tomato was so incredibly good."* She hoped her performance was a believable one.

Finally, he smiled at her and bowed a little, saying, *"Good. Great. Your main courses meal should be out in just a few minutes. If you need anything just let me know. Whatever I can do to make your night memorable, I'll be more than happy to do it,"* before he walked away.

"You really are an A+ student," Stanley said as she touched at the corners of her mouth with her napkin.

She looked up at him and couldn't decide if she was furious with him or falling harder for him than ever before. She decided to keep things light until she decided. Often, when a Liberian woman has a crush on a man, she usually does not tell that man. Many of them usually allow a stupid notion like a woman's *"self-pride"* to stand in the way of their personal happiness. This trend was being broken after the 14 years civil conflict that destroyed the country and the recent Ebola crisis that killed thousands of Liberians. Modern women in other parts of the African Continent have begun expressing their innermost desire for men they are attracted to since the explosion of the Internet and social media.

"And you are quite the inventive teacher that Liberia has produced, aren't you?" She said syllabically followed by a beautiful smile.

He raised an eyebrow and slid the small remote control

across the table before giving her a mischievous but rather a gorgeously boyish smile.

She looked at him in surprise. *"Why are you giving this to me?"*

He reached for it again, saying, *"I'm happy to take it back if you want,"* *wasting no time, she grabbed it in a split second before he did.*

"No. I think it's better if I've got this with me for the rest of the meal. Don't worry, it is in a very safe place. " She slid the remote control onto her lap and put it underneath her napkin.

He laughed and ate a bite of his salad, washing it down with a sip of champagne before saying, *"When I tell you to, I want you to press the on button on the remote."*

"Are you crazy?" She asked, positive she could never do such a wanton thing to herself. After all, it was one thing for him to drive her wild in public, but it was unthinkable for her to do the very same thing to herself!

He stared deeply into her eyes, his pupils slightly dilated, his breathing heavy and slow. *"Now."*

She stared back at him, willing herself to stay strong, to stick to the only sense of herself she had ever known, and shook her head once.

"I said now," he repeated in a clear, firm voice.

"No," she said as her heart raced straight to her throat and got stuck there.

"I'm only going to say it one more time," he said, his voice and face devoid of all expression. *"Push the button right now."*

And this time, she knew she had no choice but to obey him, although she wondered how he would punish her if she disobeyed him. Right now, she didn't have the strength for disobedience. Considering she was on the verge of coming just from the sound of his voice, she figured she may as well go for the whole damn thing. For that matter, she didn't want to look too deeply into the fact that she desperately wanted to press the button. Her finger had been trembling over the on button ever since she slipped it beneath her napkin on her lap.

So she took a deep breath that quickly turned into shallow, pressed the button and turned the machine in her panties on. As she did so, Stanley said in too low a voice for anyone but her to hear, *"I want you to keep your eyes open. Look at me while you're coming. And keep holding down that button no matter what else happens."*

Ernestine felt hot, slick liquid pool between her legs as she digested his words. So she trained her eyes on him, and every time she was tempted to shut him out, to experience this radical pleasure all by herself, he said, *"Open up, Honey. Open up. Just remember, you're in sweet Monrovia, the most entice please to be. And you're with the master of sensual romance in the sweet land of liberty, Honey."* And so she lifted her heavy lids and instinctively widened her legs underneath the table, opening everything up for the man she was falling for heedlessly.

Ernestine was on the brink of bursting into another powerful orgasm when the waiter arrived with their dishes. She was tempted to turn off the machine purring away in her labia, she began to lift her finger off the button, but Stanley's eyes held her in some sort of magnetic pull, so she continued to hold the switch down.

As she continued to detonate in her seat, the waiter set down their plates and then since they were obviously ignoring him, he stepped away from the table again without a word. Stanley whispered, "You're so beautiful, ED. I won't ever get tired looking at you if I had the chance and all the time in the world," and it was enough to make her close her eyes and fall back into her chair, holding onto the remote for dear life as she fell deeper and deeper into the void.

When she finally resurfaced, it took her several long moments to figure out what had happened, to remember where she was. All she knew was that Stanley was with her, as he had been for every one of the best sexual releases she had ever experienced.

She took in his broad grin across the table, and the expectant, slightly nervous look on his face suddenly made her want to shout out with happiness.

"WOW," Stanley said. *"That was more intense than I thought it would be."* He looked a little worried as he said, *"Are you mad at me, Honey?"*

"Nope," she said as a matter of fact. *"It was a great lesson. At least as good as one and two."* Taking a sip of champagne, she leaned closer to him across the table and said, *"I have to tell you, I can't wait to find out what you have planned for lesson four."*

Finally, the look of surprise on Stanley's face turned into laughter and he relaxed back into his chair. *"You certainly are full of surprises,"* he said with obvious appreciation. The adventure in Stanley was glad to know that Ernestine was the perfect adventurous student he'd been searching for to mentor for most of his professional writing career. His own words of advice to a group of trainers in the just ended writers' conference came back to him—if you want to teach great students, you first have to be a great teacher because only the greats produce the greatest. He wanted to make a great writer out of Ernestine whether she knew it or not. From her just ended performance, he saw a promise in her.

Ernestine just smiled a new I'm-All-Woman-So-Watch-Out smile. She waved the waiter over to their table.

"Could you pack up our food into a doggy bag so we can take it home?" She asked him sweetly. *"We just remembered a*

meeting we need to be at right away." Reaching into her purse, she threw a wad of twenty-dollar bills onto the table and begun to prepare to leave. Minutes later, the waiter returned with the change and their food.

She stood up and held out her hand to Stanley. *"Come with me,"* she said in a husky voice. They had been in the restaurant for more than two hours and didn't even know it.

He rearranged the enormous bulge in his trousers and slid the chair back to stand up. Ernestine folded her small hand into his large, warm one and a shiver ran up her spine.

She was being so naughty! She hardly recognized herself as the woman she'd been for the past twenty-nine years.

Stepping outside back into the ocean breeze, laughter bubbled up through her. Kicking off her shoes, she pulled Stanley along toward the flowering trees several hundred yards from the swimming pool of the hotel and restaurant main entrance. They walked in silence until they reached the small parking lot by the trees. By this time darkness had already taken over the small city. The light in the parking lot weren't powerful enough to illuminate everything within the vicinity.

Ernestine ducked her head to get away from a ladybug that was flying directly toward her. She pressed the remote of her car and quickly jumped in the backseat. For a moment, it seemed like something had awakened in her. Stanley quickly followed inside after her. It was like her sexual Liberian Kpelle Amazon twin sister within had been awakened by the stimulation of the vibrating panties Stanley gave her a few hours earlier.

She turned to Stanley, who had followed her into the center of the backseat, and put her hands on either side of his gorgeous face. Sitting on the edge of the seat she tilted her neck to nip at his lips with her teeth. She tasted the salty breeze on them with her tongue.

"*Honey, Honey, Ernestine,*" he groaned, wrapping his large hands on her big and soft round ass, pulling her against his erection, grinding her against him. Though he was already turned on, he did not want to get caught in any act of public nuisance or public sex in the pretentiously religious city where imams pastors, most lawmakers along with their cabinet counterpart usually have open air sex without fear of an official backlash. People making out in the backseat of their vehicles have been a way of life in Monrovia since sexual lewdness was not a major criminal offense that were not being punished under current criminal laws in the country.

She sank to the leathered backseat and he descended with her, their lips and tongues still entwined in a sensuous dance. He quickly stole a look around in the half lit parking lot when he saw the light of another car pulling into the hotel's parking lot.

"*You didn't actually think I was going to let that huge prick of yours go to waste tonight, did you?*" she asked him, mirth twinkling in her large brown eyes as she unzipped his pants and pulled out his throbbing dick.

Rolling him over onto his backseat, she crawled up on top of him, stroking the velvet skin on his meat as she did so. He reached up under her skirt and roughly pulled the motorized thong from her hips. She moved her legs to help him get the panties off.

"*Fuck me, Ernestine. I want you to please fuck me,*" he said compellingly, his voice full of needs with great lost in his voice.

She licked her lips and with great concentration kneeled above his rock-hard meat and guided it into her wet hole with her right hand. "*Stanley!*" she moaned as he slid deeper and deeper into her expanding and wanting pussy.

He leaned up to kiss her. As their lips found each other in the dark car, she began to ride him with a ferocity that was more than he could handle after already watching her explode twice in her seat at the restaurant.

Her tight, slick pussy sucked his dick so thoroughly he knew he was going to blow. Wanting to take her with him he slid his hand up under her skirt and pressed his thumb against her engorged clit while driving his left middle finger deeper into her tight ass hole.

"Oh God, damn......you feel so good, don't stop!" She cried passionately as he simultaneously pounded in and out of her and swirled her taut nub and ass. For Stanley, it was like the first time they met at his resident in the Rehab neighborhood of Paynesville. He lifted his but from the seat of the car as thrust again and again in a slow-motion fashion.

While he was still pounding Ernestine with is thirteen inch monster, an vehicle drove into the facility, directly into the direction where Ernestine had parked her car. Seeing the car's light and fearing the ultimate embarrassment, Stanley stopped pumping Ernestine, but the freak who might had been in another world continued to ride Stanley's dick without the fear of being caught. When she finally realized that her mentor was not moving, the quit riding.

"A car just pulled up next to us," Stanley whispered. He voice was deep.

"Where is the car," she asked, but Stanley only pointed in the direction of the parked vehicle. For more than 10 minutes Stanley and his student waited for the occupants of the vehicle to disembark. Out of concern, Stanley slowly moved Ernestine aside as he lifted his head up to see the car or its occupants. When he finally saw the parked vehicle going up and down, he knew right there and then that the occupants of the were involved in sexual activities.

Wasting no more time, Stanley turned Ernestine around to take her from the back. After seven minutes of continuous and intense pounding, he could no longer hold up. He ordered he to lay on her back and together, they fell into a gulf of intense pleasure, kissing each other frantically, thrashing heedlessly against each other as they climbed higher and higher on the soft backseat of their private love shack on the edge of Cape Mesurado.

CHAPTER 11

Following their big orgasm, both pairs laid in the backseat of the car for another 10 minutes. When the couple in the adjacent vehicle came out and went into the restaurant, Stanley and Ernestine put their clothes back on and stepped out of the vehicle that was now filled with the aroma of sex and their love juices.

Feeling like a victor, Ernestine shook Stanley's hand and said, *"Thank you for a wonderful lesson. It was a time well spent, I must admit,"* then got back into her car and drove away.

Stanley stood in the parking lot and watched her leave. He was unaccountably disappointed. He had hoped that maybe they had progressed beyond the handshake now; hell, he thought they had progressed far beyond a mere handshake the minute she started stripping off her clothes and he had pressed his tongue to her eager clit. He knew that she was sincere when she said, *"Thank you for a wonderful lesson."* He knew she meant it from her heart and that she had acquired knowledge that were going to help her in her writings.

He ran his hands over his hair and walked out onto the swimming pool, sitting down on one of the poolside chairs. He knew what was happening to him and it scared the shit out of him.

Good old Stanley Kla Nimely, writer extraordinaire of sensual romance, who hadn't had a serious girlfriend since his messy divorce three years earlier, was falling in love with someone he least expected—a beautiful Kpelle girl with an Americo-Liberian root. He was falling faster than he had expected. *"Maybe she had cast some kind of Kpelle Nyan Tonorn love spell on me,"* he thought as fear of commitment ravaged him some more. Spell was not the word he wanted to use—*she had taken my name or a picture of me to some Juju man or woman who had sent a cloud of confusion over me so I could fall in love with her,* he thought. Bewitching a lover for a personal reason was a practice that was very common in Monrovia and many parts of West Africa. Both men and women used the power of voodoo or black magic to control the minds of those they love or want a favor from. To counter this, many traditional men and women use portions or special objects like a piece of cloth stitched together with a gamble seed and the horn of an animal along with other mixtures usually prepared by a Juju man or woman to help them ward off evils or possessing love spells. This practice of altering a lover's mind has caused many men and women both at home and the Diaspora their relationships with their spouses or family members whenever they are under the influence of these magical spells and other supernatural forces.

One noticeable thing here was the fact that Stanley didn't have a clue how to tell the object of his affection how he felt about her. Like a pretentious pastor, he allowed himself to go along for the ride while keeping everything professional as much as possible. From how far the mentoring session has gone, it was way beyond professionalism. It was now *fuckfessionalism.*

"So much for being good with dialogues I can't even tell her how I feel about her," he muttered into the wind and let the elements carry his words away.

Ernestine drove toward her Brewerville home on the

outskirt of Monrovia from the restaurant that Monday's night still wearing the remote controlled thong, with the controls stashed neatly in her little purse along with her silk panties. A balloon of joy was swelling up inside of her chest.

Being with Stanley made her feel good. Okay, so being with him made her pussy feel incredibly good, but it was more than just the sexual rush she got whenever he was near her. He was special—there weren't that many of him in the city or even in the world, she though. He was a bundle of joy and she wanted to keep it that way.

When she was with Stanley, she felt like the best of her was actually breaking out. The walls that she had built up around her heart to protect herself from pains were falling apart, one by one, and even though she was frightened about what lay ahead, she wasn't sorry that she had embarked on this crazy ride with Stanley.

My mentor, she thought, and laughed wickedly, thinking about how upset Sheba, Queen of the Sluts in Monrovia, would be if she knew just how hot and hands-on Stanley's version of mentoring actually was. If she knew he has so many hands-on varieties to bring into the classroom, she would go to a Juju man or to a praying mother to snatch Stanley away from her.

In addition to all of the personal revelations Ernestine was having, she also felt more inspired to write than she ever had before. And as soon as she parked her car and let herself inside the door, she headed straight to her office and booted up her HP laptop computer.

Pausing for just a moment to gather her thoughts, she began to type furiously, the words coming out as fast as a hard rain. It was like the full force of the Saint Paul River was upon her as words and new ideas gushed out of her mind and were transferred through her fingers and onto the pages on the computer's monitor like magic…

….Mardea felt her innocence falling off her in thick sheets. Every time she exploded in Wilmot's arms, she changed just a little bit more. Still, twenty-one years of Catholic School training was hard to get rid of, no matter how powerful her comes were, no matter how much she loved the feel of his thick long dick between her legs and deep inside of her vagina.

All day, she had been working with the Catholic Youth Organization at the Sacred Heart Cathedral on Broad and Nelson Streets, helping the choir get ready for their Easter performance, and she couldn't help but wonder if she had fallen in love with the devil. The devil and evil things the nuns at the convent warned her about.

It wasn't the first time this thought had occurred to her. Surrounded by all of the pure, untouched young girls and the solemn nun who was conducting the practice, Mardea felt dirty for the first time in her life. As if she didn't deserve to feel the way she felt when Wilmot was in the room with her. Their Gospel of Fear which had kept her pure for decades had been corrupted by Wilmot's kisses and the powerful thrusting of his fat penis. The thoughts and images of him suspending her in midair, and bringing her down hard and fast on his dick could not leave her head. He had polluted her pureness and unclothed her of years of moral Christian virtue.

No, it was worse than that. All she had to do was think about Wilmot, think about his full lips, the way his stubble scratched her breasts, the tender skin on the inside of her thighs, and her panties instantly got soaking wet with her pussy juices.

That kind of thing only happened to bad girls. And although Mardea had made a conscious decision to stray from the moral path of perfection, she wondered if she had strayed too far. Ever since she had read in one of her favorite Catechism books that sex was a forbidden but irresistible fruit that was needed to be avoided by all of humanity until marriage, she had always been curious to eat this fruit she was being warned about. After her first two experiences with Wilmot, she came to realize that it was not as bad as the book had warned her about. It was something that made her feel good and different from all other girls of her age.

Now, as she stood in front of the door to "The Candlelight Bar and Restaurant" in Downtown Monrovia, she was tempted to turn and run as fast as she could back to the life she used to live.

Suddenly, the door flew open, and Wilmot's large, muscular body filled the frame. "Why are you skulking around outside?" he asked irately. "You know I don't like you hanging around by yourself on this Carey Street neighborhood with all these necktie and suit wearing criminals and Zokos fanning around here that they have misplaced something of value."

Mardea scowled at him. It felt so good to give in to her natural emotions instead of always caging her responses in politeness.

"Hah! That's a good one," she replied in a snotty voice. "I'd like to know how anyone on the street is going to do anything worse to me than the things you've already made me do!"

His eyes narrowed at her sarcastic comment and roughly he grabbed her by the arm and hauled her inside. Pushing her up against the wall, he shoved one of his jeans-clad thighs between her legs and pinned her arms up against the wall.

"Are you actually telling me that you think I made you grab my head so that you could rub your pussy all over my tongue?"

She whimpered as his hands tightened on her wrists. She was aware of the huge bulge in Wilmot's tight jeans pants pressing up against her hip, and she couldn't believe how much she wanted him to unzip his pants and plunge it into her until she couldn't see or breathe or even speak, just like the old blind, deaf and dumb man who often sat at the corner of Benson and Mechlin Streets in downtown Monrovia begging for money.

"Do you expect me to believe that I made you so sensitive that the slightest touch of my tongue on your clit makes you scream? That I'm to be blamed because you are so hot and ready all the time all I have to do is slide my dick into your pussy an inch and you would lose total control of yourself?"

The way he growled the questions at her, Mardea was almost afraid to respond. Frankly, she wasn't sure what the right answer was anymore.

Before she could say anything, he cursed and shoved away from her. "I got a present for you. I hate what you've made me into."

Mardea's face lit up and she started to move toward him, saying, "You did? Can I see what it is?" the look he gave her was so fierce she instinctively backed off against the wall again, as if she could hide in between the columns that held the building up. Rationally, she knew he would never hurt her—he was too gentle, too intent on giving her pleasure—but by the look in his eyes at the moment, she wasn't sure she knew him at all. "He could be one of those men that fought for one of the warring factions during the fourteen years civil war from 1989 to 2003," she thought. Again, she could not be right because news spread so fast like wildfire in this small city. If he was a former rebel fighter, one of the staff at the restaurant would have told her.

He walked behind the bar and pulled out a blue plastic bag. "If I give this to you, do you promise to do exactly what I tell you to do?"

Mardea laughed and sassed back at him, "When have I not done exactly what you've told me to do, boss man?" She felt like she was back on solid ground as she waited for him to give her the present.

"You know what? You're lucky, I am in love you. Hadn't I, I wouldn't have let you behave this way to me. You're now starting to become a complete B.I.T.C.H, just like my ex-wife," he hissed. Wilmot's definition of B.I.T.C.H was 'Being In

Total Control of Him'. He feared that the young girl was now beginning to be in total control of his mind, body and soul because he could not quit thinking of her. Wilmot hates being controlled or manipulated by a female, but the one thing he must have forgotten is the fact that women are very complex for a man to live with, and they are very difficult for a man to live without, especially when that man is straight and not gay.

He tossed the bag over the counter at her and she caught it right before it knocked over one of the tea-lights on a nearby table. "Can I open it right now?"

He shook his head. "Go to the bathroom, and when you come back out to do your job, I want you to be wearing what's in the bag."

She cocked her head at him in confusion. "You bought me clothes? What's wrong with what I have on?" she asked as she gestured to her sky blue business dress.

"Nothing," he replied, "as long as you have a thing for long dresses and Catholic nuns." He shook his head. "Just go. The bar's about to open."

As he turned back to getting the bar ready for the busy evening ahead, Mardea headed for the bathroom. Barely staving off her curiosity, she walked into the ladies room and locked the door behind her. Opening up the bag all she saw was an itty-bitty scrap of black fabric and wondered just what kind of game Wilmot was playing with her.

"He can't actually expect me to put this on!" She exclaimed as she picked up what looked to be a pair of underwear. She had heard about thongs and seen women wearing it in movies, but had never worn a pair of them herself. They seemed much too slutty and besides, they didn't seem the least bit comfortable, especially when it does not cover the entire buttock.

She wondered what Wilmot would do if she didn't put the thong on. "He'll never know," she whispered, but at the same time, she knew he never did anything without a reason, and the rapidly emerging bad-girl in her wondered what his reason was.

At the least, she knew he would make her feel incredibly good when the last customer and the other staff had left for the night and it was just the two of them. She still blushed at the thought of how she had let him penetrate her with the mouth of a large Club Beer bottle the previous night. Not that it didn't make her scream with joy, of course, it was just that the whole thing seemed a little crazy. To her, it was a total sexual escapade her working relationship with her boss has culminated into, and she relished every bit of this odyssey.

Mardea was pretty sure that being with a good girl like her was a new experience for Wilmot, even though she was getting to be more and more of an ex-good-girl with every night she spent at 'The Candlelight Bar and Restaurant'. By the looks of the women who threw themselves at Wilmot night after night—trashy hair, oversized booty and tits, too-tight jeans, caked-on makeup—she figured the only reason he was with her was because she was a novelty. She once overheard her mother and her Aunt Yvonne Cassell discussing how older men in the country were sexually exploiting young women without a flicker of tension from the government or any human rights group. Every time the subject crop up, Mardea got excited as her interest grew into experiencing sex with an older man who was more experience than many of the one minute boys that were aggressively pursuing her in their neighborhood. For now, being with someone who loved her because of her youthfulness and beautiful and also give her all the pleasure as well as appreciate the pleasure she gave in return was something she would not trade for her former live of purity and chastity. Wilmot's experience with the young girl was an epiphany many of the unprincipled men in Monrovia and men all over the world could relate to—taking advantage of young girls and boys due to their inexperience and economic status.

If his reaction to finding out she was a virgin that first

night was anything to go by, he was definitely in uncharted territory. After his release, she could have sworn he was about to apologize to her for taking advantage of her, but she couldn't stand to hear him say he was sorry about the best thing that had ever happened to her, so she kissed him before he could say the words.

That night at home, she slept like she had never slept before. The following morning feeling a little feverish and sored between the crotch, she stayed in bed all morning until quarter to 12 o'clock pm that day. Wilmot had called earlier that morning to find out if everything was okay with her, only to apologize if he had anything to do with her ailment. He was relief to have heard her say she would be at work 30 minutes before the restaurant opened for lunch.

"No, you don't have to come early if you're not feeling too well, honey. I will come to find you and bring you some medication to take, if you don't mind," Wilmot has said to her delight.

"You don't have to patronized or feel sorry for me. I am a big girl," she retorted from her end of the phone. That day after telling her how lucky he was to have her as an employee, she felt better and went to work 45 minutes early.

She refocused on the thong she was holding between her thumb and index finger. "What the heck," she said. "If he wants me to wear a thong, I'll wear a thong. And he'll be the only person who knows." It was a little exciting, she thought, for him to know she was hardly wearing any underwear underneath her ankle-length dress.

She slipped off her white cotton seamless panties and pulled the small slip of material up around her hips. It felt as if there was something firm tucked up around her vagina lips, and she shrugged, figuring all thongs came with plastic in the crotch, for extra support, perhaps?

She walked back into the bar and handed Wilmot the plastic bag. He opened it, and when he saw her white cotton underpants lying in the bottom of the bag, he smiled. Mardea headed to the back office to warm up and prepare for her shift, and when she sat down on the chair behind the desk she was distinctly aware of a pressure against her clitoris. She stole a glance at Wilmot who had come into the office, and wondered if this is what he had planned for her, but he was on his Samsun Galaxy S6 cell phone and didn't so much look at her.

Mardea smiled a small smile and felt the tips of her breasts tingling behind her white cotton bra. Now that she knew Wilmot wanted her to be the best she can be all night for his customers with a solid reminder of what was to come later pressing against her already swollen flesh, it took a great deal of effort for her to concentrate on interacting with people that were walking into the bar, and wait staff that were taking instruction from her. Mardea had to multitask all night without losing any cash. When she started Wilmot had told her that he doesn't have room for wait staff losing cash. His employees nicknamed him Ben Franklin because of his love of money.

An hour later the restaurant's public address system was playing Junior Freeman and African Soldier's "Da My Area" popular song, which had just been requested by one of the regulars, when she felt something funny happening between her legs. While singing along, she missed some of the lyrics to the song but then quickly recovered with her own creation."My area da to wear funny panties, ae yah, you know. Everybody got there are…"

Then she felt it again, a quick jolt of energy pulsing against her clit. She looked up in confusion, but she didn't lose her place in the song this time. Wilmot was standing behind the bar watching her carefully.

What the heck is wrong with these panties, she wondered

as she played into the last rousing chorus of the song. Suddenly, the buzzing started up again between her thighs, but this time she knew that somehow, some way, Wilmot was manning the controls to her pussy. She moved meticulously among the patrons while staying aware of the jolting and tingling within her panties.

As a huge orgasm overtook her, as her nipples grew rock-hard and incredibly sensitive, as her clitoris grew engorged by the stimulation of the vibrating thong, she sang louder and louder, faster and faster, hoping the booming music would mask the whimpers that escaped her as wave upon wave of pleasure shook her to her very core.

When the orgasm had finished ripping through her and the music finally came to an end, before another one began, she paused for a moment to catch her breath, staring unseeingly at the menu in front of her.

She now knew two things for sure.

Wilmot Emberson was, indeed, the devil her parents and the nuns have been warning here about.

And she, Mardea Moore, had most definitely strayed onto the path of evil....

Ernestine saved her updated document and looked up through the window of her home office just as the sun was rising in the early morning sky. She slumped back against her chair feeling equal parts pride and remorse.

On the one hand, she was writing the best damn sensual romance of her life! On the other hand, with every page she wrote she felt guiltier and guiltier about abusing and betraying Stanley's trust. The problem was simple: She may have promised not to reveal the content of their lessons to anyone, but once the words started to come to her, she couldn't stop herself. Why must she care anyway, knowing how most

Liberians do not keep their words to others. Therefore, she had promised herself not to keep her words to Stanley because it would be at her disadvantage to do such.

One thing was very clear from her story, it was her feelings she was writing about. It was just how she felt when she was with Stanley. Completely, utterly out of control and deadly in love as he unclothed her of her remaining innocence.

The phone rang loudly three times and Ernest sat straight up in bed, the covers falling to her waist. Why Am I still in bed at 4:30 pm, she wondered as she looked at the time on the cell phone.

Then, in a rush, memories of sitting in the restaurant coming violently while Stanley watched closely, flooded into her head.

I need to stop thinking about him all the time, she admonished herself. I'm starting to act like an obsessive fan, and I need to cut it out ASAP!

She threw back the covers, grabbed a short Kente pants from her closet and walked into her kitchen to make herself a cup of instant Liberian made coffee. Normally the maid leaves at 2 pm. While she was sleeping the maid tried waking her up around 12 midday that Tuesday after to remind her of a package one of her cousins had dropped off at the house earlier that day. Opening the brown envelope, she came across several magazines. The one that caught her eyes was the one that had the words EROTIC ROMANCE CONTEST written on it, and she pulled the leaflet out from the stack of envelopes and read:

Do you have an romantic manuscript that would knock our boxers and panties off our asses? If so, you should enter the 3ʳᵈ annual Erotic Romance Writer's Contest. If your manuscript makes it to the finals, your book will be read by a panel of top *editors. A secret celebrity judge will present the winner his or her award, along with a $10,000 grand prize check! Enter now and be one of Liberia's romance writers!*

Ernestine usually threw contest solicitations and other junk mails out, but that was because she knew she didn't have something that could win. She had entered several local and international contests on creative writing, but had never made it to the second round. The wheels started turning in her head.

"*No,*" she said aloud in her empty kitchen. "I can't do it. It's not right."

The wicked little voice inside her said, "*Come on Ernestine. You know you've got a winner on your hands. Stanley will never know.*"

She tried to ignore the voice, but it just got louder, saying, "*This is the entire reason he agreed to be your mentor. Stanley wants you to become a better writer. After all, isn't that the only reason why he's sleeping with you?*"

Ernestine wanted to argue, she wanted to tell her nasty inner-voice that Stanley was sleeping with her because he cared about her, because she was the perfect woman he had been looking for, but in her experience, that was never what was really going on. He was just another Liberian man taking advantage of her in the name of mentoring. They were both getting mutual benefits from the lessons—he was getting sexual fulfilment and she was acquiring knowledge while at it.

Suddenly angry at all of the ways men had used her via false pretenses over the years, she exclaimed, "*I don't owe him a damn thing! He's just my mentor and another man who loves my pussy and not me, we have a strictly professional relationship, and I need to enter this contest to further my career.*"

Using her past hurts as her guide, tapping into her failed love affairs to try and cover up the strong feelings she had for Stanley, she picked up her phone and dialed the number for CP&CG, the local publishing representative of the organization sponsoring the contest.

She needed to schedule lesson four, and she needed to do it fast. After all, she had a book to finish and there was only one way she could get the experience she desperately needed.

And it could only be found in Stanley Kla Nimely's arms and the vast knowledge he possessed.

CHAPTER 12

Being a man of his word, Stanley was up unusually early that Tuesday morning to pay a visit to the Ebola orphans boy's house next door. For the past 7 months, he had procrastinated his plan of going to the children. Maybe though, Ernestine was a major distraction that has prevented him from doing what he had told himself and his mother he would do. But on this day, things were different especially what he saw that night upon his return home from his lesson date with Ernest—the 12 year old boy and his little brother were walking back home in the middle of the night presumably after spending the evening at a market shack next to their neighborhood Total Gas Station at the intersections of Rehab and ELWA Roads selling candy and other snacks products to support themselves. When Stanley stopped his car to offer the boys a ride back home, the older brother grabbed his little brother's hand and ran with him between adjacent houses. He was thinking Stanley who never had a child of his own was one of the ritualists that were killing innocent people in this city and using their body parts for various ritualistic purposes.

Before Stanley could say, *"It is me, Mr. Nimely, your neighbor from the big fence,"* the two children had already disappeared between the houses that lined the narrow road.

That morning, Stanley woke up and waited for the 12 year-old orphan boy to begin is morning routine. When he was done lighting the coal pot to heat some water to bathe his brother, Stanley called out to him from his second floor terrace, *"Good morning, young man,"* the boy didn't answer him, but only gave him a shy wave of his hand.

"Is everything okay? How is your little brother?" Stanley asked a second and third times, but the boy only pointed in the direction of the door to their shack called house, all the while giving Stanley a sheepish look. *"Okay, don't worry, I am coming over there to see you boys right now,"* he ran back inside the house to make his way downstairs to the orphan boys' house.

Out in the yard, he ordered the watchman to open the gate to let him out. *"Is everything okay, boss,"* the watchman asked to his dismay. It was unusual for the gatekeeper to see his boss going out of the fence without his car.

"I am going right back there to see the Ebola orphan boys," he smiled at the old watchman who stood there somehow dumbfounded.

"Do you want me to come with you, boss," he asked.

"No, stay right here. I will be right back," Stanley replied as he closed the gate shut behind him.

Stanley greeted several neighbors that were walking by along the parameter of his fence as he made his way toward the orphans' home. Finally reaching the house, he saw the boy fanning the coal pot in order for the fire to catch and warm the pot containing their bath water. When the boy saw Stanley, he nearly ran into the house in fear of Stanley's unusual visit or perhaps his usual kindness.

"Hey don't be afraid, I am your neighbor, Stanley......Mr. Nimely from upstairs," he introduced himself.

"I know who you are. What are you doing here? What do you want from us," the boy asked to Stanley's dismay. He was surprised at the 12 year old's eloquence.

"I am here to visit you. I want to help you kids," he replied.

"It is too early for a visit. We are getting ready for school. You can come back later on this afternoon when we return home from school," the boy said in a strong and stern voice. His face was devoured of any emotion.

"I know you are. I have watch you kids for almost a year struggling for survival. I want to help you and your little brother," Stanley said with conviction.

"I am sorry, Uncle. We do not need your help. God will help us as he has been doing ever since the Ebola killed our parents," the boy retorted as he dropped the piece of cardboard he had been using to fan the fire under their bath water before walking back into the house to get his little. When he returned out, he was surprised to see Stanley on one knee fanning the fire under their bath water. Neighbors walking by were also surprised to see Stanley working for the orphan boys that early morning.

"Uncle I told you we don't need your help," the 12 year old said. He walked toward Stanley and tried to take the piece of cardboard out of his hand.

"I know just how you feel. I am sorry that I didn't do this early enough, but I still want to help you," Stanley said as the 12 year old and his little brother looked up at him in disbelief and playing deaf ears to his plea.

"Okay....thank you for blowing the fire to catch. I am going to brush his teeth now so we can get ready for school," the 12 year old said as he carried his brother on the side of the house to brush his teeth and wash his face.

Stanley stood by as he admired the 12 year-old's strengths of care and character. He knew as a 12 year-old, he would never have been able to do what this young boy was doing for he and his brother. As he stood there, he could not believe why society has turned its back on these orphans. From his apology to the boy, he also blamed himself for not lending a helping hand to the children. He had money and fame, he lives a life of opulence in the small community and he could easily lift the two children out of poverty, but failed to do so because of his own vanity. One fact the worth noting here is that Stanley was just a private citizen living a normal life, but was being target by the power that be because of his writing.

As he watched the young boy wash his brother's face after brushing is teeth, the 12 year-old also brush his teeth and wash his own face as he had done for his brother. Both boys came toward the pot of water that was warmed enough for the both of them to bathe with. Realizing that he was running out of time, the 12 year-old ran inside the house for an empty bucket to put the water into. When Stanley saw him bring out the bucket to empty out the hot water, he quickly took the bucket out of the boy's hand to empty out the hot water.

"I got this." Stanley told the boy as he emptied the hot water into the bucket.

"Thank you, uncle. God will bless you," the young boy said as he took the bucket of hot water off of the floor and took it into a makeshift bathroom standing several feet away from their house. The boy's words of gratitude welled Stanley's eyes with tears, but Stanley hated people seeing him cry.

"You're welcome. Is there anything you want me to do?" Stanley asked as the boy returned from the bathroom to go into the house. The 12 year-old only shook his head from side-to-side gesturing a *"NO"* to Stanley. When he came out of the house, he had a bar of soap, a body scrubbing sponge, and their regular dingy tower to wipe their skins. The boy then poured some water into the same pot and sat it back on the burning fire to warm it up for their morning tea. When he was done, he turned to his brother for their next routine.

"Let's go and take our baths," the boy told his little brother. Stanley stood there both dumbfounded as well as in disbelief at the 12 year-old level of maturity. There were not that many boys of his age that were so focused and could do what he was

doing for his little brother. After more than ten minutes in the bathroom, the two kids came out and went into their house to dress up for school. By this time Stanley had found an empty bench and was sitting on it.

"Hurry up and come outside Daniel, I have to put on your shoes before we get late for school," the boy called out to his little as he stepped out of the almost empty shack of a house with a piece of bread and sugar and a tea bag in his hands, but he was fully dressed in his blue and white school uniform. Stanley could hear the echo in the house from his location outside. During the Ebola crisis, the properties of the infected were burned to aches as a precautionary measure.

"Do you need help making breakfast, I can help. Do you want me to bring you some food from my place?" Stanley jumped to his feet like he was a servant of the 12 year-old.

"No, thank you Uncle. We have enough to eat. We're really running late for school anyway. The school is about 25 minutes walk from here," the 12 year-old boy replied. He walked over to the boiling pot of water. After dipping the red cup into the water, he dropped the bag of Lipton Tea bag into the steamy cup. He quickly walked toward a broken table by the side of the house and place the cup and the transparent plastic bag with the bread on the top.

"Daniel......, you got to hurry up and come here. Breakfast is ready," he called out to his brother a second time. Minutes later, the five year-old boy came outside wearing a hungry and an angry look on his face. The 12 year-old ran inside and brought out a little chair and a table on which he and his brother usually eat. He put his brother's black shoes on his feet and tie the strings. He meticulously put the table and the chair in place before placing the bread and tea on the mini table. He opened the plastic bag and pulled out the bread, opened it, and began to spread a plastic sac of butter he had pulled out of his pocket. When all was done and ready, he cut off a piece of the bread and gave the bigger piece to his brother as his share.

Wasting no time, the five year-old begun to gobble the bread like an hungry vulture. Kneeling on one foot, the big brother pretended to be eating his share. He would take a fake bite off the bread and then hide the piece behind his back. When the five year-old was done eating his share, the 12 year-old made his piece to magically appear from behind his back. He then gave the piece to his brother to eat, knowing he was not full by his share. The 12 year old boy always does that.

"Why do you do this? Don't you know you have to eat something in order to have something in your stomach so you can focus in class?" Stanley asked in a shaky voice. His eyes were now welling with tears from the sadness he had seen so many times.

"Do what, uncle? To let my brother eat my share of the piece of bread? It is just a piece of bread, uncle," the boy asked with a question of his own. He seemed shocked by Stanley's question.

"Yes....yes, that! I know you love him, but you need food too. What is your name by the way?" Stanley was now emotional.

"My name is Shadrach, uncle. You see, Daniel needs that bread more than I do. He is the only family member I have in this world. He's not only my brother, he's my best friend and my mother's sickly and favorite child, and my calm in the storm, as our late father used to say. In fact, I rather see him eat and live to see his twelfth birthday, just like me. I always let him have it rather than eat a piece of bread that is not enough for the two of us. I love him very much, uncle. If you could see inside my heart, you will see how dearly I love my brother Daniel, the only family God has given to me," the boy replied. He forced a sour smile at Stanley for the first time.

Trying to smile back at the boy, but instead, Stanley shook it off and replaced it with a soul searching look because this was not something he was expecting to hear from an innocent 12 year-old. Stanley bend over to try to meet the boy's eyes. *"I want to help you and your little brother. Please let me help you kid,"* he said with watery eyes.

"Let us come back from school today, and then, we will talk about it. But you have to first tell our aunty and see what she says," the boy replied as he carried the utensils and coal pot back inside their little shack. When he came out, he had his bookbag along with his brother's bookbag in his hands. After locking the front door, he motioned his brother over to come for his bag.

Stanley wanted to say something, but didn't know how to begin in the first place. He wanted to tell the boy how sincere he was about helping him and his five-year-old little brother.

"If you let me help you boys, things will be different from now on. You will eat what I will eat. You boys will be the children that I have never had. I will do my best to be a good father to you boys," Stanley said as tear streamed down his cheeks. Upon seeing Stanley's tears, the five-year-old began to cry as well.

"Don't cry Daniel. You know what mama said about men crying, right. Big boys don't cry. They cry within and don't let others see their tears," Shadrach comforted his little brother. He turned to Stanley whose eyes were red like fire.

"Please let us go to school now. When we come back, I will take you to our aunty who lives near the market. She looks after us, but she's also afraid to come in our house because of the virus," the boy promised Stanley who was now wiping away his tears.

Following his interaction with the children that lasted for almost an hour fifteen minutes, Stanley returned to his house and begun to hatch out plans on how to keep his promise to the orphan boys and to his mother. Later that morning he called his mother and told her about his visit to the orphan boys home. Mrs. Namely was very glad that Stanley who never had a child of his own was thinking on adopting the two children. When Stanley hung up the line with his mother, he got an unexpected call from Ernestine. Their short conversation got him excited as well. At least, he had something to laugh about and look forward to after crying his heart out that early morning.

Stanley was pleased that Ernestine had called him to arrange lesson four so quickly. *Maybe she likes me a little bit after all,* he thought to himself. He thought it was the act of God that Ernestine had called after he had taken advantage of her more than once. He did not to appear like the typical opportunistic Liberian men who prey on women's weakness or use their social statuses to exploit women and men.

The only problem was, he hadn't quite figured out an appropriate site for their lesson on sex in new locations because the boys situation was weighing heavily on his mind.. Dodging her questions on the phone, he told her he'd pick her up at noon on Thursday and surprise her with their destination.

That late Tuesday morning, he ran through the options again in his head. He thought of his favorite adult sex club, 'Adam and Eve's Playground' off the Monrovia and Cape Mont County Highway was too predictable, and there was no way in hell he'd let any man gets his hands on Ernestine. At Adam and Eve's Playground, everybody belongs to anybody. This secret facility was really lovers' paradise or perhaps, sin's paradise. The proprietor, Jordan Porompyae, a personal friend of Stanley, believes in free love and sexual liberation as a way to satisfy a person's insatiable sexual appetite. At the main entrance of the secrete cabin, he had an engraving up on the wall that *reads, "The first act of free love, is to believe in free love as a means of total sexual revolution of the body, mind and soul."* There were also several sex clubs overtly operating within the capital, suburbs and in other parts of the country. In fact, there were dozens of strip and sex clubs on the Monrovia and Robertsfield Highway, as well as the Monrovia and Bomi Highway. Stanley thought that doing it in his car, parked outside over a beautiful panorama like Red Hill in Paynesville overlooking the city of Monrovia, was too much like being in high school. Having a quickie in a dark alley on a busy street in Monrovia was straight out of his latest novel, so that was out of the question. He needed to think of a place and he needed to do it quick.

With only fifteen minutes to go until he was supposed to be at Ernestine's house, he still hadn't come up with a good location for their lesson. *"Where is the one place she'd never think about having sex?"* he asked himself in frustrated tones.

Then the answer came to him in a flash, so he smiled, grabbed his keys, and hopped in his red BMW M4 convertible, turning up David Mell's *"I Will Carry Your Load"* song so loud that he could feel the bass drum vibrating in his seat as eyes of passerby at the Du Port Road Market rubbed against him and his car. Passing by the Du Port Road Cemetery, he made ha hard right on the road that bypasses the main Paynesville Red Light Highway leading to the Paynesville Red Light Market. Thank God, the government had paved most of the side streets and installed traffic lights on most of the streets within the capital since the Mount Coffee Hydro . At the Benson Hospital section of the road, Stanley made a left turn toward the main highway. Once he drove pass the Red Light business district on to the newly constructed Freeport and Red Light Highway, Stanley began to pump more gas in the 6 cylinder twin turbo engine of the M4. He was running between 70 to 95 Mph as he weaved in and out of traffic. Lucky for him, there was not traffic at this hour of the day—people were still at work shoving papers in government's offices, serving customers at retail outlets, and crunching numbers in hot accountant firms in the city and in other places around the hot country.

Meanwhile, on the newly constructed Somali Drive

Gardnersville Road was much larger and less congested driving toward the Freeport of Monrovia. Know time was against him, he was driving between 70 and 80 mph. At the Freeport, he made a hard right turn onto the United Nations Drive toward Brewerville. Lucky him, there were no traffic at the Duala Market and Caldwell's intersections. Thank God for the new traffic light and the newly constructed bridge over the Stockton Creek leading into the Township of Caldwell.

In no time, he reached Ernestine's house and realized how beautifully she was dressed. Wasting no time, she jumped in the front seat of the convertible and with one roar of the engine of the German-made sports car, they were on their way to start lesson four. In no time he drove his way out of the traffic-congested Duala Market corridor toward the Freeport of Monrovia. At the Freeport of Monrovia, he made a quick left turn on Somali Drive, as he headed toward the famous Paynesville Red Light where was about 25 minutes earlier. In less than ten minutes, he was at the Paynesville Red Light market. Once the traffic light changed to green, he made a quick left turn toward the Monrovia and Kakata Highway. Once he was out to the usual traffic congestion, he looked at her and said, *"We're going to the Urey's farm zoo in Careysburg."*

"Wulki Farm zoo? Are you really taking me to Wulki Farm in Careysburg? WOW!" Ernest had a curious look on her face. She knew that Stanley was very strategic. He had a reason for every lesson plan.

Ernestine turned to him with a look of utter surprise. This was the last place she would have thought about going to for lesson four. After driving for about twenty minutes, they reach their destination.

Stanley pulled into a vacant parking spot as he stepped out of his BMW M4 that always gets attention in the impoverished city. She followed him into the park. *"Yup,"* he said, nodding happily. *"The zoo."*

She shook her head and chuckled. *"You have got to be kidding me Stanley. I'd like to know one thing that's sexy about the zoo."*

He pulled her close and said, *"You,"* before kissing her hard on her lips. Grabbing her hand, he said, *"Let's go and look at the chimps and the crocodiles on the other side of the zoo."*

Ernestine raised an eyebrow, but followed after him. *"You're the teacher, so I guess you know best,"* she said, but he could tell by the sound of her voice that she thought he was completely coo, coo. He gently held her left hand as they walked past other visitors mainly made of school children and fewer adults.

The zoo's chimps habitat and crocodiles pounds were completely deserted at noon on this Thursday and as they walked hand-in-hand, Stanley thought again how much he loved being with Ernestine. She was funny, witty, smart, and incredibly passionate about her newly found career. For a moment, he almost wished they were done with their lessons so that he could finally tell her how he felt about her, without feeling like a total jerk for taking advantage of their teacher and student relationship.

Then he thought about what he had planned for the day and grinned. No, he certainly didn't want to give up any of the time he'd be spending exploring Ernestine's body. And he sure as hell wouldn't trade the satisfaction he'd already received from showing her how to let herself go, how to explode with every fiber of her body and soul.

They walked past the crocodile pounds and ponies fence, stopping to admire the brawny beasts, finally arriving at the donkeys' depot. One of the ponies was being ridden by a young girl from the J.J. Roberts United Methodist School.

Since this was the only farm housing different types of animals, it had become the favorite place for class trips for the various schools in and around Monrovia.

Stanley wanted to have Ernestine to take a horse ride so she can get a firsthand experience of what it's like to get on the back of one of the powerful beasts in the world. He wanted her to feel that up and down motion on her pussy lips and deep inside her female organ.

"Wait here for a second," Stanley said as he went up to one of the caretakers of the zoo and said a few words to him while covertly slipping him a twenty dollar bill. As it was in Liberia, everybody paid some type of bride or took a bride one way or another. If one wants to get ahead of a line in public places, all that person need to do is to slip a few American Green Back into the hands of the person in charge. The country was a hotbed for everything criminal.

Mission accomplished, Stanley was grinning ear to ear when he waved Ernestine through the gate that held the ponies and horses into captivity.

She started to walk toward one of the smaller, unoccupied ponies that looked like a cross between a horse and a donkey, but he redirected her to a bigger and a full grown horse. From the animals' physical appearances, it seemed like they were all underfed and needed serious medical attention. No matter the physical conditions of these beasts, the farm's management still used them as local cash machines with little regard for their health and dignity.

"We're going to ride on the back of this bigger one. You will sit on the upper back while I'll sit behind you on the lower back," he said, and he thought he saw a tiny hint of a smile appearing on the corner of her luscious lips as she mounted up on the back of the animal. When she turned her back to cross her left leg over the horse, her short skirt flipped up and revealed

to him her big, fat round ass, and smooth pussy lips peeking between her slightly parted thighs from the back.

His dick went instantly hard in his pants—straight from 0 to 60 miles of erection per second. His innocent student hadn't worn any panties at all! Like many women living in Europe and the United States that do not wear any panties during the summer heat, many women in Liberia had adopted the habit of not wearing panties during the heated Dry Season. Many of them had the notion that the less garment a female wore during the hot Dry Season, the better their pussies will breathe and remain fresh for love making.

He stood down from behind the horse, holding onto the harness and cleared his throat, finally managing a husky voice he said, *"Did you forget to put something on this morning when you were getting dressed?"*

Ernestine blushed and said, *"I might have forgotten a couple of things, actually."*

Suddenly he noticed she wasn't wearing a bra either. He could discern the faint outline of the areolas of her firmed breast beneath her light pink tank top. As he stared at her chest in continued amazement, her nipples grew hard and pronounced, and it was all he could do not to rip the thin fabric off her body and suck at her nipples like a hungry newborn baby who came into the this unforgiving world screaming for food.

He rearranged his pants to accommodate his throbbing bulge and climbed up and sat behind her on the back of the beast. Once he was comfortably seated behind her, he grabbed onto her tightly that his knuckles got purple. He gave a thumb's up to the caretaker and the horse began to move slowly within the perimeter of the fence.

"You seem a little nervous today," he said as he rubbed his thumb in a circle on his belly and her thigh.

She nodded, but didn't quite turn around to meet his eyes. Finally she looked up at another rider approaching them and said, *"You're right. I am nervous today."* Then she laughed and said, *"Which is crazy! You'd think I'd be perfectly calm around you after the three lessons we've had so far, wouldn't you?"*

Stanley nodded absentmindedly as he pushed his body closer to her as if he was trying to get a better posture of the horse. *"I'm a little nervous too,"* he murmured as he slowly slid his hands down her skirt. He looked around to see if anyone was looking at the goings on. Realizing no one was watching them under the hot sun, he further buried his hand deeper down into her skirt.

"I need some hand-room down here," he said softly and as she sucked her flat stomach in to give room to his invading hand. He slid his right hand down the mound of her pussy, positioning his middle finger right over her already swollen clitoris. Her head fell back and she moaned softly. He fondle her clit a few time, even though he wanted nothing more than to bury his face between her legs, hoping the waiting would intensify her arousal.

Even though his hand was on her clit, she was already so wet her juices were soaking his fingers. Gently he slipped his pinkies into her dripping honeycomb and her moans grew louder. Her hands pulled the rope causing the horse to pick up speed into the wrong direction. He wanted to take her to his car so he could pull his face down to her impatient clitoris.

"Hold on to that rope, Honey," he demanded. He saw her warring with herself, but then she reached out and grabbed the rope that had almost fallen from her grips. He told her to direct the horse further up in the field where no visitor was.

"Good girl," he whispered as he bit the back of her neck and dug his long fat fingers deeper into her wet slit. He thought about a scene he had created in his new book, *"The Black Mamba"* that he was now fine-tuning. It was a scene

in which Tony and Elizabeth were caught by a local church group having sex in the Paynesville Town Hall Park. Stanley laid several kisses behind Ernestine's neck, and then worked his right hand up to her breast and gently cupped it before squeezing her already rock-hard nipple between his fingers. And it felt damn good to both of them!

Her nipples jutted out at his hand which was now safely concealed under her blouse and he couldn't resist their beckoning. Slowly, he inserted his middle and index fingers deep inside her wet and ready pussy. The sensation send a chill up her spine and then to her brain. He quickly looked around the vicinity to see if anyone was watching from behind bushes or the security booth, realizing there was no one, made him feel like he was the luckiest man on Earth. He therefore continued with what he was doing—orally stimulating Ernestine in the strangest place anyone would imagine.

"Stanley, I don't think we should—" she began to say, and he cut off her protest with a hot kiss to her neck and her ear. He wanted to tongue kiss her, but he did not want to attract any attention to them. He slowly moved his wet fingers to her flat stomach and caressed it a few time.

"—I'm in charge of this lesson," he said sternly when he finally pulled away from her slightly bruised neck.

She said, *"I know you are, but....,"* and he kissed her neck again, gently this time just on the corners of her right earlobe.

"Won't you trust me, sweetheart?" he asked her, his tone now gently cajoling.

She smiled tremulously and he returned his attention to her succulent tits under her shirt, finally bared in all their God's given glory. He leaned his full weight against her back as he pulled his fingers out of her wet pussy. The swelling in his pants was ready to explode if he didn't do something about it. *"Let us go back to the gate where the caretaker is waiting for our return, Honey,"* he softly whispered in her.

Not wasting any more time Ernestine pulled the rope to the left, directing the horse toward the starting line. At the caretaker, there were others in line awaiting their return for an afternoon horse ride. Stanley climbed down and then helped her get off the animal. Their evidence was all over the saddle—her hot pussy juices were smeared on the material. Stanley quickly slid his hand over the saddle and cleaned her come and vagina fluid before anyone took notice. He then quickly put the hand he had cleaned the surface with into his pocket.

Stanley led Ernestine back to the parking lot, toward his car. Fifty feet to his car, Stanley was stopped by one of his fans who wanted an autograph from the sex icon. He signed the lady's paper and they were both on their way out of the farm.

He drove toward the direction of Kakata, in Margibi County. At the police checkpoint, in an area known as Fifteen Gate, he made a hard right turn toward the Firestone Natural Rubber Company plantation. Five minutes into their drive, he saw an abandoned unpaved road where he made a quick left and parked his BMW M4 convertible under the thick grove. Once they were out of public view, he opened the trunk of his vehicle and pulled out a mat and a beach towel and spread then out on the hard ground.

He removed his shirt and took a deep penetrating look at Ernestine Johnson who was also staring at him. *"Come over here, you beautiful creature. We're going to finish lesson four right here,"* he said kneeling on the towel like an American Football champion who has won a trophy in the National Football League, Super Bowl final.

She slowly walked toward him as her tits moved from side-to-side under her shirt. He slowly reached out and grabbed her, pulled her to him and softly kissed her belly button. Stanley then rubbed his face across her succulent breast, letting her nipples slide in and out of his mouth, driving his tongue across them, forcing whimpers from Ernestine with every stroke.

Finally looking up from her breasts, he noticed that the area had lots of butterflies and plenty of shades as well as trees to hide them from any would be traveler. As he slowly pulled his hands out from beneath her ass and reached for the hem of her skirt to lift it up, she whimpered, *"Yes, Stanley. Please!"* And opened her legs wide so that he would have easy access to her swollen and wet pussy. He ran the tip of his thumb up and down her moist folds, steering clear of her most sensitive spot. She tried to maneuver her hips so that he'd be forced to touch her clit, but he teased and circled, all the while avoiding the one place that was dying for his touch.

He slid one finger into her and took one of her huge tits into his mouth. He sucked her nipple in the same rhythm as he moved his long finger in and out of her.

Ernestine's head thrashed back and forth and she let go of her own head to wrap her hands around the back of his head, holding him tightly to her breasts. He could feel the tension in her body, felt the muscles beginning to convulse around his finger, and knew she was about to explode.

Hastily he removed his finger and, with his lips still sucking gently on one of her breasts, Stanley moved to a sitting position on the towel spread out on the hard earth, bringing Ernestine's body with him, so that she was straddling his hips, her knees spread out apart in a ninety degrees angle.

Her slender fingers moved to unbutton and unzip his khaki slacks, until the full length of his hard dick sprang free. *"Wow! Your black mamba is already up and ready for action,"* she said comically as if Stanley had given her a nickname for his manhood. More often in every relationship between a male and female, it is the lady who often names the penis of her lover, and Stanley knew this for a fact. Hearing her call his dick that name of one of the character from his book, he felt, obliged to live up to the legend of his hero from his imagination.

She wrapped her hand around the hot length of him, positioning herself above him so that the head of his penis was just at the entrance of her incredibly wet lips.

And then, with a sound of deep satisfaction, Ernestine lowered herself down onto his enormous cock, taking in each and every inch of his monster. Her pussy spread out and received his every length and girth with a joy any sexually aroused female can imagine.

Stanley was overwhelmed by the sensation of her tight, wet pussy enveloping him. He looked up from her breasts, and pulled her head down to capture her mouth in a hot, tongue-thrusting kiss.

Ernestine was in charge of their lovemaking as she rode up and down on Stanley's dick, milking it with her tight, throbbing muscles. A flash of satisfactory smile went across his face.

"I can't hold on anymore," he gritted out through clenched teeth and as he began to come, she began to scream, her muscles convulsing around his cock. He drained every last drop of his sperm deep within the woman he had fallen in love with. He covered her scream with his mouth and as they rode toward ecstasy together, their lips and tongues mated in a frenzy that matched the mating of their bodies.

As their convulsions came to an end, they kissed, their caresses growing tender and softer. Stanley finally fell to the ground on the towel while Ernestine came crashing after, just like the story of Jack and Jill.

"Honey, I," Stanley began to say, but right as he was about to declare his feelings for her, regardless of their mentoring, a rubber truck drove by their hideout sending the butterflies flying in different directions.

Quickly, Ernestine slid off his lap, pulled her tank top back up over her breasts, and laid next to him on the towel. She kissed him tenderly as he caressed her some more. After she did so she looked at him with undisguised amusement and said, *"You might want to zip your pants back up before something jumps from the bush and bites it."* He locked eyes with her, wondering if what had just transpired was really true. He could not tell if he was actually falling in love with her by the day or if he was falling in love with her sex. She reminded him of his ex-wife—when they met the sex was good until something went wrong along the road, until her church got involved into their marriage.

He surfaced from his daze and made his fumbling fingers obey her commands to zip his pants. He wanted another round of hot sweltering sex, but he did not want to appear greedy, he did not want her thinking that sex was all he had on his mind. He forced a smile and then French kissed her. He knew if he went slowly, there might just be more opportunities at the end of his mentoring since he'd seen a promise in her eyes.

Coincidentally, both of their cell phones rang as if someone had synchronized the call to distract them from whatever they were doing that afternoon. *"Did you enjoy the lesson,"* Stanley said as he walked toward the car to get his phone. Ernestine also got up and ran to get her phone from her purse.

After her conversation with the caller, Ernestine looked at Stanley with a twinkle in her eyes and said, with a fairly straight face, *"Oh yes. More than you can ever imagine. In fact, it's safe to say, I'll never look at the Wulki Farm and Firestone Rubber Plantation the same way again."*

And with that, she headed back to the BMW M4 convertible and threw herself into the front passenger seat. Stanley picked up the towel and threw it in the trunk of the car and jump into the driver seat.

With a roar of the 6 cylinders engine, they headed back toward Monrovia a city that is in dire need of a true lover what will give her the needed attention she so deserves. The two lovebirds sat in silence for the rest of the ride home, perhaps wondering over what had just happened.

CHAPTER 13

When Stanley dropped Ernestine off at her Parker Corner home in Brewerville, she was torn between inviting him in and running to her computer to write down the next scene in her book. Before she could ask him inside for a drink, he looked at his watch and said, *"I've got to get going. Thanks for a great afternoon,"* and sped off, leaving her standing in front of her nine-foot fence feeling more than a little bereft. Like an angry child whom toy had been taken away from her by a disciplinarian father for a bad behavior, she pushed the gate open and quickly walked in without returning a *hello* from a smiling neighbor who lives across the street a hundred feet away from her fence. In fact, the house had previously belonged to Ernestine's parents, but she had inherited the beautiful house that was built on a five acres land from her grandparents back the 1980s.

Being the only child from both loving parents, she was spoiled—rotten, she was given everything any only child could think of. Disappointingly to her highly successful parents, she had majored in English and Literature at the University of Liberia instead of going into medicine like her father. Ernest Johnson, her father, was a renowned medical doctor in the country. As for Christina Clarke-Johnson, or C.J. as she was commonly called by her closed friends, was a successful White Collar Criminal Defense lawyer who had defended more than two thousand clients accused of corruption and economic sabotage by the Government of Liberia and financial institutions as well as corporations. But again, as good parents, they accepted their daughter's career choice without imposing on her. Ever since she graduated from college, Ernestine never found a job in her field. Instead, she worked full time as a teacher at a local school in Sinkor while she wrote young adults novels in her spare time. On the creative writing end, Ernestine had successfully written and published more than five book through a local publishing house, Wahala Publishing located in Central Monrovia. None of her books made her any profit besides giving her the fame she deserved.

The truth was, no matter how much she tried to pretend she didn't have feelings for Stanley, no matter how much she wavered back and forth about the emotional extent of their relationship, she now knew with 100% certainty that she was in love with him. The man had her to the neck and she could not lie about it. She wanted him as a lover, she wanted him for keep, she wanted his big long dick to pleasure her some more and always. But for now, she was disappointingly aware that she did not own him—there was no strings attach. In fact, she was aware of the man's history—he was a heartbreaker who was afraid of commitment. Like herself who hates being controlled by another human being, she knew the man she was dealing with believed in free will such that he did not want to be controlled by another person, let alone, a woman that is easily influenced by him or others.

After their incredible sex play on top of the horse at the zoo on Wulki Farm in Careysburg and their big orgasms among the rubber trees at the Firestone Natural Rubber Plantation Company, they had spent the rest of the day eating barbeque fish and baby back ribs as well as drink cold beer at RL Johnson Resort in ELWA. The pair also took a long stroll along the beach that late afternoon—it was like two lovers that were fallen in love all over again. At least that's what Ernestine thought it seemed like. With every minute that passed in Stanley's company, Ernestine fell harder and harder for him.

He was funny, gorgeous, brilliant, and the most sexually intoxicating man she had ever encountered on the African Continent. Ernestine was sure she would never meet anyone again who would make her feel so incredibly good, so wonderfully happy. Stanley Nimely was one of those last God's send Liberian men that any woman would instantly fall for, would love to take home to her parents and say, *"Mommy and daddy, this is the man I am going to marry. This is the man I want to spend the rest of my life with."*

All of that only served to increase her guilt over her deception. Every time she wrote another scene with Mardea and Wilmot, she was elated by how far she'd come as a writer. But at the same time, another part of her, the part that is controlled by the hands of God, was horrified by her dishonesty.

To a moan, she shook her head in frustration knowing that every scene in her book mimicked her encounters with Stanley. No matter how badly she tried to be original and organic she knew deep down in her heart that she was directly copying from Stanley's playbook.

She went inside her house, sat down in front of her computer and booted it up, holding her head in her hands, trying to figure out some sort of compromise she could live with. Her thoughts were running a million miles per second.

What if I tell him about the story after we've cemented a strong relationship with each other outside of his mentoring? What if I refuse to have sex with him? What if he learns of my dishonesty and realizes that I am only coming along for the ride as a means to a selfish end? She thought widely without knowing what to do.

If he wanted to have a real relationship with her, then by the time she told him about the story she had written, he'd just laugh and kiss her, telling her she was silly for even worrying about it in the first place. Unlike some Liberian men that hate being competed with by the spouses, Stanley might be quite the opposite. Being as exposed as he is, and being from a working class family he would definite prefer a highly successful work that would complement his success. That is, if Ernestine is that woman he will win his heart and his love.

She wasn't going to keep it a secret from him forever. Just until she entered the contest and got some feedback on her writing. Just until she and Stanley communicated with each other about their feelings. Just until he commits to satisfying her innermost desire, especially the lust she felt deep within her soul for him.

Feeling slightly better about what she was doing, she opened up her computer, navigated to her saved document and began to type the words she had been writing in her head all afternoon and leading up to the evening.

……*"Have you ever been on a real motorbike? I am not talking about the Pam, Pam or the Kee Kee that you see throwing people down and injuring commuters around here."*

Mardea looked up from the bar at Wilmot who was standing by the front door of the bar. "Are you kidding me? I've never even been in a poor-man's convertible, neither have I gotten in a poor-man's Limo before," she replied, referring to the transport bikes referred to in the country by locals as Pam Pam.

"We're gonna open a little late today," he said, gesturing for her to come to him. "Let's go."

Wilmot held the door open for Mardea and tapped his booted foot impatiently while she serenely closed the lid on the ice cooler, stood up and walked toward him.

He led her around the back of the restaurant to his Harley Davidson he had brought from the United States and handed her a helmet. She swallowed nervously and didn't put the helmet on.

"I'm not so sure about this," she said, but his was already on and had revved up the engine. "You'll be just fine," he said, "just keep your arms wrapped tightly around me."

Mardea felt like she had no choice, but to do as he asked. It was always that way with Wilmot, she mused. Him telling and her doing, just like the good girl she once were. To Mardea, it felt like being on an Armed Forces of Liberia, AFL boot camp where all the recruits were forced to say "Yes, sir to their drill sergeants or superior officers."

"One day the tables are going to turn, Wilmot. Knowing that the perfect girl I once was is no more, and is gone forever, I will start becoming that bad girl that you want me to be. One day you will know, it is just a matter of time," she said, but he couldn't hear her over the rumbling of his bike's engine.

She slipped onto the seat behind him and wiggled her hips tightly up against his muscled rear end and thighs. She ran her hands up and down his chiseled abs through his t-shirt and reveled in his extraordinary masculinity.

And then they were off, flying down Broad Street of toward the Johnson Street Bridge. The wind whipped at her hair and with her body wrapped around Wilmot's, she felt perfectly in tune with the world around her. Every person who walked by them seemed to be smiling. The sky was bluer with passing clouds. The sun was hotter in the African sky than it has been in previous days, but sitting behind the man who taught her everything made the weather to feel cool and just right for the little Catholic school girl.

Of course, her pussy was completely soaked. It was such a frequent occurrence, she had stopped wearing panties altogether.

As it was, whenever she was with Wilmot he was always ripping them off her ass in his haste to thrust his huge dick into her or to press his lips to the sensitive nub between her legs.

She had only worked for him for a month a two weeks, but already she knew she wouldn't have it any other way. Wilmot was a drug she never wanted to get off from, no matter how wrong anyone thought he might be for her, no matter how dictatorial he might have been seen by others, she was hooked on him. No one could help her get out of what she was now in, not even her parents nor the nuns that took years to mode and steer her in the path of righteousness. Wilmot was one of those bad boys parents often warned their children especially girls to stay away from.

Mardea had gone home once to visit her parents at their Paynesville home, and she couldn't believe how hard it was for her to pull her weaved-in hair back and sit quietly at dinner. All night while she was with her parents she wondered what Wilmot was doing, wondered what he would have done to her at the end of the evening after he locked the door to his bar and restaurant. For her, home was no longer a place to be because there were no more fun for her at the place that once brought her solace. As it now appeared, she was getting all the funs and loving touch from 'Wilmot The Bad Boy Emberson', the man who opened her eyes to the eighth wonders of the human's world.

After catching her in a daydream more than once, her mother pulled her aside in the kitchen to ask if anything was wrong from the look on her face. Mardea knew she had to get back to the city right away, back to the man whose caresses had become as important to her as breathing.

Eventually, after riding for more than fifteen minutes through Bushrod Island, the old Bong Mine's Bridge, crowded Duala, and over the Saint Paul River's Bridge, the small road dead-ended into the old Hotel Africa back parking lot in Virginia. Wilmot slowed down the bike and drove into the back of an abandoned villa home that once beautified the hotel's facility. Mardea shivered with anticipation, hoping Wilmot was going to start touching, licking, and biting her soon.

I am a slut, she thought. Totally a big Wata Police Catholic School slut who loves to get fucked everywhere and at any available time. But by now, after so many nights of falling to pieces in Wilmot's arms, she was too far gone to care about something that would have bothered her deeply in her past life. For now the old things have passed away as her life had become anew—not caring about what the hell the world had to say about her. As her father usually says, "No matter what Jesus Christ did, people still talked bad things about him."

He pulled off his helmet and his one-inch black with speckles of gray hair gets cooled by the wind from the ocean's current. She took off her helmet and shook out her long weaved-in burgundy and black Brazilian hair, trying to finger-comb the knots out to no avail as the wind lashed out against it. Still balanced on the bike seat she leaned her head back and closed her eyes, letting the gentle breeze wash over her and blow through her hair.

Wilmot stood up and got off his bike, turning around to face her as he straddled the seat once again.

"Oh!" she exclaimed nervously when she opened up her eyes. His face was directly in front of hers, his eyes hot with needs.

He bent his head down and captured her lips in a sweet kiss. Reaching under her skirt, he ran his hands slowly up her calves, past her knees, up to her thighs.

Working his hands up her thighs, he finally reached her hips, he stopped kissing her and gave her a searing look. "You're not wearing any panties, sweetheart," he said questioningly.

She gave him a half-smile, saying, "I was wondering when you'd notice it, my darling."

He growled and kissed her again, hungrily, slipping his large callused hands beneath her ass, lifting her off the seat and onto him. She felt the thick bulge in his pants and reached for the button of his jeans.

He chuckled softly. "We're in public, you know we are," he said.

Unable, unwilling to stop herself, Mardea worked at his fly. "Isn't that the point we're out here, Mr. Wilmot Emberson?" she said syllabically, calling him by his full name for the first time.

By then she had his pants undone and as his dick sprang free into her hands, she was pleased to find that he wasn't wearing anything underneath his jeans. No brief, no boxer, not even a piece of fabric made in the Republic Guinea, their next-door neighbor.

As she stroked the dark skin on the head of his powerful rod of a dick, he groaned, saying, "What did you do with my little nun?"

"Wow! Your prick is so big today. Did you do something to it? It is already hard and ready for action, huh. Today is my first time seeing it under the light of day," she moaned passionately.

Mardea wriggled onto Wilmot's lap and gasped as his hot flesh probed her drenching wet pussy lips, stretching her open to fit all of his meat inside. Finally, after she had taken in all ten inches of him, after he was sheathed to the hilt within her, she looked him in the eye.

"I love you Mr. Emberson. I really do love you," she said, and then instinctively rode up and down on his manhood, faster and faster as her orgasm swelled up to overwhelm her.

Wilmot kept the bike steady while she took him in and then slid him out until just the tip of his dick was still within her. He pulled her down on him again, so deeply she could feel his balls press against her ass cheeks. At the feel of him swelling impossibly bigger within her, she went over the edge, crying out his name as her inner muscles clenched and milked his dick hard.

He buried his head in her long hair and roared, "Mardea! Oh, Mardea...Shhhiiitttt!" as he shot his sperm inside of her, crashing his hips into hers as hard and deep as he could. For the past two weeks, Wilmot has stopped using condoms on Mardea. He knew he was first to enter her untouched vagina and he was sure she was not sleeping around with another man like some of the young women in the city. Even if he thought she did, it was not something Mardea was thinking about doing. As far as she was concern, no other man could make her feel the way that Wilmot makes her feel. Mardea knew she was not going anywhere, and Wilmot was not as well. He loves her youthfulness and her innocence of sex and foreplay turned him on whenever he was alone. She was the perfect girl any big shot would love to have and to keep.

They held tight to each other until their heartbeats returned to normal, and then he slid her off him and zipped up his jeans pants. Without a word, he handed Mardea her helmet, put his back on, and started the engine.

Mardea blinked back tears as she position herself behind him. When they were joined together she realized she could no longer deny how much she loved Wilmot and was unable to hold back the words.

"I love you, Wilmot."

But now, they were heading back to the restaurant and he hadn't said anything. Not, "I love you too," or any kind of comment at all in response to her open and honest statement of her feelings for him. With a sinking feeling low in her belly, she wondered if she had done the wrong thing.

Maybe, she thought with sudden sorrow, loving the devil is nothing more than a one-way trip to hell. The path her parents and the nuns had always warned her to stay off......

Ernestine finished writing her new scene and as she reread it, she had a spark of insight about the piece of the puzzle between her and Stanley that she had been missing all along.

It was one thing for her to learn to enjoy taking pleasure in Stanley's arms—lots and lots of pleasure!—but it was another thing entirely for her to lead the way.

Her path was suddenly crystal clear and she wanted to jump for joy. Lesson five was going to be different than the previous four lessons, for one big reason.

She was going to be the teacher this time, and at that, she was not going to hold back. She had decided to make the best use of this once in a life time opportunity. Like a greedy and corrupt Liberian cabinet minister, she was going to amass the most wealth of experience than she had with the previous four lessons.

The following morning, feeling very good about her ability to get her story fluidly on paper, the decided to fast track the next lesson. She was not sure if Stanley would make time for her since lesson four was just a day old. Having self doubts, she finally pick up he cell and dialed Stanley's number.

"Hi, my darling mentor," she said. Her words send a love chill down Stanley's spine. He was so confused by his new title "darling" that he could not articulate him with a simple "Hello".

Chocking on his word he said, "Hi.....hello....hello how are you." He begun to perspire in his palms again. A classic sign of nervousness. After listening to Ernestine for five or maybe ten minutes about how she really appreciate his help and the difference his guidance has made in her writing. When he finally hung up the phone, he could not remember what he and Ernestine have discussed. All he remember was agreeing to meet with here at his house for lesson five. Since this lesson was out of his control, he did not know what his student had in store for him—*she better be good*, he thought.

The following day, Ernestine was up early in the morning; she proofread her story, and did her routine Yoga exercise. Based on agreement made from the previous day, she grabbed her car keys, and locked the front door behind her. The gate man swung the front gate open and she drove toward town. If everything went according to plan, she wouldn't be coming home tonight.

At his Rehab Road residence, Stanley sat in his living room and stared blankly at the big screen 60 inch high definition LED TV. *"I'm such an idiot,"* he told himself, taking a large swig from the beer he'd pulled out from the six-pack inside his refrigerator. Stanley didn't like the taste of the locally brewed beer; rather, he preferred imported beer, especially Heinekens.

"She was going to ask me to come inside, probably to her bedroom, and I acted like some stupid sixteen-year-old boy! Maybe I will have a chance with her tonight" He gave his head a quick slap with both hands. *"Fuck, fuck, fuuuuuuck,"* he said for a second and third times.

He shook his head at his stupidity. He couldn't believe how nervous he gets around Ernestine whenever it comes time to wrap up their lessons. Stanley was very good at his game but it seemed he did not have this one under control. He was still afraid she'd say, *"Thanks so much for everything, and by the way, I never want to see you again, you pervert."* He was really feeling her, but he didn't know if she had the same vibe for him, if she was really gravitating toward him with the same frequency and magnitude as he. His fear of rejection still lingers when it come to Ernestine.

He wanted so desperately to tell her he was in love with her, even though he had only known her less than three months. No matter how he tried to frame it in his mind, he felt like a total fool for bringing such powerful emotions into their mentoring sessions. As it was, the fact that they had mind-blowing sex during each of the lessons was a little weird, but at least they had an upfront agreement about it: Whatever happened during their lessons, stayed in their lessons. Everyone in Liberia does it, teachers at the various schools and universities, government's officials, even employees and bosses at local and international corporations and NGOs, they all engaged in some form of mutually understandable sex that lived outside of those professional entities. As people always say, *"This too is Monrovia, a city where money is power and sex is a means to an end; and the only place where only the corruptly wise enjoy the fruits of the land while the poor suffer, live, and die in eternal poverty."*

If only they had made some sort of agreement about their emotions. Something like: If I fall in love with you, I can tell you how I feel and you'll say you love me too.

Stanley sighed heavily and flipped the top off another bottle of cold beer. Getting drunk was the sucker's way out of his situation, but since that's what he was, he drank up his frustrations with self-indulged reservations.

A sudden knock on his door startled him out of his not-quite-drunken-enough stupor. He plopped the beer bottle down, sloshing sticky liquid all over the coffee table, and dragged himself to the front door.

"Probably the neighborhood watch team kids are out collecting cash for their midnight coffee and bread," he muttered as he turned the doorknob. Stanley had been drinking all afternoon up to the early evening. He might have lost tack of time for the impending lesson.

"Hey Stanley!" Ernestine said, as she stood on his doorstep looking more glorious than any angel he had ever seen in an

American movie. *"Could I come in?"* She asked girlishly as he stood there stupefied.

He nodded and stepped aside dazedly.

She was still wearing the short yellow skirt and pink top from their jaunt to the zoo at Wulki Farm and at the rubber plantation. She looked tastier than ever, especially since the zippy night air had puckered her nipples up beneath her thin cotton tank.

Still in his foyer, she turned to him with a determined look in her eyes, and said, *"I hope I am not intruding on your privacy. The reason I am here this late is because I was thinking about lesson five, and all of the wonderful lessons we've already had. I think we need to shake things up a little bit for this last lesson. What do you suggest?"*

He stood there completely out of words. He wanted to say something, but could not get the air out of his belly through his lungs and then out of his mouth. It was like someone had hit him with a jackhammer between his balls.

"So, for lesson five, which I believe you told me was going to be about role playing, I'm going to be the teacher and you're going to be the student." She said without any condition—in fact, she had planned this all the way from her house several hours ago.

Like a military officer standing at full attention, Stanley's dick stood up at full attention as he took in her words. He was speechless, stunned that she had magically appeared on his doorstep, mesmerized by her beauty, and bowled over by how she wanted to reverse their roles. His mouth drooped open at what he'd just heard from Ernestine, the woman he has fallen in love with, but was afraid to tell.

Not waiting for any response from him, she walked out of his foyer and down the hall, until she reached the door of his second master bedroom. Stanley had designed the house with 2 equally proportional master bedrooms. She looked over her shoulder and said, *"You don't want to be late to class, do you? Cause I hear that the teacher spanks her students when they're bad or late for class,"* and then disappeared into his bedroom.

It was like Stanley was in a twilight zone from all that were playing out in front of him. By the time he snapped out of his fog and ran down the hall to the goddess who awaited him, Ernestine was nowhere to be found in his bedroom. Hearing the water running in his adjoining bathroom, he peeked his head into the doorway and saw a blessed sight only God can reveal to a faithful servant who asked for it. The sight of her in the bathroom was like a miracle that only happens when a devoted person prays sincerely to his Heavenly Father or whom, or whatever that individual's source of comfort, power and or solace is.

Ernestine was leaning over his enormous spa bathtub, setting the jets speed of the tub, and completely naked. It was like a sight from a Hollywood movie. Stanley liking to live in comfort and style, had furnished the house to his taste and intimate desire. He had created his own American lifestyle in Liberia where majority of the people lived on less than $2.50 United States Dollars a day.

He reached for the hem of his t-shirt to pull it off over his head, but she whipped around and said, *"Keep your clothes on."*

He stopped with the shirt mid-way up his torso. *"Huh?"*

She walked up to him and pressed her full breasts up against his chest. *"You heard me. I want you to keep your clothes on until I tell you otherwise,"* she said, and then spun around and gingerly dipped a toe into the soapy water. Slipping into the tub, she stretched out fully, with her nipples jutting proudly out of the water. They puckered tightly as cool air blew across them.

"*Soap me up,*" she said, and Stanley immediately gathered up a small washcloth and a bar of a locally-made herbal soap off the holder by the tub.

"*Kneel on the bath mat,*" she directed him, and again he did as she instructed. Then she crossed her legs in the tub and wiggled the toes on her right foot. "*Start here,*" she said with a smile flashing across her face.

Incredibly aroused by the way she had taken charge of their lovemaking, Stanley thought his dick was going to explode in his pants. Though he had lived in the U.S. where he had sex with many different races and nationalities of women, he could not remember which one of those women ever made him to feel this way. He wanted to ask Ernestine if she had ever lived in the U.S. or Europe because he felt that no local Liberian woman possessed the enormous romantic talent she had. How was he going to ask her such a stupid question when the civil conflict had exposed Liberians to so many things, including sex, crimes, lies and dishonesty, innovation and all of the things that make a country tick like a working clock? Holding back his question, he obeyed his teacher's every command. He wet the small, soft terry cloth towel, slid it over the bar of scented herbal soap until it foamed, and rubbed it over the arch of her foot, making her moan with pleasure.

He worked the cloth diligently up her right leg, leaning over the rim of the sunken two-person tub to touch every inch of her smooth chocolate skin, running the cloth past her kneecap, across the top of her thigh. And then, just as he got to the apex between her legs, he stopped, lathered up the towel and started with her left foot, mirroring his actions on her left side.

"*Wash my pussy, student. I need you to make me fresh, clean and ready,*" she said as he got closer and closer to her mound.

Stanley held back a grin and obeyed her again, pressing the cloth firmly into her pussy lips, rubbing it back and forth over her clit, watching her nipples grow engorged as she got more and more aroused, watching the pulse in her neck beat wildly as she closed her eyes and arched her back.

"Yes! There! Don't stop! That's the spot right there! Oh, oh, oh, oooohhhhh. Oh shiiiiit, I love it!" she cried as she began to come underneath his hand, beneath the small towel he rubbed forcefully against her swollen clitoris.

He wanted to kiss her, but he knew she was in charge of this lesson, so he continued to rock her pelvis in the palm of his hand until her breathing returned to normal and she opened her eyes again.

"Take off your clothes and get inside the tub," she said evenly. He was surprised by how controlled she was, considering she had been screaming and wriggling just moments before.

Like a starving man, he quickly stripped off his t-shirt and jeans and then stepped into the water. He stood in the tub, his dick thick and rock-hard and ready to plunge into Ernestine's wet pussy. As he watched her eyes take in his arousal, a thick spurt of sperm spilled from the tip of his penis.

"Do me doggy style, Stanley. I want to feel your big prick thrusting deep inside me," she said, and turned over so that her breasts were pressed up against the cool tile surrounding the tub and her big and soft ass was flared up from the rim like the top of the Putu Mountain in Grand Gedeh.

Stanley kneeled behind her and said, *"If the teacher insists, who Am I to refuse,"* as he reached one hand around between the tile and her torso to cup and squeeze her breasts and the other around to swirl her swollen clit.

And then he did what he'd wanted to do since the beginning of lesson one, and rammed his big dick hard into

Ernestine's warm and wet pussy.

His balls were swinging into her thighs and she reached around to cup them in her right hand. *"Harder, Stanley. Harder!"* She demanded as she pushed her ass tighter to his hips, squirming and moaning while he thrusts deeper and deeper into her sweetie pum pum.

He couldn't remember the last time his dick had been so distended, so engorged. As he felt his cock begin to contract, he pressed his palm against her swollen, firm clit and pumped his hand against her mound.

She cried out, *"Damn your prick is so big and sweet, Stanley. I think I want it all to myself. I never knew a dick could feel so good and sweet like this, for real."* He spread her butt cheeks apart with both hands as rammed her hard and fast. Her suction-like gripping pussy milk his dick at every assault.

"Oh my God, Honey, you're so hot, so wet. You may this dick anywhere you wish. It is all yours," Stanley groaned as she screamed, *"Harder, there, now! Oh shhhhiiiitttt!"* in ecstasy.

The water was tepid by the time she wrung the last drop of come out of him. They untangled their bodies and got up to take a shower. As he soaped her up, he kneeled between her legs, asking *"Are we done with all five lessons now?"* She didn't get a chance to answer because another huge orgasm overtook her.

As he dried her off with a thick white towel, she smiled at him and said, *"Thanks for the five great mentoring sessions,"* and kissed him softly on his lips, letting her tongue merge with his.

Pulling back from her mouth, Stanley said, *"Honey, there's something I need to tell you,"* at the very exact time she said, *"Stanley, there's something I've been meaning to say to you."*

They laughed and kissed again. *"You first,"* he said, and tried to get his heart to stop pounding so damn hard in his chest as he waited for her to speak.

Suddenly looking shy and unsure, she forced herself to look into his eyes and said, *"First of all, I want you to know how much I've enjoyed working with you this week."*

He smiled and waited for her to finish. *"And even though I know these were just supposed to be lessons for me to write better erotica, the truth is..."*

Her words fell away and Stanley swallowed hard once again.

Taking a deep breath she started again. *"The truth is, Stanley, I'm in love with you."*

Stanley had never been happier. He put his arms around her waist and spun her around in a circle in his large bathroom, their towels falling into a heap on the floor.

Breathless with joy, he said, *"Ernestine Honey Johnson, I love you too, and it's been killing me not telling you all these past weeks. I am all head over heels for you, my love. I really do love you more than you can imagine. I have been dying to get it off my chest and for some unknown reason, it has become a nightmare that has haunted me night after night when I am in solitude. You see, Love can sometimes be like the air we breathe. If we hold our breath in for so long, we will suffocate and die. I have been dying slowly by holding back my intense desire for too long. "*

She reached her hands up around the back of his head and kissed him passionately. He swept her up into his arms and walked methodically with the beautiful animal into the master bedroom, and laid her on his king-size bed. He looked down at her lying in his fluffy master bed as thousands of thoughts raced through his mind. He could not believe he was back in love once again.

Within that instant he realized that in his bedroom is where she belonged. In fact, this was all he ever wanted to do to the stranger he had fallen in love with. Stanley could feel something suddenly leaving his body, his head, his heart and his mind. It was his depression that was leaving his state of being. He felt relief from all the glooms and isolations that had made him a sad and lonely man for more than five. Deep down within his heart, he knew he had found love and he would soon be walking tall just like the man he used to be more than half a decade ago. With Ernestine in his life, he was sure his self-esteem would be restored and his sense of humor and sophistication would reemerge. Like the phoenix of old rising from the ashes of a ferocious incineration, he was rising from societal's inflicted death and nothingness that have engulfed him for years. He was now traveling onto an everlasting sure of peace, love, and romance like never before, so he thought. Stanley knew that Monrovia, the city he so loved would soon find a true lover like him, especially with an impending election on the horizon in which an unknown and a powerful, patriotic and a diminutive personality like Alexander B. Cummings is participating to be elected as the country's next president. Being born and raised in Monrovia, Stanley thinks if he's elected, he could be a perfect partner to restore the city's faded glory, but for now, his focus is to give all the love and attentions to the only woman he loves in the world and leave the current state of Monrovia up to Alexander Cummings, Benoni Urey, Charles Brumskine, George Weah, and thirty other politicians.

"Nothing is ever going to come between us. You're my angel without wings, and I like the way Monrovia has made you," Stanley said thickly and Ernestine covered his mouth with hers before he could see the guilt and worry in her eyes.

…I will try my utmost best to tell him about the story soon, she promised herself as she sank deeper into the comfort of Stanley's arms—something she had longed wanted to be able to do aside from their occasional spicy sex. For the next eleven hours, the pairs had each other to themselves.

they made love more than six times in different places within the house and using various sexual positions. Being in his mid forty, Stanley performance was not bad at all, especially given the fact that he had been with someone he cared so much about. For now, he has come to believe in the transformative power of true love and warms he body, mind, and soul.

CHAPTER 14

Ernestine thought back on the incredible night she and Stanley had spent together and smiled, happier than she had ever been in her entire life. She had taken charge of her own sexuality for once in her life, and told the man she loved how she felt. And to add to the perfection, he felt the same way about her! It was a feeling every human being craved for—to know and be assured that the man or woman you're in love with feels the same way about you—loves you unconditionally.

She had wanted her to spend the weekend with him, and she was tempted, but she wanted to finish her story first so that she could overnight it to the judges at the publishing company in Central Monrovia. The judges would do the preliminary qualification for every entry into the competition before forwarding it to the hosting organization in the United States. Making an excuse about some errands, she promised to be back in his bed by the evening, for another all-night fuck session and orgasm carnival.

Sitting down at her desk, Ernestine knew exactly how her story about Wilmot and Mardea needed to end.

......Wilmot watched Mardea walked up and down among patrons in the restaurant and the bar, and reminded himself again that his relationship with her would never last, that they came from different worlds, that he would eventually be tire of

her body. He knew that he had no future with her—only sex brought them together.

He laughed out loud at how bad a liar he was. He was full of shit…real bullshit! Any fool could tell that he was completely, irrevocably, ridiculously in love with the angel-faced little Bassa girl who walked so primly up and down in his establishment. Between her and his ex-wife, he would choose Mardea over her and over any female he had slept with for the past three years. She was young, innocent, and most importantly beautiful. Her vagina had not been explored by any other dick besides his—she was so tight that he sometimes found it difficult to penetrate her.

Mardea is a girl who looked like a nun, but fucked like a she-devil or one of the hookers from the back of Flamingo Bar and Night Club in Sinkor Old Road, adjacent Symthe Road. His friend who was the Speaker of the House of Representative in the Liberian government, whom also had a crush on Mardea when he first laid eyes on her, told Wilmot that she was sexually exotic and wanted to test-drive her pussy if Wilmot didn't mind. The big shot comment made Wilmot to severed friendship with him. Gangbanging or orgies sex was a common practice among wealthy and public officials in the country. Women didn't mind inviting their friends into their husbands' or boy friends' beds. For Wilmot, he wouldn't allow another man to laid hands of his young pride.

As he served a trio of overly made up, cheaply dressed women sitting at the bar trying to get his attention, he winced and thought about how they used to be just the kind of women he would take home and fuck all night. Now, just the thought of being with any woman but Mardea disgusted him. Mardea was now his world and he promised himself never to do anything to hurt her.

He hadn't known the meaning of good sex until the first time his tongue laved her clitoris, until the first time he sank his dick deep into her tight, virginal pussy as she screamed his name, her muscles tensing around his thick penis.

By the time the bar and restaurant closed that night, he had never been more ready to lock the doors and take Mardea into his arms. When he looked around the bar for her, she was nowhere to be found.

"Damn it!" he said, angry at her for leaving him alone when he needed her most. Walking into his office, he found a note on his desk, so he picked it up and read, "Wilmot. As a good Catholic girl I've never stolen anything in my life, but I took the keys to your house and I'll be waiting there for you, if you want to join me. Mardea."

He stroked the prickly stubble on his chin and wondered what she was up to. They had been in his house only once, on the way home from the bar, before he dropped her off at her apartment in Mamba Point. She knows damn well we only fuck here, in the bar, he thought angrily.

He didn't want to take her to his bed where he had screwed so many other, meaningless women. Mardea was special. And so much hotter than anyone else he had laid in the past. She was not just any Bassa girl, she was intelligent, homegrown, beautiful, and most importantly, a Catholic who had a deep family value.

He drove his Harley Davidson motorcycle home as if he was an America Hell's Angel, the biker gangs that are found in many American cities. He stomped loudly up his front stairs, hoping he was scaring her just a bit. She was going to get the spanking of her life from him once he got inside, and his dick hardened as he thought of her soft flesh beneath the palm of his hand. He could already see her ass turning blue and purple under his assault, and could taste her come on his lips.

He turned the knob and the door opened. "Mardea," he called, but got no answer. She wasn't in his living room or the kitchen, so he walked down the hall and heard the water running in his master bath.

When he walked into the room, his little nun was lying naked beneath the pouring water, smiling wickedly.

He was so angry and so aroused he growled, "What the hell are you doing?" She just sank deeper into the water and said, "I want you to soap me up."

"You what?" he exploded.

She shook her head at him and pinched her lips into a tight line of disapproval. "You heard me," she said crossly. "You are going to soap me up."

"Hell no! I'm not going to," he said, and she rose up angrily out of the tub.

"You big jerk," she cried as water poured off her naked body. "I'm asking you to do one simple thing, and all you do is use blasphemy!" She made a fist and said, "Now get over here and do as I say!"

Wilmot leaned against the door, crossed his arms, and said, "Make me do it if you think you have the power to."

Narrowing her eyes at him, Mardea took a deep breath and stepped out of the tub. Walking toward him, still blessedly naked in her birthday suit, she grabbed a towel off the rack and threw it onto the floor in front of Wilmot's black boots. Kneeling in front of him she undid the button on his jeans and unzipped the zipper, letting his half hard dick spring free of its overly tight confines.

Mardea had never taken him into her mouth before. Because she was such a novice, he'd never forced her to blow him. He was always happy to sink into her tight, wet pussy every night instead.

He was shocked by her new brazen behavior. His arousal was so acute he was afraid he'd shoot into her mouth the minute she so much as kissed the head of his dick.

Running her fingers up and down his penis, she stuck the tip of her sweet little tongue out and licked him once, twice, and then suddenly sucked in several inches of him, moaning as she did so.

Instinctively she reached between his legs and cupped his balls, massaging them as she throated his dick as well as any professional courtesan might have. She slowly inserted her index finger into Wilmot's ass. This caused an instant burst of sensation to surge through him like a powerful lightning bolt. Wilmot knew he was a goner, but he couldn't do anything about it, so he just threaded his hands into her silky black hair and pulsed deeply into her mouth, gratified as she swallowed every last drop of his sperm.

He didn't know how long it was before he was done shooting into the back of her throat, but his legs were shaking. He didn't have the strength to fight her, to show her that he was the boss, so he let her pull him into the tub.

He lay back against the rim and she straddled him and kissed him on his mouth, tasting his lips, playing with his tongue, nipping at his bottom lip.

"Mardea," he said, "I've got to tell you something."

Her face fell and her lips quivered slightly. He couldn't keep himself from laughing out loud. In male dominated Liberia, most women live at the mercy of their partners. Did she actually think for one minute that he'd break up with her? Didn't she know he loved her more than life itself? Or more than many African presidents and their officials love corruption?

"Stop laughing at me!" she cried and pounded his chest with her right fists.

He grabbed her hands and held them still, saying, "What I wanted to tell you, you little fool, is that I'm in love with you."

Mardea grew completely still, then said, "Say that again?"

He reached for her face and pulled her down for a hard kiss. "I love you, Mardea. I really, really and truly love you. I know we are separated by years and youth, but we are banded by love and connected by faith, if you didn't know that. I love you so dearly," he growled as he took her lips again. Already hard, he plunged his dick deep within her soaking wet pussy, taking immeasurable pleasure in filling her pussy with his thick and hard dick, in shooting his sperm into her womb, in hearing her cry out his name.

Later, as she lay on his chest, with her head in the crook of his shoulder, she said, "I love you too, Wilmot. I really want to marry you," and he smiled and said, "Thank God. It is something worth considering after being consumed by loneliness for a long while. And I don't care what the world or your parents may say. I will not let this artificial distance of age separate us. Mardea, I will move my world just to be with you no matter where you are. I will take you for my wife and love you forever and ever, even to the end of the world, I will go. I will do anything for you. I will rub your back, wash your hair, I'll do anything for you, Mardea. I don't care what people may say. I'll cook your food, buy your clothes, paint your nails, you're my world, I will go to the limit, to make you smile. If you'll let me share your world, I will love you forever. I have nothing out there to run after anymore knowing God has brought a woman like you in my life. Even if I die while loving you, I will search for you on the other side through a thousand worlds, and five million lifetimes, until I find you and love you all over again. And believe me baby, I will find you no matter where you go! And when I find you, I will love you for all eternity." Wilmot look Mardea deep in the eyes with tears almost rolling down his cheeks. He took a deep breath wanting to say something, but the words couldn't come out. After several minutes of silence when he recomposed himself, he begun to speak again, "And when… and whenever we get home from work, I'll run you some warm bath water like you just did tonight. I'll put some bubbles and

some scented bath oil inside. I know you like bubbles. I will
slowly wash you up, and I'll dry you off with some Turkish
Cotton Towels. I'll then lotion your body down with some
Versace Pour Femme Luxury Body Lotion, and massage you
until you fall asleep in my arms. And if you'll like, I'll braid
your hair. I know you'll like that too, honey. It has been a long
way coming, my love. I think we were made for each other at ·
different times by the same Heavenly Creator you were taught
to worship at the convent," That evening, Wilmot vowed to go to
church again the next day, to give thanks to God Almighty for
the woman He had brought into his loving arms......

Ernestine saved her newly updated file, quickly proofread
it, and then printed it off for the contest. Sealing the envelope,
she went to the headquarters of CP&CG on Carey Street
in Central Monrovia to submit her entry. At the publisher's
office, she was then an e-mail with instructions for submission
of an electronic copy of her manuscript.

Driving back home, she encountered several thousand
people wearing T-shirts with the picture of Alexander
Cummings, an unknown politician running for the
presidency of Liberia. For the most part, many observers
think he might not even be qualified by the National Election
Commission or get a 2% of the vote in the election. Finally
passing the throng of supporters of the unknown business
man turned politician, she made her way toward the Johnson
Street Bridge for the United Nations' Drive in Vai Town.
Getting at the Freeport of Monrovia, she met a group of
demonstrators demanding that the government brings down
the price of imported commodities on the market. After being
stalled at the Freeport and witnessing the theatrical display of
insanity by a group of low thinking citizens, she was finally on
her way to her beautiful home.

Knowing Stanley was waiting for her to come back to
his house, she put the contest out of her mind, stuffed her
deception and guilt away from her heart, and got in her car to

drive straight to heaven for some out of this world delights.

The next three weeks were the most amazing weeks of Ernestine's life. She and Stanley spent nearly all of their time together and had even begun to collaborate on an Romance novel. Were it not for the black cloud of her dishonesty hanging over her head, she would have felt complete joy in being with Stanley, the master of romance, sex and relationship.

The problem was, every time she had an opportunity to tell him about her manuscript, she couldn't bring herself to do it. He was so damn good—so sweet and loving and tender— she hated thc thought of ever seeing anything but love in his eyes.

Ernestine was desperately afraid he'd leave her if he found out how she had betrayed the promise they'd made to each other. What had happened in their lessons was supposed to forever stay in their lessons, but by writing Mardea and Wilmot's tale she had broken that pledge. She was afraid, she hadn't live up to her oath of secrecy. To her, she was exhibiting the typical behavior of true Monrovian—double standing, unloyal and never to be trusted no matter what is promised

As the days dragged by and she didn't hear a word from the contest judges, she began to irrationally hope that her entry had gotten lost in the pile of rejection at Clarke Publishing Herring Publishing Group. Or perhaps, if she were lucky, the judges had hated it so much they just threw it away or shredded it and placed it into the recycle bin.

If Ernestine had it all to do over, if it meant preserving Stanley's love, she knew she never would have written the manuscript in the first place.

Over the past few weeks she had spent every night at Stanley's house. Every day more of her clothes appeared in his closet. This is a typical behavior of most Liberians and Africans females—marking their territories by leaving their underclothes, skirts or anything that would warn another female of their presence in a home. He wanted her to move in with him so as to help him raise the two orphan boys who he was paying, but she told him it was a little too early for such a big commitment. Each time she thought of Stanley's *"Please move in with me,"* words, she would recall her late mother's stern warning *"Do not move in with any man, if that man is not your husband. If you disobey and do, that man will never marry you. As the saying goes, "If he cannot buy the cow, do not give him the milk." Do not move in with a man if he's not willing to engage you for his wife or show you the true love only you deserve in this world. If you do, your replacement will be right around the corner because you will just be another disposal asset to him. Never move in with a man who does not respects you as well as sleeps around with a multiple sex partners. If you do, your home will be a scene of continual conference hall where people would be judging cases every week due to domestic conflicts and other abuses. Do not cohabit with any man whose mother is involved in his relationship. If you do, just be prepared to know that she's going to be the other woman running your home right under your nose. Listen to these words, my child and be that morally strong woman I've trained you to be."*

A voice in her head said, *"You would move in with him in a heartbeat if he knew what you had done and said he loved you anyway or if your mother did not warn you about men like him."*

Ernestine shook the voice off, and tried to stick to her story about needing more time. He was getting harder and harder to put off with each passing day, as they discovered depths of passion and love in each other's arms that neither had dreamed was even possible in this sun-drenched part of West Africa. For some, love was a one-way street with the man leading the way while the woman followed. As Ernestine had come to learn, love is mutually agreeable where both parties' happiness and pleasure are at stake.

Her heart sank into her stomach as she saw the light blinking on her cell phone atop the dining table by the kitchen. She did not recognize the number at first, but reluctantly took the call from the strange number.

Feeling like she was suffocating, could not believe her ear when the voice said, "This is Stella Herring from Clarke Herring Publishing Group. May I please speak to Honey Lauren?"

"Yes, this is she. This is Honey," she quivered with excitement as she ran and sat on a chair and braced herself for the news from the lady on the other end of the phone.

"Ms. Lauren," the lady breathed hard in the earpiece of Ernestine's mobile device. She then continued to speak, *"We are pleased to inform you that you are the Grand Prize Winner of our 3rd Annual Romance Writer's Contest! We hereby request your presence at the awards ceremony on July 21st. We are certain you will be thrilled to receive your medal and a $10,000 check from our secret celebrity judge."* The lady waited for a few seconds to hear Ernestine's reaction, but none came.

"Are you there, Ms. Lauren?" the caller asked, but Ernestine seemed to be having an out of body moment. After almost ten seconds of utter silence, she responded.

"Yes..., yes, I am still here, but this sounds and looks very surreal to me. I think I am dreaming," Ernest replied with excitement followed by a loud shout.

"No you're not dreaming. This is actually happening now. We are here rejoicing for you at our office here on Carey Street. Congratulations," the caller declared.

"Thank you, thank you very much. I can't believe it, I can't believe it. Oh my God, this can't be real," she repeated with more excitements and celebrations.

"You're welcome, Ms. Lauren. We'll be looking forward to seeing you on July 21ˢᵗ at the Golden Key Hotel in Paynesville City," the caller said finally before hanging up the phone. For a moment, Ernestine was in a state of denial.

Seconds later, Ernestine jumped up from the chair and screamed, *"I won! I won!"* and ran into the kitchen to call Stanley. She stopped as everything came crashing down on and around her.

"Shit!" she exclaimed.

Tell him now, her rational African female inner-voice nagged her.

"He'll leave me if I tell him," she said aloud and her words reverberated off the shiny counters in her state of the art Italian kitchen.

Unwilling to risk his love for her, Ernestine decided not to tell him about winning the award. And now she needed to think of a good excuse for why she was going to be busy on Saturday night of the 21ˢᵗ of July.

"Damn it," she muttered as she went back into her living room pick up the pieces of papers that were strewn all over her carpeted floors. *"I wish I had never entered this stupid contest in the first place,"* she declared as she began to compose her newest lie in her head. She knew she could pull this off. She knew he loved her and might forgive her of any wrong she has done. Ernestine believed that true love conquers every adversity, even if the beloved is in the wrong. She believed that if Stanley truly loves her, he would forgive her of any wrong doing because love triumphs over, the lies, the bad, and the ugly, but when she recalls her dead father's warning, she became more frightened. When she was twelve years old, her that told her to always remain true to herself and to always do the right thing, even if no one was watching her. This piece of advice had cause her a lot of emotional harms in her love relationship with men she gave her heart to. With Stanley

being on the receiving end this time, ripped her apart. As for now, she needed to be creative in finding the best excuse that would wouldn't raise Stanley's suspicion of any kind.

CHAPTER 15

"Baby," Ernestine said as she lay in the crook of Stanley's arm, *"I have a family matter to attend to this Saturday."*

"Oh good. I've been dying to meet your family." Stanley's said with excitement. Know she had lost both parents a few years back, he wanted to meet her other family members. Beyond telling him about her mother and father, she didn't say if she had other siblings or uncles and aunties. All he knew of her family was that they had a lot of properties in Monrovia and in various places around the country that they didn't have deeds for.

Inwardly she cursed herself for saying the wrong thing. *"Actually,"* she said, *"it's a private matter. I promise to tell you everything once things are ironed out, but for now, the lawyers have insisted we keep it within the family."*

Stanley kissed the top of her head. *"Sounds serious. Are you sure you don't want me to come along for moral support?"*

"Definitely not! I am sure you don't want to be in the middle of a bitter family land dispute," she exclaimed. Realizing she had been far more fervent with her protests than was necessary, she stroked her hands through his short black hair that complemented his muscular chest. Trying to keep her tone light she said, *"Hey Boo, Boo, you'll finally get a day*

without me. I'll bet you've been dying to hang out with the guys to drink beer, and eat roasted meat and fish at Brenda Samuels' shop in Congo Town, huh?"

Stanley chuckled. *"Honestly? No. I haven't been the least bit interested in hanging out with the guys. In fact, Emeka Obiamiwe, Prince Freeman, Moses Dekai and Lester are mad at me because I have been busy with you lately."*

"Really?" she asked in an uncertain voice.

"Are you kidding me? You're all I need. You're the woman I want to share my bed and my dreams with," he replied. *"Only a madman would choose Club Beer, wisecracking Brenda, roasted meat and fish over a beautiful woman like you."*

Ernestine tilted her head up and kissed him softly on the lips. *"I love you so much, S.K. Nimely. Just the thought of you turns me on every time."*

Stanley had planned on asking Ernestine to the Romance Writing Contest ceremonies where he had been invited as an official guest, but he kept forgetting. As one of the big faces of Erotica Romance in Liberia, he was bonded by loyal to the trade to be present. By the time he learned she already had unbreakable plans, he figured there was no point in mentioning it at all.

Three weeks later, July 21st appeared on Stanley Nimley's calendar. He and Ernestine had spend the night together, but she had to rush back home to prepared for her fake family meeting she had told Stanley about. Stanley missed her presence and he wished she and he would go to the award that evening. Due to the love he had developed for her, he felt they had now become a conjoin twins, but he knew sometimes a family matter takes precedence over romantic relationship. He knew that a lover can leave a person, but family will always remain no matter what.

Stanley spend the whole day going over his speech and

rehearsing moves and other things he would do at the event. At 12 o'clock midday, he went drove to town to collect his tuxedo he had dropped at the Montgomery Dry cleaners on Lynch Street a day earlier. Once he got home, he went over at his adopted children's house next door to make sure things were in perspective. He had brought in contractors to renovate their house and change the furniture and appliances with new ones. Realizing he had only two hours to prepare and drive to the program, he jumped into action. Since the hotel was about three and a half miles from his home, he was not in a hurry. When he finally did get dress for the occasion, he jumped inside his Mercedes C Class with Judi Clarke Swaggeristic blaring for the surround sound speakers. Pulling into the hotel's parking lot, it was about thirty minutes to show time. Stanley is a believer of time.

Backstage that Saturday evening, where all the guests and celebrities were relaxing for their turns to the stage, Stanley clipped on his bowtie and evened up the sleeves of his tux jacket. Looking at himself in the mirror on the wall, he saw a man in love looking back at him. How he wished Ernestine was here to see him up on stage. His memory when back to the first day he saw her at the We Care Library on Carey Street and then at the writers conference at the Grand Royal Hotel in Sinkor, on Tubman Boulevard. From the first day he met her to the day they first made love, he knew she was special. She was a diamond in the rough, only awaiting the excess to be chipped away and be polished to his desire tone. His eyes were clear and bright, a smile was permanently plastered on his face, and he was thrilled to know that he and Ernestine were going to share the rest of their lives together.

He had planned on asking her to marry him. In fact, he had dropped by Classic Jewelry on Broad Street that very afternoon and purchased one of the biggest diamond rings he could find.

He couldn't wait to slip the expensive solitaire gem on her finger, knowing she'd be in his bed, in his heart, for all eternity. He knew from their very first encounter, she was the woman he had been searching for. She was the cure for the depression that had ravaged him for so long. With Ernestine in his life, his world would be different and he had promised himself to give her everything she had ever dreamed of and even more, true and unconditional love.

Kerkula Jensen stuck his head inside the little room where Stanley was sitting. *"Hey Stanley, I thought you might want to check out the winning manuscript before you present the award to the winner."* Kerkula put the thick bundle of pages on the table nearest the door. *"It's pretty fuckin' hot. I can't wait to get a look at the woman who wrote it when she walks up on stage tonight."*

Stanley cocked his head to the side. *"You don't recognize the writer's name?" "I think it's a pseudonym. Nobody in Liberia would name their daughter Honey Lauren."*

Honey? Stanley felt a squeezing sensation in his chest, but brushed his sense of foreboding aside. Of course Ernestine hadn't turned herself into Honey Lauren.

Then again, he had never asked her if she wrote under a pseudonym.

She would have told him if she entered this contest, he knew she would have. They told each other everything—all of their dreams, fears, and hopes for the unforeseeable future.

He shook his head to clear the insanity from it and picked up the manuscript. *"Thanks Kerkula. I'll take a quick look at it. See you out there."*

"I'll save you some champagne," Kerkula said and then loped off down the narrow walkway in the hall.

Stanley shut the door behind Kerkula, sat down on the leather sofa in the small dressing room and read, *"Mardea was a good girl..."*

Ernestine walked into the beautifully decorated ballroom of the Golden Key Hotel in Paynesville City outside Monrovia and slid her hands over her red silk dress, smoothing out invisible wrinkles. She was incredibly nervous about accepting the award for her story, The Angel From Hell. Yet again, she wished she had told Stanley about it, so he could lend her the moral support she so desperately needed on this very special night.

A stunning medium height black lady greeted her at the doorway. *"Good evening and welcome. And you are?"*

"I am Honey....Honey Lauren," Ernestine replied with a big smile.

"Oooh wow, how exciting it must be for you. I am very impressed by your work!" the woman exclaimed as she spontaneously gave Ernestine a hug. *"Stanley Nimely was.....or if is your mentor this year, wasn't he?"*

Ernestine nodded. *"That's right."*

The woman leaned in closer and said, *"Decontee was spitting nails for weeks after losing out on the chance to work with him. I hear you nabbed him the minute he walked into the conference hall that day at the Royal Grand Hotel."* Unknowing to Ernestine, Stanley was swirling out of control among other writers in the city. She thought soon their relationship would make national headlines in the gossip happy country.

Grinning, Ernestine said, *"Pretty much,"* liking the woman immensely and feeling a great deal more at ease. She knew how things played out between the woman and her at the conference that day. She often refers to her as Sheba Queen of the Hopo Joe sluts—for she carried herself about like one of those lose women that people often referred to in Liberia as sleepy Martha.

"I'm Ama Malakpa," the beautiful big breasted woman

said with a shake of her perfect black ringlets. *"Stanley was my mentor last year and I learned so much from him. I'll bet you did too. That man is God's send, and I wished I could do it all over again."* She winked at Ernestine.

The smile froze on Ernestine's face. *"You worked with Stanley last year?"* she asked, striving for an even tone.

Ama Malakpa winked a second time. *"He's quite a hunk, isn't he? That man is…oh my God, I don't have words to describe him. No wonder he's the best in the business."*

Ernestine felt all of the color rush out of her face just as a loud buzzing started in her ears. *"He is,"* she said quickly. *"Could you point me to the ladies room, please?"* Ernestine asked. Her eyes spitting fire, and hands shaking at her side.

"Sure thing, honey. It's just down the hall to the left. You don't look so good all of a sudden," the woman added, clearly concerned.

"Probably just something I ate," Ernestine lied before spinning around and practically running down the hall. She was panting as if she'd been running—almost hyperventilating as she doubled her paces down the hall. It seemed like she was about to get a panic attack.

Once she had locked herself into a stall in the lady's room, she let the tears stream down her face. *"I can't believe I'm such an idiot. I feel like such a cheap good for nothing hoe. I am such a slut,"* she whispered. *"Of course I wasn't the only female apprentice he's ever had."* She sniffled and rolled some toilet paper into her fist, dashing it angrily at her face.

Painful memories crashed down around her. Walking in on her first boyfriend in his one bedroom apartment on Clay Street while he screwed the President of the Student Government Association of Cuttington University. Bravely letting her next boyfriend have sex with her, only to have him tell her she was a cold fish in bed and that the anal sex he really wanted was not forthcoming from her. Swallowing her pride as she found signs of her latest boyfriend's affair, and realizing it was with the woman she thought was her best friend.

And now Stanley. He had probably slept with every woman in the room on a *"mentor/apprentice"* basis.

"Damn him! To hell with him anyway. I don't give a shit about him no more. He can fuck anyone he wants, I don't give a fuck! He's just a user, and I used him too." she exclaimed.

Her tears ran dry and she heaved in a shaky breath. *"I'll show him,"* she declared. *"I'm going to accept this award, shove it in his face, and move on with my beautiful life. With or without him."*

She unlatched the bathroom door and made her way to the mirror. Quickly fixing her makeup, she strode into the banquet hall and tried to ignore the voice in her head that said she could never live without Stanley by her side. But again, why will she allow herself to get hurt knowing the history of Stanley—he was a complete heartbreak who wore his feeling under his feet. Since his divorce, he has had this fear of commitment, but since Ernestine walked into his life, everything has changed for the Romance King who didn't see any good in all of the women before Ernestine Honey Lauren Johnson stepped into his world.

The words played in endless repeat in Stanley's head and swam before his eyes.

"....He hooked his fingers into the edges of her cotton panties and slowly slid them off her fat and soft chocolaty ass."

"Suddenly the buzzing started up again between her thighs, but this time, she knew that somehow, some way, Wilmot was manning the controls to her vagina."

"You're not wearing panties,' he said. 'I was wondering when you'd notice."

"I want you to soap me up....."

Stanley ran his hand over his hair and dropped the manuscript back onto the table in front of him. He had read the words, but he still couldn't believe them.

Ernestine had detailed their lessons act by act, scene by scene, in her book The Angel From Hell. He couldn't deny that it was a powerful writing, and yet the hole in his heart was so deep he could hardly feel anything at all.

"She promised," he said aloud in the small room and closed his eyes, wiping away the moisture that had crept beneath his eyelids.

"Damn it!" he exclaimed as he punched his hand into the table. Some of the papers, pens and materials crumbled beneath his fist just as one of the event's organizers knocked once at the door to the little room.

"What!?" Stanley said in a gruff tone.

"We're ready for you," said the voice from the hall.

"I'll be right out." Stanley replied as he fixed his tux around his large shoulder.

He had thought he was special to Ernestine, but now he wondered if he was just a fool for believing that she truly loved him. For all he knew, she was going to take her new knowledge and find another *"mentor",* one who knew more than he did, who could give her things he couldn't afford. But then, Stanley was the best in all of Liberia. The only man who wrote what he felt without fear of a backlash from anyone.

Stanley took a deep breath and tried to compose himself. And then he stepped out of his little dressing room and down the hall to greet the person he loved most in the world, wondering what the hell he was going to say to her when they finally came face to face.

The MC said, *"Thank you for coming to the 3rd Annual Romance Writer's Contest awards ceremonies! We had some incredible entries this year, but for the first time in the history of this contest, our judges at Clarke Herring Publishing Group, voted unanimously for the winner. Here to present the $10,000 check to our winner is none other than Liberia's number one best-selling author and the master of romance, sex and eroticism, Stanley Kla Nimely."* The ballroom exploded with loud applauds as the MC announced the name.

Sitting out in the audience, Ernestine was hardly aware of the raucous hoots and hollers from the crowd. *"Stanley is the surprise celebrity guest,"* she said to herself. She could not believe her ears.

She looked around for the nearest escape or exit, but knew that she couldn't take the coward's way out. Not this time. Even if she ran tonight, he'd find out that Honey Lauren was her pseudonym, that The Angel From Hell had been inspired by their astonishing lovemaking. It was finally time for her to face the punishment.

Stanley took the stage and she could see him scanning the crowd, looking for her. His eyes locked with hers and she forced herself not to look away. She didn't know what she expected to see in his eyes—pain, hatred maybe—but not the awful blankness that radiated down to her in the audience.

Her stomach heaved, but she swallowed the bile back into her throat and clasped her hands tightly in her lap, her spine as straight as rebar, straight like the Salala Gate.

"Writing is a funny thing," he began, as he looked out over the large, well-dressed crowd with a small smile. *"We think that we can separate ourselves from the stories we weave, but no matter how much we lie to ourselves, there is always a piece of us in there. Somewhere, some way, somehow, we can never disguise what's in our hearts. Our writings are reflections of us,*

of what we are, what we stand for, and what we have in our hearts and minds. Like our politicians that lie to us to get our votes ever four, six and nine years without delivering one single campaign promise, we as writers only lie to that part of our brain that cries for neutrality, but ignore that tiny voice while crafting our malices and vanities. More often, what we write is what or who we are," he locke eyes with Ernestine for a second time without giving her a small smile as he usually do.

"About thirty minutes ago, Kerkula Jensen handed me a copy of the winning manuscript. Truth is, folks, I couldn't put it down. It was compelling. It was sensual. And most of all, it was honest. One of the very best for a newcomer." He paused as a quick smile flashed across his face.

A tear began to slip down Ernestine's cheek, and she shook her head, whispering, *"Stop, Stanley. Please, stop."*

"It is with distinct pleasure that I award this year's Romance Writer's of the Year Award to Ernestine Johnson, for her forthcoming erotic romance novel, 'The Angel From Hell'. She has written this beautiful piece under the nom de plume or pen name as Honey Lauren." Stanley announced followed by another flash of smile.

The applause was deafening as Ernestine unsteadily rose to her feet. Strangers reached out to shake her hand in congratulations. She smiled and murmured thanks, but she was held prisoner by the intensity of Stanley's gaze.

I love you and I'm sorry, her heart cried out to him, but by the look in his eyes, she knew he was lost to her.

Wiping away the tear that had rolled down her cheek, she carefully climbed the small flight of stairs up to the podium where Stanley was standing and holding the a small golden statue, an award certificate, and the check in his hands.

"I'm sorry," she mouthed to him, but he ignored her, his face devoid of all emotions. For the first time since their

relationship, he looked different—he was stonewalled.

Putting the check into her trembling hands, without touching her, he stepped back into the shadows. Fearing her knees were going to buckle beneath her, Ernestine clutched at the podium and held on for dear life.

Looking out at the rapt crowd who was waiting for her acceptance speech, she swallowed nervously.

"Hi," she said softly into the microphone, surprised by the volume of her voice through the speakers.

"I, uh, want to thank the judges for..." She cut herself off, shaking her head, her face crumpling. *"The truth is, I am accepting this award with a heavy-heart. I hope I was the angel you all see me to be on this particular night. I'm sorry,"* she cried as a sob escaped her. Holding her hand over her mouth to quiet her weeping, she ran off the stage and down through the tables and chairs in the banquet room. She continued to run through the lobby and out into the hot July evening ocean air in the hotel's parking lot, not stopping to breathe until she tripped in her high heels and landed hard against a car.

Clutching the car for support, she sobbed and gasped for air, hating herself more and more with every passing second.

She felt a warm hand on the small of her back through her thin silk dress. *"It's a wonderful book, Honey,"* Stanley said as he gently rubbed her back.

She shook her head so hard, her gold clip fell out of her hair and clattered to the pavement. *"No. It's not. I'm sorry. I'm so sorry."* She sniffled and wiped her nose with the back of her hand.

"Sweetheart," he said, his voice tender, *"I love you."*

She finally turned around to face him, anger mixing with her sorrow as bile of jealousy surged through her GI tract toward her throat and her mouth. *"Is that what you told Ama*

Malakpa last year?"

"What does Ama Malakpa have to do with this?" Stanley reply was mixed with surprise.

Ernestine crossed her cooled hands across her chest and held onto her shoulders, rocking slightly back and forth as if to comfort herself.

"What kind of lessons did you set up for her? Were they hotter than ours? Is this what you do to every female you take advantage of in the name of mentoring?" Ernestine's asked to Stanley's surprise.

Giving her not chance, he said, *"God no! I edited a couple of her manuscripts and then passed her off to my agent. Let's go so you can ask her yourself."*

Ernestine knew the look of shock and disbelief on Stanley's face was pure and she felt like an even bigger fool than before. *"Of course you didn't,"* she said quietly, all of the fight back out of her. *"I understand if you never want to see me again, Stanley. But all I want to tell you from the bottom of my heart is, I am very sorry for betraying your confidence,"* she said, staring at the dirty pavement between them.

He slipped one of his fingers underneath her chin and forced her to look him in the eyes.

"Honey, I won't lie to you. This hurts like hell. I thought you knew you could tell me anything. Anything at all. I am not letting this insignificant inconsequential mishap of yours stand in our way. I loved you before tonight, I love you now and will always love you," he said softly.

"I do, but—" she protested, but he quieted her by pressing his thumb over her lips.

"The truth is I'll love you until the day I die, no matter what. So if you think I'm going to let the content of one of your future best-selling novels get in the way of our future, you're

very much mistaken. It's gonna take a whole lot more than a few hot love scenes to change the way I feel about you, sweetheart. You're the woman I have been praying to God earnestly for. Only God knows the joy you've brought back into my life," He spoke candidly from his heart—the deepest truth a man can speak from the secret confines of his wounded heart.

New tears had formed in Ernestine's eyes, but this time, they were tears of joy. She launched herself onto him, wrapping her long legs around his waist and kissed him with all of the love in her heart. He too kissed her right back

"Oh baby," she said when they stopped devouring each other's lips for a moment, *"I love you so much until it hurts me for not meeting you so long ago,"*

Stanley just smiled and held her closer to him, heedless of the stares from the strangers as they walked by. He knew the news of him kissing Ernestine would spread fast across the city and even the country like wildfire. Liberia had too many busybodies and less busy people. Therefore, they were servicing as citizen journalists.

"Thank God we both share the same feelings for each other," he murmured as he bent his head and captured Ernestine's lips in a kiss that went straight to her soul.

"Now, let's get home so that I can punish you for your very bad behavior. You just don't know how happy I am for you knowing that your writing career is about to be taken to another level, not only in the country, but internationally," Stanley smiled as he pulled her along to a romantic ecstasy which he hopes she would remember forever.

After their public display of affection for each other, he walked Ernestine to her came and opened the driver's door like he always does. When she was finally behind the driver's seat, He walked back to his Benz and fired-up the engine and set off for home as his Crown Jewel came driving after on the dark ELWA highway.

And so it was that Stanley finally got to enact the scene he had been choreographing in his imagination since the day he first lay Ernestine naked upon the bed in his guest bedroom and tasted her sweet vagina. He knew that Ernestine was the only cure to his internal illness.

Stanley sat down on the edge of their bed, still wearing his tuxedo. *"Come here,"* he said. Ernestine couldn't hold back the smile on her lips as she walked toward him.

"What could you possibly be smiling about," he said, trying and failing to hold back his own grin, *"when you are about to get spanked until your ass is purple and stinging?"*

Ernestine made a show by demurely lowering her eyes. *"Forgive me, oh benevolent one. If you will forgive me of this mishap, I'll be forever your lover for life. This is a true plead coming from the heart of a loving African woman—a true Monrovian, to be exact."* She looked up at him through her long lashes. *"I am a very bad girl, and I deserve to be punished."*

"Lie across my thighs," he ordered.

"What about my clothes?" she asked him, gesturing to her ankle-length red silk dress.

"Leave your clothes to me. Now get over here." He ordered her like a Catholic school principal.

Hiding another smile, but unable to disguise the twinkle in her eyes, Ernestine draped her body, face down, across the tops of Stanley's thighs.

Through the smooth, thin silk of her dress, he rubbed her round, soft and fat ass.

"No panties? Damn, Honey, you're a freak," he said hoarsely.

In a subservient voice she said, *"I wouldn't dare wear panties. Not when you're already about to discipline me."*

"Good girl," he said, licking his lips.

Unexpectedly, he ripped the seam of Ernestine's dress open from her knee to her waist. She gasped and he said, *"See how upset I am with you?"*

She nodded and waited expectantly for his onslaught to begin. Already, her pussy was moist and swollen, ready to be touched, sucked, and fucked. Her nipples were hard with anticipation for his touch, for what this Kru man had to do with her.

Again, he rubbed the palm of his right hand on her booty, warming up her chilled flesh. *"You have such a beautiful butt. I can never get enough of it,"* he murmured. He lifted up his hand and then brought it down firmly on her round globes.

Ernestine gasped again as pleasure and pain got all mingled up inside of her into an immediate need. He brought his hand down again and liquid dripped from her wet pussy onto her thighs.

"Am I hurting you?" Stanley asked her, his voice hot with need.

"A little," she said in a small voice, equally wracked with the need to be possessed by the man she loved.

He ran his hand down her ass cheek to the very top of her thighs and then slid an index finger inside her swollen pussy. *"What about now?"* he asked, his breath coming in quick bursts. *"Am I hurting you now?"*

Ernestine nodded again. *"Yes,"* she said, *"I need more."*

Abruptly, Stanley ripped the dress all the way up to her shoulders. She was completely naked underneath and he lowered her to the soft rug in front of his bed. She looked up at him with love in her eyes.

"Now for the final punishment," he said, as he unzipped his

pants and let his huge, throbbing dick spring free.

"Please, Stanley, I need this right now," she begged him, her hands moving to fondle his meat, to pull it towards her ready pussy.

Settling himself between her legs, he pushed into her wet, hot pussy, inch by inch until half of his trunk disappeared inside her penis purse.

"Stanley," she moaned, her head thrashing on the floor.

"Oh God," he roared as she moved her hips slightly, taking him all the way to the hilt. Roughly he grabbed her hips, and plunged his long rock-hard dick in and out of her wet lips, feeling her muscles contract around him as her pleasure spiraled out of control.

Right before they came, Stanley forced their bodies to go completely still. Holding her hips in his hands, watching the rise and fall of her breasts as she panted beneath him, he said, *"I love you Ernestine Johnson. Don't you ever forget it again. You're the woman I've been looking for after all these years of fruitless search. I don't care what the world thinks of us or say about us, I will love you forever, even to the edge of doom. If I'll be a fool to take the first plunge in falling in love with my apprentice, let me surround my wealth, and status to love, the mother of peace of mind and happiness."*

He plunged into her hot folds, and she milked him dry as a soul-shattering orgasm rocked through them both.

The next day, they wrote their latest lovemaking into their new tale of erotic romance and then headed back to the bedroom after attending to the orphan boy by their house for another round of *"research"*. They both knew that because of the explosion of social media, Liberians were beginning to embrace their kind of writing—only it was being done in secrecy by those in the churches, mosques, government and the academic arenas. As the veil of censorships were now being dismantled in countries across Africa, erotica was taking a root as there were various forms of lovemaking going on in every village, in every city, and in every home across the continent and in many of the movies being produced on the continent.

When Stanley's book, *The Black Mamba* finally hits bookstore in Monrovia, across the continent, the United States, Europe, and around the world, it was an instant hit. Stanley was now thinking of proposing to his beautiful Ernestine who had restored sanity in his life, but he had planned to do it in grand style for all to see.

As he sat and looked out his home office windows at the beautiful butterflies and at birds chirping up in the mango tree by his window the following morning, he began to look back at his life, at the many roads he'd traveled on up until now. Realizing how lucky they both had been in finding each other, he smiled at the long and perilous journey to where they now are. He put down the cup of hot coffee he had in his hand and slowly open the window to let in fresh morning air.

Simultaneously taking in a burst of fresh air through his mouth and nostrils, and with his eyes closed, Stanley said out loud as a way of self-reminder of his own philosophy and deep conviction about life, love and relationship, *"In the unlikely that is called hope, there is nothing false about true love. True love is an unknown force that looks in death's eyes and say "I will live again no matter what you have done to me or what anyone thinks of me." True love is mightier than poverty and forgiving than God Almighty who often warns us about those we love, but do not love us in return. True love will always triumph whether we like it or not. True love will never let us fall because, like a mother, she holds us in her unchanging and protective arms. WOW! Love truly does heal. Even the most wounded and broken hearted can be healed by the power of true love. Never give up on love because it will always find its way back home where it belongs. Like me, my beautiful city will one day find her true love who will heal her wounded hear and revive her broken spirit."*

Being a fully committed man with a beautiful girlfriend to please and two boys to raise, Stanley's life will never be the same. For now, all he has to do is to pray for his beloved country and the people in his city to elect a president that will restore the faded image of Monrovia, the only face of Liberia known by the world.

GLOSSARY OF LIBERIAN WORDS

1. Wata or water police: A female or male prostitute who has no pimp.
2. Hopo Joe: See Wata police.
3. Kpatawe Waterfall: A natural waterfall found in Bong County within the area bearing that name
4. Polaris: A street walker, sex addict, a whore.
5. Bracket or bracketed: to meet or to have met before
6. Kpelle: A native tribe found in Liberia, Guinea, Ivory Coast, and parts of Central and East Africa
7. Sande Society: is women's association found in Liberia, Sierra Leone and Guinea that initiates girls into adulthood, confers fertility, instills notions of morality and proper sexual comportment, and maintains an interest in the well-being of its members throughout their lives
8. Lofa County: One of the fifteen counties of Liberia
9. Sapo National Park: is a national reserved park in Sinoe County, Liberia. It is the country's largest protected area of rainforest and it is the only national park, and contains the second-largest area of primary tropical rainforest in West Africa.
10. Saint Paul River: One of the seven major rivers in Liberia
11. Kakata: The administrative capital of Margibi County
12. Margibi County: One of the fifteen counties in Liberia
13. Pem, Pem or Kee Kee: The local name given to commercial bikes in Liberia

14. Kru: A native tribe found in Liberia, Ghana, Sierra Leone, and many West and Central African countries in Africa.
15. Grand Gedeh: One of the fifteen counties in Liberia
16. Nimba: One of the fifteen counties in Liberia
17. Bong: One of the fifteen counties in Liberia
18. Maryland: One of the fifteen counties in Liberia
19. Grand Cape Mont: One of the fifteen counties in Liberia
20. Couso: A slang that means cousin or a very closed friend.

List of Hanging Out Places (bars, night clubs, entertainment centers) in and around Monrovia

Name of Place	Location
1. Exodus Night Club (Facebook)	Gurley Street
2. Déjà vu	Airfield Short Cut
3. Pepper Bush	Warren Street
4. 704	Du Port Road
5. Musu's Entertainment Center	Oldest Congo Town
6. Samoa Bar	Airfield Road
7. KTC	Matadi
8. New Creation	Bong Mines Bridge
9. Royal Plus	Paynesville
10. View Point	72nd Junction Somali Drive
11. Destiny	Capitol Bypass
12. Delta Boo	GSA Road Junction
13. Flamingo	Sinkor
14. Sharks Business Center	Sinkor Airfield
15. Freddy's	Duport Road
16. Embassy Club	Tubman Boulevard Sinkor
17. Old Folks	Airfield Sinkor and other areas

www.ingramcontent.com/pod-product-compliance
Lightning Source LLC
Chambersburg PA
CBHW070326260626
47160CB00003B/958